VENOM ON THE LEVELS

An addictive crime thriller full of twists

DAVID HODGES

Detective Kate Hamblin Mystery book 10

JOFFE BOOKS

Joffe Books, London
www.joffebooks.com

First published in Great Britain in 2022

This paperback edition was first published
in Great Britain in 2022

ISBN: 978-1-80405-327-0

This book is dedicated to my wife, Elizabeth,
for all her love, patience and support over so many wonderful
years and to my late mother and father, whose faith in me to one
day achieve my ambition as a writer remained steadfast throughout
their lifetime and whose tragic passing has left a hole in my life
that will never be filled.

AUTHOR'S NOTE

I served as a police officer from constable to superintendent for thirty wonderful years, but not in the Avon and Somerset Police area where the action of this novel takes place. The story itself and all the characters in it are entirely fictitious and are not representative of any of the personnel I worked with. At the time of writing, there is *no* police station in Highbridge. This has been drawn entirely from my imagination to ensure no connection is made between any existing police station or personnel in the force. Some poetic licence has been adopted in relation to the local police structure and specific operational police procedures solely to meet the requirements of the plot. But the novel is primarily a crime thriller and does not profess to be a detailed police procedural, even though the policing background, as depicted, is broadly in accord with my own recollections of the many years I spent in the force. I trust that these small departures from fact will not spoil the reading enjoyment of any serving or retired police officers for whom I have the utmost respect.

David Hodges

BEFORE THE FACT

She was scared. Very scared. She kept looking behind her through the swarms of mosquitos and other flying bugs for signs of pursuit as she stumbled along the narrow trail through the forest. Back towards the safety of the compound. But she saw nothing save the boles of the trees soaring upward towards the light from the dense undergrowth. Some, she knew, like the giant kapok tree, achieved a height of two-hundred feet and a breadth of nine to ten feet. It was like being among the columns of some massive cathedral, but at that moment she was in no mood to appreciate their magnificence.

The sticky heat of the day was at its height, and it had already started to rain again. The percussion-like thudding of the heavy drops on the dense foliage had combined with the constant buzz of the millions of insects and the rich, melodic chorus of the multitude of invisible songbirds to create a euphony of sound. This was frequently punctuated by the weird whooping calls of the howler monkeys and the harsh, discordant cries of the toucans and parrots high up in the forest's canopy.

It was a primaeval, alien world and nothing like the soft, sun-dappled patchwork of fields and woods of her native

Oxfordshire. Yet the multifarious voices of the Amazon held little real fear for her, even though she knew that this exotic wilderness sheltered some of the deadliest creatures on the planet. The rainforest's flora and fauna were what she had come to this vast country with the rest of the team to document, and the fear that was driving her in such a panic back towards the safety of the compound had nothing to do with dangerous reptiles or venomous snakes and spiders, but another even more dangerous creature that walked on two legs. Man. Or in this case one particular man.

Her affair with him had been a big mistake, she realised that now. Had she known how badly things were going to turn out, she would never have allowed it to happen in the first place. But then the benefit of hindsight was something that had eluded mankind ever since time began. In her naivety she had been drawn to her handsome man of the world like a moth to the proverbial flame. This was in spite of her feelings of guilt over the fact that he was already married. It was only after nearly a year consorting with him that she had sensed there was another less palatable side to her new-found love.

Even when he was wearing that haughty, enigmatic smile that had first attracted her to him, she had sensed the cold ruthlessness behind it. The darkness lurking in the depths of those calculating brown eyes that could harden so suddenly at the merest hint of a threat to his wellbeing. She had promised herself so many times that she would end the relationship. Walk away from him for good. But it had never happened. Her resolve had always melted away as soon as she was in his bed. She should have known he would take the news of her pregnancy badly. After all, he had a wife and family back home and a respected professional standing to protect. If his infidelity were ever to become known, the resultant scandal could ruin him.

His reaction to the news when they'd met at the spot in the forest they always used for their secret assignations had been carefully controlled. But after a long pause his hooded gaze had radiated menace and his face had become a cold mask, suddenly drained of colour.

'You stupid little bitch!' he'd rasped in scarcely above a whisper. 'How could you let this happen?'

Like a fool, she had reminded him that he was equally to blame and that she expected him to stand by his obligations or face public ridicule.

That was a big mistake. His hand had gripped her tightly by the throat, almost choking the life out of her. 'Get rid of it,' he'd warned. 'Or I'll get rid of you.'

She had managed to make him release his grip by scratching his face with her long nails. Then she had taken to her heels as he'd reeled backwards, clutching at his wounds. But she knew he would come after her. He had too much to lose.

She stopped for a moment, a stitch in her side as she gripped a projecting tree branch to steady herself and turned again to study the forest behind her. The buzzing and rustling seemed to have intensified and a large, green-coloured lizard darted across the track almost under her feet and disappeared back into the forest. But there was no sign of the man she feared. Maybe he had given up on any pursuit.

Then, moments later, she saw the back wall of the compound through the trees ahead and stumbled into the central courtyard round which the individual rondavel-style guest rooms were grouped.

She didn't go to her room immediately but went straight to the little bar the team had set up. She was shaken and had to have time to think. Threatening him had been a stupid thing to do. She realised that now, but it was too late to take it back. Ordering a stiff G & T, despite the warning voice in her head reminding her of her pregnancy, she considered her options. She could report what had happened, of course, tell one of the team. But what had she actually to report? A verbal threat and a minor physical assault, neither of which she could prove. She had examined her neck in the toilet mirror, but there were no visible injuries. Just a slight flush, which could have been due to the heat. If she did report the incident, everything would have to come out. Her affair. Her pregnancy. The fact that she had cheated with another woman's husband. What would it achieve? Nothing except dismissal from her job, loss of accommodation and public humiliation.

She downed her drink in two panicky gasps and ordered another.

The plain fact was, there was nothing she could do. He held all the aces. Okay, so a blood test could ultimately establish paternity, but that was something to consider at the right time which was months ahead. The only option open to her right now was to carry on as if nothing had happened and review the situation once she was on home turf again. True, that meant continuing to work with the arsehole until then, but as they were all due back to the UK in a couple of days, it wasn't too long to wait, was it? Even if he'd meant what he'd said in his warning, she didn't think he would try anything on her in the meantime. The risk was too great and the last thing he would want was a police investigation and the possibility of ending up in a Brazilian prison.

No, sit tight, girl, she said to herself. Just play along with him and get through the next couple of days. If not for yourself, for the baby.

Her decision made, she nodded a brief 'goodnight' to her colleagues already now assembling in the bar for pre-dinner drinks, complaining of a headache and the need for an early night. She then headed across the courtyard to her room.

The door was ajar when she got there, and she frowned. She always shut it to keep out the creepy-crawlies when she went anywhere. She inwardly cursed the carelessness of the domestics the team had hired to service the rooms.

There appeared to be no unwanted 'visitors' inside when she scanned the interior and closed the door behind her, and she saw that the mosquito net was already in place around the single bed. At least someone had done that job properly anyway.

Kicking off her shoes, she stripped and made for the primitive shower with which each hut was provided, making do with the weak flow of water the outside generator pumped up from the adjacent lake. It was nowhere near the luxurious shower she was used to back home. But when she emerged twenty minutes later she felt a lot better and even considered dressing and joining the others for dinner. Then she decided against it. She wasn't in the least bit hungry, and she baulked at the prospect of making small talk for the next couple of hours with so much on her mind.

Unwisely pouring a third G & T, from the bottles on a side table, she unfastened the mosquito net and slipped into bed, turning slightly to plump up the pillows. It was then that she froze. Something was in the bed with her. Something that was now crawling up her leg under the sheets. It felt fairly large and had several legs. A spider. It had to be.

Knowing the lethal nature of some of the arachnids in this part of the world, she gritted her teeth and tried not to panic, forcing herself to stay perfectly still. But she could feel the perspiration on her skin and was conscious of a sudden tell-tale dryness in her mouth as she used all her willpower to stop herself screaming.

The thing reached her naked thigh and began crawling across her stomach. Now it was on the lower part of her left breast, where it suddenly stopped. She held her breath. Could it feel her heart throbbing? Then it was on the move again on to her shoulder and down her arm. If she could just wait until it got to her hand and crawled off her on to the sheet . . .

She kept her head perfectly still but couldn't help herself turning her eyes as far as she could in their sockets to see what was there. At which point the creature stopped again, halfway along her wrist. She found herself staring at a brown hairy body, about two inches long, with a leg span of around six inches, and dull soulless eyes that studied her fixedly. She felt sick with terror. A Brazilian wandering spider. She recognised it immediately. The most venomous and feared arachnid in the world. And it was at this point that it reared up aggressively, with its front legs raised in the air and the reddish hairs around its fangs exposed.

Knowing what she faced, she hesitated no longer. She flicked her wrist to one side to dislodge the spider, and simultaneously threw herself sideways towards the edge of the bed. Only to become entangled in the mosquito net. Even as she desperately tried to claw herself free, she felt the thing running up her back on to her shoulder. Two agonising needle-like jabs penetrated her neck a second before she tumbled out of the bed on to the floor. Her shrill, bubbling scream carried with it an abject sense of terror and loathing as she tore the spider off her and crushed it into a sticky, quivering mess in one hand.

She managed to crawl to the door of her room, moaning and sobbing as the burning pain from the bites increased in severity. She knew that the lethal neuromuscular toxins would spread rapidly through her body to attack the central nervous system. This would ultimately result in convulsions and death unless she could get antivenom treatment. But when she reached up to grip the door handle it would not open, no matter how much she tugged and pulled on it. It was as if it had been locked from the outside. Now losing control altogether, she screamed for help at the top of her voice. But her cries were lost in the sudden cacophony that erupted from powerful speakers as the team's amateur DJ in the bar opposite began his usual evening gig.

Outside the stricken woman's bedroom door, the man in the Hawaiian top and shorts, who had inserted the key in the lock a moment before, tapped his sandal-shod feet on the wooden floor of the decking in time to the music as he coolly smoked a cigar and waited for her cries and frantic struggles to cease.

CHAPTER 1

Kate Lewis detected a strange atmosphere in the general CID office when she turned up for her first day's duty at Highbridge police station after her fortnight's enforced absence. Her colleagues were welcoming enough, commenting that they were glad to see her back after her sick leave. There were plenty of indulgent nods and smiles too, but she sensed a kind of reserve. An awkwardness, as if they felt uncomfortable in her presence.

Something was going on behind her back, she was sure of it, and she was determined to find out what. But she was not given the opportunity at that precise moment. Even before she had hung up her coat, the short, stocky office manager, Ajeet Singh, approached her with a grave look on his bearded face. 'Sorry, Kate,' he said, 'but we've just had a call from the superintendent's secretary to say you're to pop upstairs to see the old man as soon as you come in.'

Mystified and not a little worried by this unusual summons, coming as it did on top of her peculiar reception from her colleagues, she looked for some sign from the secretary when she entered her office as to the reason for the imperious summons. But June Cavendish remained impassive. She merely gave her a nod over the top of her laptop and flicked her eyebrows towards the inner sanctum.

'You're to go straight in,' she said.

Kate found her boss seated behind his desk shuffling papers when she entered the office after a barked 'Enter' in response to her knock.

There was a leather chair placed in front of the superintendent's desk. Throwing her a brief glance over his rimless spectacles, he waved a hand towards it. She studied him curiously for a moment as she sat down.

A rotund, balding individual with a neat military moustache and a permanent puckered frown, George Rutherford was a former army major and one of the last of the old guard. Nicknamed 'Birdie' for his passion for golf, he had a reputation as a straight-laced, traditional copper who did things exactly by the book. A man who had little time for the 'brave', new, politically correct regime which saw its role more as a social service than an enforcement organisation, charged with the job of feeling the collars of criminals. But at fifty-five years of age and nearing the end of his service, he was past his sell-by date as far as the hierarchy at police headquarters were concerned. They were looking for any excuse to dislodge him from his post and encourage him to retire so that they could replace him with a younger officer.

Kate had not had much to do with him. She was much too low in the rank pecking order. But from what she had seen of him, she'd always found him to be a gruff, though fair 'guv'nor', but one who was short on the sort of effective interpersonal skills which were expected of senior managers in the new style police service.

He looked a little out of his comfort zone sitting across from her now and his level of discomfort as he seemed to chew over what he wanted to say was even more pronounced than that of her colleagues downstairs.

'So, you're back with us again,' he growled, stating the obvious. 'How did the therapy go?'

She shrugged. 'Fine, sir,' she replied, thinking of her two weeks' recuperation and counselling at the holistic centre near Taunton which had been paid for by the force. 'It enabled me to relax, and it also put everything in perspective.'

He grunted. 'Good. We were very worried about you when you were found unconscious in your car at the motorway service area on your way back from that job in Pembrokeshire.'

She nodded. 'Some sort of latent reaction to the concussion and trauma I suffered on that last case, I was told. The hospital did say it might happen.'

As she spoke, her mind flashed back to the scrapyard near Bridgwater when the psychopath she was pursuing shut her in the boot of the car and left her for the gaping jaws of the car crusher. She could still smell the inside of that boot and the corpse of the scrappie proprietor crammed in beside her. Still remember her total panic as she had slammed her head repeatedly against the boot lid in a frantic bid to get out. Despite the recent counselling she had received, she still suffered from the nightmares, but she didn't tell him that.

'I feel okay now anyway, sir,' she added, 'and the police doc has given me a clean bill of health.'

He looked slightly dubious. 'So you're fit to resume work?'

'Very much so, sir, and I can't wait to take up my acting detective inspector role next week.'

He made a face. 'Ah, yes, that . . .' He hesitated and sat back in his padded swivel chair, twirling his spectacles in the fingers of one hand and staring at the picture of the queen on the wall beside Kate, avoiding her gaze. 'The thing is . . . ah . . . there's been a change to that while you were away.'

Kate tensed, unintentionally leaning forward slightly to study him. 'Change, sir?' she asked. 'I don't understand.'

He threw a quick glance in her direction, slipped his spectacles back on and began sifting through the papers on his desk again. 'I'm afraid that's not going to happen now. I've decided DS Woo at Bridgwater will take over the role instead.'

'Charlie Woo?' she echoed, thinking of her old friend and former Hong Kong policeman currently on CID at Bridgwater. 'But . . . but you told me I had been appointed. It was all agreed by Headquarters.'

He grimaced. 'Yes, well, I've been on to ACC Personnel, and she agrees that this would be the best course.'

Her voice was cracked and didn't sound like her own. 'Can I know why, sir? I am the most experienced DS on this police area and am already through the promotion board, so I am eminently qualified.'

'Yes, yes, but you've had a nasty experience and have been quite ill. I felt you should be given some time to get back into things.'

'But I'm fully recovered now,' she persisted, her eyes hard and angry. 'Even the doc says so.' She took a chance and added, 'There's more to this, isn't there, sir?'

He shifted his position in his chair and issued a heavy sigh, this time meeting her gaze. 'Well, I didn't want to go into that just now, but you've left me no alternative. The fact is some disquiet has been expressed by HQ for a while about your approach to your work—'

'My approach? With respect, sir, I have one of the highest detection rates in the force.'

His left cheek developed a tic of irritation. 'Yes, yes, yes, but detective work is not just about collars. It is also about teamwork. You have shown a tendency to constantly go against orders and procedures to do your own thing. I believe your superiors have already brought this to your notice. I know there have also been occasions when your conduct would normally have led to disciplinary action had you not achieved such a successful result in the end.'

She went to say something else, but he waved her to silence, and it was apparent that he was in full flow now.

'Take this last case of yours, involving the so-called "Stalker". Your reckless behaviour nearly cost you your life. Twice, if my memory serves me correctly. On both occasions, it was because you disobeyed instructions and went off on a one-woman crusade.'

He removed his spectacles again and polished the lenses with a white handkerchief.

'Your own colleagues call you "Maverick Kate", I believe. That has serious implications for cohesion on a small department like yours. I have no doubt you are an excellent detective, but as a sergeant, you have to be more than that, and as the DI, a lot more. So, I shall be looking at you in future to see if you can meet the challenge of proving your ability to handle the responsibilities of the next rank. Do that, and I will have no hesitation in recommending you.'

Kate had nothing to say. She was stunned. But she knew deep down that his criticisms were justified. When he returned to shuffling his paperwork, she took that as a sign that the interview was over. Quietly leaving the room, she made her way downstairs, hardly aware of anything save the hot, heady feeling of shock and despair.

The canteen was practically empty. She found a table in the farthest corner and sat down with her hands clasped round a steaming cup of black coffee. The humiliation of it all. She would never be able to face any of her colleagues again. It was obvious now that the grapevine had been in overdrive. They had all known about what was going to happen before she'd even walked in. Yet no one had said a word. And where was her husband and partner, Hayden? He had said nothing to her about what was in store when he'd picked her up from the therapy centre the previous night. Yet he must have known. Her whole world had collapsed. She wanted to die. It was then that she made her decision. She had no option but to resign. Slipping into the uniform briefing room just down the corridor, she grabbed a form from the nest of document drawers just inside and put her decision into immediate effect with a handwritten report. Ten minutes later she dropped a sealed envelope into the 'in' tray on June Cavendish's desk, ignoring the secretary's quizzical glance as she did so, and returned to the canteen for a second coffee.

* * *

Hayden Lewis, Kate's detective constable husband, was naturally attracted to the smell of food and his ability to consume vast quantities of it was evinced by his more than generous waistline. It was perhaps inevitable that he would visit the police canteen sooner or later and he materialised while she was still sitting in her corner.

Dressed in a shabby grey suit and scuffed suede shoes and sporting a head of unruly blond hair that looked as though it had never seen a comb, the eccentric former graduate and public-school boarder was either oblivious to his untidy appearance or just didn't care. As those around him knew only too well, he was incapable of smartening himself up anyway. It was part and parcel of his genes.

Kate saw him coming and watched his clumsy progress between the empty tables with a feeling of angry resentment. Not because of the state of him, but because of the way she believed he had let her down.

'Thought I might find you here, old girl,' he said with his plum-in-the-mouth way of speaking and dropped heavily into a chair opposite 'Sorry about the Acting DI job. Jolly bad form for them to treat you the way they have after what you've been through.'

She took a gulp of her coffee. 'Is that what you call it?' She choked, her eyes wet with tears. 'Jolly bad form? I can think of a more colourful description. So why didn't you tell me what was going on, you deceitful prick? You must have known. Everyone else in the office seemed to know.'

He winced. 'I *didn't* know — not until this morning after you'd gone in to work and Charlie Woo rang me.'

'Charlie told you I was about to be shafted?'

He wriggled in his seat. 'He was, er, embarrassed that it had happened but had been instructed not to say anything to you before you were told officially.'

She released her breath in a derisive snort. 'So everyone knew except me? And my own husband chose to say nothing at all?'

He grimaced. 'It was too late by then. You'd already left.'

'So how come you didn't even pick up a whisper before that? The whole nick must have been alive with gossip.'

He scowled, his own resentment showing. 'In case you've forgotten, I've been on an equal opportunities course at Taunton while you've been away, and I only got back yesterday in time to pick you up from that therapy place.'

The hurt in her expression faded and she looked away from him, feeling small and regretting her outburst. To hide her discomfort, she drained her coffee slowly, but then changed tack, determined to revel in her misery.

'The thing is nothing has gone right for me since the day CID moved from the downstairs office up to this floor to give uniform a bigger briefing room. It's almost as if my luck changed overnight.'

He released an incredulous laugh. 'Oh come on, you can't be serious. That move was years ago. Anyway, how on earth could a departmental move to a different floor have anything to do with the way things turned out for you? Next you'll be saying there's a little green gremlin sitting on your shoulder piling on the agonies.'

'You can scoff, but I happen to believe in good and bad luck. Things were going so well when I first joined the department. I got promoted to sergeant in record time and there was every prospect of my making DI within a couple of years. Then the department moved house and almost over-night my career took a nosedive. You forget that I was due for acting rank once before, but had it knocked on the head at the last minute. Now it's happened all over again.'

'And *you* forget that we were all actually still on the ground floor when you faced those horrendous, unfounded accusations of running out on your colleagues after Andy Seldon and Alf Cross were blown to bits in their surveillance van on "Operation Firetrap". I can't think of a worse position to be in than that, can you? So bad luck has got nothing to do with what's happened to you. We all make our own bad luck and that includes you.'

She stiffened. 'What did you mean by that?'

He started to say something else, then bit his lip and said nothing.

'Go on,' she challenged, 'what were you going to say?'

He made a face. 'Just that, well, don't you think you have, er, brought a lot of this down on your own head? I mean, you've been warned enough times about your tendency to sort of do your own thing instead of working as part of a team.'

She gave a hollow, unamused laugh. 'Oh you mean, this "Maverick Kate" label someone's stuck on me? Thanks a lot for taking their side.'

He flushed angrily. 'Oh grow up, Kate, for goodness sake. I'm on your side and always will be. But you really have to face up to the criticism you've received. You *do* regularly go off on your own during crime inquiries instead of taking the team with you and, as a DS, you need to change your ways in that respect, or you will never make DI.' He took a deep breath, conscious of her open-mouthed stare after his uncharacteristic rebuke. 'Well, I've said it now, so I'll leave it at that.'

Her face twisted into a bitter grimace. 'It doesn't matter now anyway,' she snapped. 'I've resigned.'

'You've done *what?*'

'The envelope is with the super as we speak.'

'That was a downright stupid thing to do.'

She shrugged. 'That isn't what you would have said a short time back. You were urging me to chuck it all in then, remember?'

'Yes, but that was when I had a job offer at my old public school. It was an excellent opportunity.'

'So, it's okay for you to want to leave when it suits you, but not me?'

He shook his head irritably. 'That's not it at all. You're twisting things. *Then* I had another job to go to. What are you going to do if you leave the force? In your thirties with no other outside experience? You'll be lucky to get a job on the checkout counter at Tesco.'

The barb went in deeply, and Kate glared at him. 'That was a cheap shot.'

He reddened, looking down at the table. 'Sorry, I didn't mean to say that. I know you have a degree, and you should find another job easily. But you won't earn the salary you are getting now, especially with all the "x's" you get on top of your pay as a DS.'

She shrugged again and blew her nose into her hand-kerchief. 'It's too late now anyway. The guv'nor will already have read my report.'

He fidgeted, head down, inspecting the tabletop and playing with an abandoned sugar lump in the bowl.

'He won't.'

'Sorry?'

He looked up and grinned. 'I said he won't.' Reaching into his inside pocket, he produced a crumpled envelope, finishing, 'I thought you might do something silly like this, so I forewarned June Cavendish. She rescued it from the guv'nor's "in" tray while he was out of the office.'

She half-rose in her chair, her eyes blazing. 'You did what? You have no right.'

She had raised her voice and a couple of community support officers on a table near the counter glanced across at them.

Hayden made a face. 'Sit down, Kate. You're attracting attention.'

She glanced across at the other table and reluctantly slumped back in her chair.

Hayden leaned across the table. 'All I'm asking you to do is sleep on it tonight. Don't do anything rash without think-ing things through first. If after you have done that you still want to chuck it all in, I'll go along with your decision, but give it some thought first. Don't do it in hot blood.'

She hesitated, starting to calm down when she saw the sense in what he was suggesting.

'One night?'

'You've got it.'

She released a long, trembling sigh, which was still filled with intense emotion.

'One night then, but that's all. No more than that?'

'I wouldn't expect anything more. Now "get up them stairs", as they say, and settle back into things. No one is going to take the mickey out of you. There'll all be feeling pretty sorry that this has happened.'

She shook her head. 'No can do, Hayd. I can't face anyone at the moment.'

'So, what *are* you going to do then? You'll have to work a month's notice if you go through with your resignation anyway. You can't simply hide away down here for four weeks.'

'I might just report sick again. Leave on ill-health grounds. Mental trauma and all that.'

He snorted. 'You mean, take the coward's way out? That's not the Kate Lewis I know.'

She bit her lip, caught up in an agony of indecision — and it was at that precise moment that the station's public address system blasted. 'Mobile to attend Moat House, Westhay. Report of intruders on premises.'

Hayden stared at Kate fixedly, half rising in his chair and flourishing an ignition key in front of her, his apparent eagerness to respond completely out of character. 'Well? Are we going to that or are you just going to sit here and hide in your corner?'

She met his aggressive stare but continued chewing her lip.

'Well?'

She released her breath in a sharp hiss and jumped to her feet. 'You shitbag!' she exclaimed, snatching the key from his hand, 'But I'm driving.'

'That's my girl,' he said and chuckled as he stumbled after her in the direction of the door.

CHAPTER 2

Westhay Moor was a wild, swampy tract of marsh and peat bog on the Somerset Levels, close to the small village of Westhay and just a few miles from Burtle where Kate and Hayden had their own small, thatched cottage. Sparsely populated and criss-crossed by numerous drainage ditches, or *rhynes*, the area was a haven for wildlife, particularly its variety of birds, and home to a national nature reserve which had been declared a site of special scientific interest.

The satnav directed Kate down a rutted lane, marked 'No Through Road'. This eventually came to a halt before a high wall and iron gates set in brick buttresses on the other side of a partially overgrown ditch. One of the buttresses carried a brass plate bearing the name 'Moat House'. The gates were wide open and there was a quaint stone lodge with a pointed roof like something out of a child's fairy tale just inside.

'About time someone cleared out the moat,' Kate commented drily.

Driving through the entrance, they followed a tarmac driveway which meandered between mature willows to a large grey house with ivy-clad walls and tall Victorian style chimneys. Several cars were drawn up on the gravel hardstanding outside, one of them a marked police patrol car.

Hayden's eyes lit up when he spotted the white sports car parked alongside a black BMW. 'Gordon Bennett!' he exclaimed, 'It's a Mk II Triumph Spitfire. These models were first produced in the mid-sixties. But it looks immaculate.'

Kate grimaced. She knew from past experience how easily Hayden could be distracted by the sight of a vintage or veteran motor car. Sometimes she wondered whether it would have been more natural for him to have had an eye for a pretty girl, like most men, provided he only looked, of course, but that wasn't her Hayden. For him, the sexiest thing on earth was a classic motor car and there was nothing better than that.

'You dragged me here, Hayd,' she snapped. 'Forget the car, will you? Concentrate on why we came.'

'Sorry, old girl,' he replied mildly. 'Keep your stripes on. Just looking.'

The front door of the house opened as they got to it and a short muscular man in his thirties with curly blond hair, wearing a suede coat and fawn corduroy trousers, bounded out. He was carrying a bunch of keys in one hand and almost collided with them.

'My apologies,' he said with a boyish grin. 'In a bit of a hurry, sorry.'

'DS Lewis, Highbridge CID,' Kate said, flashing her warrant card.

'Howard,' he replied, 'Howard Dunbar. Can't stop. Just go in, will you. They're all in the kitchen at the back.'

Then he was striding across the hardstanding to the sports car and climbing inside. Hayden turned to watch the car reverse, then roar away down the drive. His face registering an expression of pure joy until Kate's elbow found his ribs.

'Burglary, Hayd?' she exclaimed. 'Remember?'

Pushing through the front door, they found themselves in a long hallway. Doors opened off on both sides and there was an ornate staircase at the far end rising to the upper level. They followed the hallway to a door tucked into a corner beside the staircase which stood ajar.

A uniformed police constable was standing just inside talking to a middle-aged man in a pullover and grey flannels. He turned at their approach.

'Ah, Sarge,' he said, almost with a sense of relief, 'this is Professor Hubert Dunbar. He called us.'

Dunbar grunted, but there was no warmth in the expression on his hard, lean face as Kate introduced Hayden and herself, and his dark eyes fastened on Kate like a serpent contemplating a prospective meal. Then he smiled and she rather wished he hadn't. The smile was just as cold and failed to reach his eyes.

'Good of you to come,' he said, though Kate detected a note of sarcasm in his tone. 'I'm afraid that whoever was in here is long gone now, but he certainly made a mess.'

Stepping past him into the room which lay beyond, she found herself in a large ultra-modern kitchen with an ornate tiled floor and floor-to-ceiling grey units. There were low-level, stainless-steel lights over a central island, a triple stainless-steel sink, and an imposing black range cooker. Going by the apparent age of the house, it was clear that the room had undergone substantial renovation to bring it up to twenty-first-century standards, and that must have cost a pretty penny.

Dunbar waved a hand towards the double window over the sink. Kate saw that one of the windows was wide open, with the pane smashed.

'Our domestic found it when she came in here this morning,' he went on. 'Must have happened during the night, but my wife and I wouldn't have heard a thing as our rooms are upstairs on the far side of the house. No other members of the family seem to have heard anything either. Or so they claimed at breakfast this morning.'

Kate carefully approached the sink unit and saw that the window catch was in the open position and some jagged remains of the glass were still visible along the edge of the wooden frame. Broken glass, some with black tape still attached, littered the work surface and the sink bowl itself.

She also saw that most of the drawers in the kitchen units had been left open and the contents dumped on the floor in front of them, indicating an untidy search.

'Apart from the tape, not a very professional job,' she commented. 'A "pro" opens drawers bottom to top to save time having to close them again, and to avoid opened drawers getting in his way during the search. But these have obviously been opened higgledy-piggledy. Your burglar showed a bit of nuance by taping up the window before putting it in to deaden the sound of the breaking glass, but this was certainly a rushed, haphazard job. Any idea what's gone?'

Dunbar snorted and nodded towards a wine rack in the corner. 'For a start, two bottles of rather nice Châteauneuf-du-Pape red wine at forty odd quid each. Plus, I'm told, a couple of loaves of bread, a big truckle of cheddar cheese, and four pints of milk. On top of that, there's about a hundred quid in small notes and loose change gone. It was in the locked drawer over there which the burglar seems to have forced, obviously realising that if the drawer was locked, it had to have something of value inside.'

Kate noted the drawer he was indicating, which was still projecting from the cabinet. Even from where she stood she could see that the front was hanging off.

'Why do you keep money here in the kitchen?' she asked.

'It's for our domestic, Dorothy Matlock, to pay for sundries.'

'Your domestic?'

'Yes, she's an excellent cook. I employ her to prepare our main meals and shop for what is required, since no one in this house seems even capable of boiling an egg. She also does a weekly house-clean for me. She lives in The Lodge close to the main entrance.'

'A hundred pounds is a lot of money for sundries.'

'I have very expensive tastes and I am also cursed with a family of gannets, Sergeant.'

'Any idea who may have been responsible for the burglary?'

'Probably a drug addict looking for cash to, what is it they call it, feed their habit?'

'Why would you think that?'

'Well, nothing else seems to have been taken and there's no indication that the intruder went anywhere else. Furthermore, it's what these junkies do, isn't it? You know, break into isolated houses like this on the off-chance of finding any money that's lying about.'

'It was likely one of the hippies, or naturalists as they call themselves now,' another voice chimed in.

Kate turned quickly to face the speaker. A thin, bespectacled youth in his late teens or twenties, with lank, shoulder-length, black hair, dressed in a creased, fawn T-shirt and green, combat style trousers.

'And you are?' she asked.

The lad blinked owlishly at her. 'Julian,' he said.

'My youngest son,' Dunbar explained in a weary, patronising tone that seemed to dismiss him as an irrelevance before he could say anything else.

'The more intelligent one,' Julian said with a smirk.

His father scowled. 'I've got two sons for my sins,' he added tersely. 'Julian and Howard. Plus Angela, a tiresome, neurotic daughter, who is permanently away with the fairies and insists on calling herself Cloud even though her real name is Angela. All of them a damned nuisance.'

Kate nodded without passing comment. 'So, what's this about hippies or naturalists?'

'There is a whole gang of them at Mason's Farm,' Julian went on.

Kate raised an inquiring eyebrow. 'Mason's Farm?'

Professor Dunbar released his breath in an irritable hiss. 'Yes, it's a derelict property that backs on to my land. You probably passed the track leading to the place without realising it when you drove in just now. It was the site of one of those drug-fuelled hippy type gatherings about three months ago. A few of the participants returned there after your colleagues had cleared the main rabble out and they have been nothing but a dratted nuisance ever since. Holding wild, noisy parties, thieving from our barn and threatening visitors.'

Mention of the issue seemed to wind him up further. 'About time the local police did something about them instead of just talking of court eviction orders and such like. We have to pay rates for this place, you know.'

Seeing the way the conversation was going, Kate quickly steered things back to the break-in.

'You say they have been stealing from your barn. What else has been taken?'

'Oh, tools, petrol for the mini tractor and other bits.'

'Did you report the thefts?'

'Not much point was there. No idea when the stuff went missing. It was just there one day and not the next. We didn't notice it at first.'

'Ever actually disturbed any of them on your property, sir?'

He stared at her for a moment, as if thrown by the question. 'Well, yes, a week ago. But not me personally. It was my gardener, Josh Matlock. Caught one of the damned hippies sleeping it off in our barn. Some long-haired, bearded yobo covered in tattoos. Josh chased him off with a pitchfork. Should have run him through with it.'

Kate ignored his last comment. 'We'll need to speak to Mr Matlock in due course to see if he can give us a description.'

'That's easy enough. He lives in The Lodge by the main gates. Married to our domestic, Dorothy Matlock. I "inherited" them both when I bought this place about three years ago. Sort of job lot. But Josh is my general handyman as well as the gardener. Can turn his hand to anything. Useful chap to have around. I believe he's home at the moment repairing a mowing machine.'

Kate nodded. 'We'll pop and see him when we leave here. In the meantime, can you ensure that this crime scene is left exactly as it is until we can arrange for our scenes of crime team to give it the once-over? I'll also need a statement off you about the break-in and a list of what was stolen, especially the make of the wine if it is not the usual run-of-the-mill stuff. I'll get someone to take that statement off you before we go.'

Dunbar frowned. 'As long as I can carry on with my work in the annexe in the meantime. I am in the middle of a research project at the moment, and I wouldn't want to be disturbed once I've returned to it.'

'I don't think there would be any need to disturb you in another part of the house, sir, provided your intruder hasn't been in there too.'

'As far as I know, he didn't go anywhere else. Just the kitchen. But I can soon check it out. I was on my way there when I was told about the break-in.'

'And where exactly is this annexe, sir?'

'Well, it's not strictly speaking an annexe as it's not joined to the house. We just call it that. It was originally a stable at the side of the house. The last owner was well into riding and equestrian sports. Not my thing, I'm afraid. I had it converted and it's now my main place of work.'

Kate nodded. 'And what sort of work is that, sir, if you don't mind my asking?'

He treated her to a thin smile. 'Rather than trying to explain, let me show you, Sergeant. I think you'll be intrigued.'

But as it turned out, 'intrigued' was the last word Kate would have used to describe it.

CHAPTER 3

Leaving the kitchen at a brisk stride, Dunbar led the way out the back door and across a courtyard enclosed by a high wall with a gated entrance to the right. There was a single-storey brick building on the far side and as they reached it, Kate noticed a sign attached to the wall by the door which read: 'Danger. Keep Out'.

'Danger?' she queried.

Dunbar's thin smile returned. 'You will see,' he said.

Unlocking the door, he ushered Kate and Hayden into a large, square room boasting a single window in the centre of the far wall which admitted the only natural light. Dunbar flicked a switch and strip lights blazed from the ceiling, revealing what at first sight appeared to be a rather extravagant office.

A laptop computer and printer occupied the top of a large wooden desk in the far left-hand corner, and there was a freestanding photocopier beside it with rows of filing cabinets and overfull bookcases crammed with books, filing boxes and sheafs of papers lining two of the other walls. All the usual equipment to be found in the office of almost any commercial business in the country and hardly worth a second glance.

But what brought a certain incongruity to this otherwise unremarkable office scene, and immediately arrested Kate's attention, was firstly, the expensive looking microscope standing on a side table to the left of the desk, together with some sort of electronic box equipped with a floor pedal from which different coloured wires trailed. There was also a Bunsen burner and a plastic tray holding a number of what she knew from her school biology days to be pipettes and microscopic slides. Beside the table were two tall refrigerators and a pair of steel cabinets. The door of one cabinet was partially open to reveal shelves filled with racks of glass test tubes, syringes, beakers and a whole assortment of similar equipment.

'This is a lab,' she blurted suddenly.

Dunbar raised an eyebrow. 'Very good, Sergeant,' he remarked with a patronising tone.

'What do you do here then?'

'I'll show you, if you like,'

Back-tracking slightly, he led the way to an internal door set in a shallow recess just past the cabinets containing the laboratory equipment.

'This used to be the tack room. Saddles, bridles, that sort of thing,' he said, opening the door and ushering her through, 'and it suits my purpose admirably.'

The room beyond was much smaller than the first and appeared to be windowless. It was lit solely by some kind of suffused greenish light provided by a double row of strip lights. The unexpected humidity hit Kate as soon as she stepped inside, and she was conscious of an unpleasant musty smell. In one corner of the room, a tall cabinet displaying a blue light in a recessed panel produced a consistent electronic hum. In another, wire cages stacked one on top of the other held dozens of white mice, which scampered erratically in every direction on a solid floor covered in sawdust. Beside the cages was a large glass cabinet with several shelves each accommodating hundreds of different insects, including what Kate thought to be crickets and cockroaches.

More curiously, the whole length of the wall directly opposite the door was occupied by a number of what looked like large aquarium tanks, each supported on a steel frame and containing a variety of exotic looking vegetation.

'Terrariums,' Dunbar said at her elbow, as if reading her mind. 'All temperature controlled, of course.'

'I see. So, what's in them?'

'Why don't you take a look?'

Kate shrugged and approached the nearest one curiously. Only to step back quickly with a sharp intake of breath.

The huge spider had emerged from a hole in a deep layer of substrate and was crouching there motionless, with one leg resting against the glass. Light brown in colour and covered in hair, the tarantula was almost the size of her hand.

Dunbar grunted. 'Ah, *Theraphosa blondi*,' he commented. 'A good choice. She's what's commonly called a Goliath tarantula of the family Theraphosidae. I got her from the forests of Suriname. We call her Susie.'

'You've given that horrible creature a name?' Kate exclaimed, backing away.

He sighed. 'Oh, this one's quite a darling,' he said. 'Despite her size, she's harmless really. Her bite is no worse for us than a bee sting. That is not the case for her prey, of course, which usually consists of insects, rodents, lizards and such like. Hence the cockroaches, crickets and other insects you can see in the glass cabinet and the mice in the cages which are also used for experimental purposes.'

'You mean you actually feed those poor little things to . . . to that?'

He shrugged. 'Spiders have to eat too, you know. I sense you'd be against that as well?'

'I'm against all forms of cruelty.'

'Would you rather we used human beings or dogs for our toxin research instead?'

Kate didn't answer. She realised just in time that she was not there to express an opinion, however deeply felt it was. He was simply trying to goad her.

Receiving no response, he shrugged and continued. 'The terrarium to the left of Susie is occupied by Helen, though she is being a little coy at the moment and staying in her burrow. She is of the genus *Cyriopagopus lividus*, commonly called a Cobalt Blue. If she deigned to show herself, you would see that she is a particularly beautiful tarantula with a distinct blue colouration. But she is very aggressive and has an extremely painful bite. Not the sort of 'girl' you would want to take liberties with. She comes from Thailand, and I was lucky to find her. Cobalt Blues are not that common.'

Kate shuddered. 'And the other terrariums,' she said, 'do they all contain poisonous spiders?'

He sighed. ''Fraid so. From left to right, we have Freya, a rather nasty funnel-web from Australia. Then there's Lisa, a Redback, also from Australia. Next to her are firstly, Theresa, a Black Widow, then Linda, a Brown Recluse. Both from the United States. A bite from any of these ladies would be lethal to a human being. But my prize specimen is Martha, in the far cabinet, reputed to be the most dangerous arachnid in the world.

'She is of the genus *Phoneutria*, which means 'Murderess' in Greek. A very apt name, I can tell you. Otherwise known as the Brazilian wandering spider, she is from the jungles of the Amazon Delta, and she proved to be a devil to catch. Come, let me introduce you to her.'

Kate shook her head vigorously as her mind flashed back to an old woodshed from her childhood. It had been at the bottom of her stepfather's allotment and for years it had dominated her nightmares. 'No thanks. I'll skip that if you don't mind.'

He tutted. 'For goodness' sake, Sergeant, you only have to look. The creatures can't get out of their terrariums. The lids are fully secured, for obvious reasons.'

In the light from the study which spilled through the doorway behind him, Kate could read the contempt written into his expression, and she realised he was laughing at her. Worse still, his son, Julian, suddenly pushed past them both.

Hands thrust in his pockets in an obvious act of male bravado, he approached the glass cabinet Dunbar had indicated and peered inside.

Gritting her teeth, Kate was left with no option but to follow his example, and she was relieved when she got to the terrarium to see that the spider was not in evidence. She guessed that, like the Cobalt Blue, it was hiding deep in its burrow at the bottom of the long pipe that was just visible poking up through the luxuriant undergrowth covering the thick layer of substrate. She wasn't in the least bit disappointed by the fact and was quite happy for it to stay there. But that wasn't to be.

Giving her an unpleasant sideways sneer, Julian tapped sharply on the terrarium. The response was almost immediate. Kate sprang back with an involuntary cry as a large hairy body virtually exploded against the glass as if from nowhere and remained there, quivering with rampant aggression.

Brown like the tarantula and covered in hair, the spider was not as big as its near neighbour and its intimidating posture probably made it look much larger than it actually was. But with its two front legs raised against the glass, exposing a patch of scarlet hair as it swayed from side to side, it was certainly big and ugly enough for Kate, and she felt physically sick.

'That was a stupid thing to do,' Dunbar snapped at Julian. 'You could have frightened her and made her more difficult to handle in future.'

'Only a joke,' Julian replied sourly.

Dunbar's voice was low and menacing. 'Get out!' he said. 'And I mean now!'

With a sheepish smirk, his son slouched away. Dunbar shook his head in resignation. 'Sorry about that,' he said. 'Sometimes I don't think he'll ever grow up.'

He cleared his throat. 'She's a big girl, wouldn't you say?' he said proudly. 'These arachnids can reach a length of about two inches or five centimetres and a leg span of around six inches or fifteen centimetres, but she's a bit more than that already. See the beautiful ventral markings on her front legs and the challenging way she rears up to expose the patch of scarlet hair where her fangs are located. She is a truly magnificent creature. I am delighted to have her.'

Kate stared at the spider with a kind of horrible fascination but kept her distance from the terrarium. 'Why on earth do you have these things?' she breathed. 'They're dangerous. I assume you have some sort of import licence?'

He nodded. 'Of course I do. It is a legal requirement and as a professional arachnologist, I take my responsibilities very seriously. My particular specialism is the study of toxins produced in the venom of the global arachnid population, which can vary according to species. Some toxins, for example, can cause necrosis in human beings, which is the destruction of body tissue. Others will attack the neuromuscular system. Still others will do both. But however the venom works, it is thought that some of the components of the toxins might actually have specific benefits.'

Kate stared at the spider and grimaced. 'I can't think that the poison in that thing's bite would be of any benefit to anyone,' she said.

He cleared his throat. 'Not in its raw state, no,' he said. 'The bite of a Brazilian wandering spider is likely to prove fatal to a human being if not treated with antivenom almost immediately afterwards. It is regarded as the world's most deadly arachnid, because of its aggressive nature and the potency of the neurotoxins in its venom. But it is known, for example, that a component within the venom can raise the level of nitric acid in the body and thereby increase blood flow, suggesting it might ultimately be of value in the treatment of erectile dysfunction in men.

'More generally, arachnid venom is believed to contain many millions of bioactive peptides. These are strings of amino acids which can have a significant impact on human health in such areas as the digestive, cardiovascular, immune and nervous systems. Research is currently being undertaken in relation to a protein found in the venom of the Australian funnel-web, for example, to establish its value in the treatment of serious nervous system disorders, like stroke and epilepsy. Then there are the likely environmental benefits in the use of other components from spider venom for effective pest control in agriculture.

'Research is still ongoing in all these areas, globally, and I mention them merely to illustrate my point that there is an upside to the toxins in spider venom as well as a downside. Continued research in this field is therefore absolutely vital to medical and environmental science generally and not just to provide more effective antivenom protection against spider bites. This is where I and other scientists like myself come in.'

Kate turned away and joined Hayden in the doorway. 'And to carry out your research you physically handle these creatures?'

'Have to, I'm afraid, in order to extract the venom from their fangs. It involves anaesthetising the arachnid with carbon dioxide, then delivering an electric shock to it by means of the kit you probably noticed outside in the lab. This causes it to vomit and after separating the venom from the vomit, we collect it in a glass capillary for analysis and experimentation. It's a very delicate process and it is also very time-consuming, involving multiple extractions over a lengthy period.'

'*Nice.* Rather you than me.'

'Aha,' he chuckled, 'spoken like a true arachnophobe.'

She ignored the blatant dig. 'So, what if you were accidentally bitten by one of your little "patients"? Taunton Hospital is quite a distance from here and there's no guarantee they would have the antivenom you would need.'

He nodded. 'All covered,' he said.

Ushering her back to the main room, he opened a metal cabinet to reveal several pairs of thick gloves and Perspex visors on the lowest of two high shelves, with at least two pairs of green overalls, hanging on hooks underneath. 'Full protective clothing is worn when any of the arachnids is being handled,' he said, 'and I also have those.'

He indicated a row of glass tubes in a wooden rack next to a narrow cardboard box on the shelf above. 'Antivenom in respect of each of my spiders and all clearly labelled. There is a hypodermic in the box beside them for the necessary injection, should I or my assistant ever need it, and the cabinet is left unlocked in case of just such an emergency. You will appreciate that immediate action in the case of an accident is absolutely essential.'

'You mentioned an assistant?'

'Yes, Sam, er, Dr Samantha Lawrence. She's off for a couple of days. Visiting a sick aunt or something, I gather. She's a well-qualified biologist and venomologist who's been with me for around six months now. Her expertise in the field is invaluable.'

Kate turned for the door, anxious to be out of the room. 'I'm sure she is, sir,' she said, thinking of the fangs of the Brazilian wandering spider. 'But let's hope neither of you ever need that hypodermic.'

Leaving the annexe a few minutes later, Kate spotted the uniformed constable hovering in the hall of the main house and sent him back to the laboratory to take the necessary statement from the professor while she paused for a few moments in front of the house to take several deep breaths of clean fresh air.

'So, what was all that about with the beasties in the terrariums?' Hayden asked at her elbow. 'I never knew you had a phobia about spiders.'

'It goes back a long way,' she replied. 'I'll tell you about it one day.'

'But you still look as white as a sheet. You okay?'

'I'm fine, honestly. Now let's get SOCO out here to look at the crime scene and while we're waiting for them to arrive, it might be a good idea to try and track down this gardener, Josh Matlock, and see what he can tells us. Then I think a trip to see our hippy friends would be in order.'

Hayden was secretly delighted that her mood seemed to have lifted now that they were back on another investigation.

Albeit that it was a very minor job. But he couldn't resist a little dig. Glancing innocently at the ground, he kicked a stone away with his foot and cast her a sly glance. 'Not resigning just yet then?'

She unlocked the car door. 'Don't push it, fat man,' she said tightly.

CHAPTER 4

There was no reply when Kate rang the old brass bell at the front of The Lodge, but not to be put off, she and Hayden went round the back of the cottage and found the gardener in his shed.

Josh Matlock was a short, plump man in his early sixties with sparse ginger hair and a matching moustache. He was dressed in dirty, green overalls and wellington boots. He looked none too pleased to see them, turning quickly and scowling when Kate coughed and tapped lightly on the wide-open door with her warrant card held out in front of her.

'Highbridge CID,' Mr Matlock,' she said, 'DS Kate Lewis and DC Hayden Lewis.'

Matlock straightened up with a grunt from the big garden mower he was bending over and wiped his hands on an already oily rag. 'Keepin' the job in the family then, be we?' he growled, obviously referring to their shared name.

Kate didn't confirm or deny it. 'We're investigating a burglary at the house,' she went on.

He nodded. 'Aye. Heard all about it this mornin' from young Julian. Got in through the kitchen winder, I hear. Not surprised.'

'Why do you say that?'

33

He shrugged. 'Darned hippies next door al'ays creepin' 'bout the place like. Seein' what they can nick.'

'We hear you chased one of them off recently.'

'With a pitchfork. Caught him dossin' in the big barn at the back of the place. Lyin' there bold as brass, he were. Soon made off when he seen me, I can tell you.'

'Did you get much of a look at him to give us a description?'

'Looked like all the rest of them weirdos. You know, jeans covered in painted flowers, black waistcoat, no shirt mind, and one of them things tied round his head—'

'Bandana?'

'Aye, that's it.'

'What age do you think he was?' Hayden asked.

Matlock studied him for a moment, as if sizing him up. 'Weren't no kid, like, I'll say that. In his thirties, I reckons. Covered in tattoos, he were. Flowers, birds, fish, the lot.' Now he chuckled. 'Had a bloody silly goatee beard too. Looked a right dickhead.'

'Did he say what he was doing in the barn?' Hayden continued.

Matlock grinned. 'Didn't seem too keen on chattin'. Not with me pitchfork halfway up his arse.' He broke off. 'Beggin' your pardon, missy.'

Kate tightened her lips to conceal the smirk. 'Would you recognise him again if you saw him?' she asked.

'Maybe I would and then, maybe I wouldn't.'

'Can you show us this barn?'

He scowled. ''Appen I could, though I don't know what good that'll do you.'

He wiped his hand on his overalls. 'C'mon then, missy. I ain't got all day. Busy man, see.'

He led the way back down the driveway towards the house, but turned sharp left across the hardstanding, then right down a wide track running between the right-hand wall of the house and an area of scrubby woodland. At the end of the house it was joined by a six-to-seven-foot-high wall, with the roof of another building projecting above it. Kate guessed they were skirting the perimeter wall of the courtyard enclosing Professor Dunbar's laboratory.

Then the wall itself ended and they crossed a piece of open ground strewn with the rusted remains of farm machinery, heading towards a dilapidated barn with a threadbare thatched roof in the far corner which backed on to more scrubby woodland.

'Feller must've used that path through the wood to get from Mason's Farm to here,' Matlock said, pointing at a gap among the trees. Stopping briefly before the barn's heavy double doors, he raised a long wooden arm slotted into a pair of wooden hooks that held them shut and pulled one open to let them into the building. 'Path goes all the way through them woods, past the old bird hide on the edge of the lake, then on to the farm. Last owner, Colonel Buxton, had a thing about birds when he lived here. Had the hide built just so he could watch the marsh fowl.'

Childhood visions of the old shed came back to Kate again, and she hesitated before following Hayden into the gloom, noticing the same musty, decaying smell that she remembered from those long-ago days which sent an unpleasant shiver down her spine. The barn contained nothing but rotting bales of hay, a small tractor and an old garden excavator, both of which gleamed with newly applied oil. A paraffin lamp stood on an upturned beer barrel to one side of the doorway and at the back there was a wooden staircase ascending to what had obviously once been a hayloft with a wooden rail running the length of it. Thick cobwebs hung from the roof, and their sticky weaves stirred slightly in the draught from the open door. To the right there was another narrow opening lacking a door. This accessed a second room which Kate found to contain just a workbench, an old, rusted bed frame with broken springs and a stack of paint tins.

'Satisfied, then?' Matlock said. 'Feller were lyin' on some old sacks just over there. Didn't stay long after he saw me, though.'

'Is there anything else you can remember about the incident?' Kate asked.

Matlock hesitated and smoothed his moustache with his finger and thumb. "Tain't my place to say.'

'Your place to say what?'

He shook his head firmly. 'Nowt. Me and the missus always keeps ourselves to ourselves. It's best that way. Gossip don't help no one.'

'Anything you tell us will be kept in the strictest confidence.'

He thought about that for a moment, then added, 'All I'm sayin' is that the feller in the barn weren't alone.' He pointed to the second room. Someone were hidin' in there, I'll be bound, though I didn't bother to look. And matey boy hisself weren't in the barn for just a doss neither.' He treated them both to an extravagant wink. 'He were pretendin' to be asleep, but I reckons he were there for somethin' a lot more personal like.'

'Such as?'

He turned back on them. 'G'day to you, Sergeant. I 'spect you can find your own way back.'

'What do you think he meant by that remark, "something a lot more personal"?' Hayden drawled on their way back to the house. 'He rather left things up in the air.'

Kate shook her head irritably. 'Didn't he just. Bloody annoying. He obviously saw more than he's letting on.'

'The way he winked, suggested to me that he was probably being discreet about things, maybe protecting someone or just not wanting to get involved. The hippy had probably been with a woman in there.'

'Shagging, you mean?'

He frowned. 'There you go again, resorting to gutter language. I think you do it deliberately, just because you know it annoys me.'

She tutted. 'Right now, Hayd, I couldn't give a toss about what annoys you and what doesn't. We're here to investigate a burglary, however minor it might be, so just concentrate on that, will you?'

'Fine, *Sergeant*,' he retorted sarcastically. 'Anything you say, *Sergeant*.'

SOCO still hadn't arrived by the time they got back to the house, but they found a young woman of about twenty-five sitting on the doorstep. She was wearing tatty jeans and a skimpy denim top and was drinking from what turned out to be a can of cider.

She hardly looked up as they approached, and Kate gave a discreet cough. 'You must be Angela?' she said, hazarding a guess.

Pale blue eyes, framed by a mass of curly fair hair, stared at her over the rim of the can. 'I am called "Cloud" now,' the girl corrected. 'And you must be the coppers Daddy called in.'

'Highbridge CID,' Kate confirmed.

'This burglary is a load of crap,' the girl added. 'Crap reported by a crappy family.'

Kate raised an eyebrow. 'You think your family are crappy? That's not very nice.'

'They're not a very nice family, that's why. Julian is a psycho who creeps around all the time spying on people, Howard has his head so far up his arse he can't see daylight, and dear old Daddy is a total weirdo. I mean, have you seen what he's got in the annexe?'

'The spiders you mean?'

She shivered, much as Kate had done earlier. 'What sort of creep keeps those horrible things as pets?'

'They're hardly pets. He's using them to study toxins for the benefit of science.'

'Yeah, so he says, but I think he secretly loves the horrid little shits. Always has done. In fact, I think he is a lot like one of them himself. You know, cold, calculating and totally lacking in any sense of empathy.'

'That's a rather unkind description of your own father.'

'You don't know him or what he's capable of.' Then she added, 'Those things in the annexe are dangerous, you do know that, don't you? One bite from any of them could be fatal. What if one were ever to get out? Can you imagine it? No one would be safe in this house with something like that on the loose.' Her eyes widened. 'Just think, you could be lying in bed fast asleep when it slipped into your room, climbed up the coverlet and scuttled towards you, fangs dripping in anticipation—'

'Yes, yes, yes,' Kate interjected. The other's lurid description was a little too much for her own vivid imagination to handle under the circumstances. 'But I'm quite sure he takes every precaution.'

The young woman stood up and slipped a cigarette between her lips.

'Maybe he does, but you can never be certain about anything, and his work has already cost one life.'

'A life? How do you mean?'

Angela Dunbar lit up and accidentally blew scented smoke into Kate's face, apologised, then waved it away. 'No one's told you about Gillian George, then?'

'Gillian George?' Kate shook her head.

'Well, I don't suppose they had any reason to, and Father certainly wouldn't mention her. But you ought to ask.'

'So, what about her?'

Dunbar tapped her nose confidentially with her forefinger. Then with a smirk, she simply strolled away without saying another word, trailing smoke.

Kate didn't call after her for an explanation. There was little point and though intrigued by her remark, she had little opportunity to pursue things further anyway as the SOCO van chose that moment to pull in next to the CID car. Kate showed them through the house to the kitchen past a watchful Professor Dunbar. Then after a quick brief, she and Hayden left them to it.

'So, what next, MacDuff?' Hayden asked with a grin. 'We seem to be creating quite a few ripples in a very muddy pool.'

Kate nodded. 'There's certainly some interesting undercurrents bubbling away beneath the surface here,' she acknowledged, 'but they're nothing to do with us. We're here to investigate a burglary, so let's get on with doing just that, and I think our next step is to have a chat with Professor Dunbar's hippy neighbours.'

'Not walking there on that path Matlock pointed to, I hope.'

Kate smiled to herself, well aware of Hayden's aversion to any physical activity that didn't involve eating.

'Don't worry, Hayd,' she reassured. 'I think we'll drive there. We don't know what sort of a reception we might get.'

'In that case, "let there be love",' he said solemnly, quoting the old sixties hippy slogan and raising two fingers in the familiar peace sign.

* * *

They almost missed the track, and it was apparent why they had not seen it on the way in. It was badly overgrown with large trees and scrub and the fingerpost which had originally carried the direction sign had been broken off, leaving just the first part of the name.

There was a grass strip down the centre and as they followed it into a gloomy tunnel, they could hear the undergrowth scraping along both sides of the CID car.

'Good job it's an old motor,' Hayden commented. 'The new scratches should eventually blend in with all the others.'

Kate winced as one of the front wheels found a deep rut and churned for a second before coming out of it. 'Obviously our hippy squatters don't venture out much. At least, not by the main entrance.'

As she spoke, the track broadened out slightly and they emerged from the gloom on to a rough gravel area virtually overgrown with calf-high weeds. In front of them a ruined, grey, stone house minus much of its tiled roof reared up starkly against a backdrop of derelict sheds and open fields. An old green coach reminiscent of the glory days of the charabanc was parked to one side of the house, drawn curtains visible in the windows, and a decrepit looking green VW Camper van covered in hand-painted pink flowers stood alongside it. Several wigwam-style tents had been pegged into the ground on the other side and as they drove up, a number of figures dressed in jeans, a variety of garish tops and bandanas or floppy hats materialised from the ruins of the house.

One long-haired man with a distinct goatee beard, wearing a black waistcoat but no shirt, stepped in front of the car forcing Kate to come to an abrupt halt.

'Welcome, sister,' he said in a slightly amused, educated voice. 'Are you lost?'

Kate produced her warrant card and held it up against the window. He half-turned towards the motley collection of souls staring at the car from a short distance away. 'It's the fuzz, people,' he shouted back. 'One's a tasty chick.'

Kate climbed out of the car, forcing him to step back quickly. 'And you are?' she asked, noting the multitude of tattoos on his bare arms and chest and catching the distinct smell of patchouli oil off his clothes.

He grinned. 'A free spirit.'

She nodded, expecting that sort of response. 'And what name does this free spirit go by?'

'You can call me Adam if you like.'

'Adam what?'

'Adam whatever you like. Eve didn't need a surname and we don't deal in identities here either. They are the devices of Babylon.'

Kate sighed, well familiar with the term. She knew from her drug squad days that it was a reference to corrupt institutions or government and was an import from the Rastafarian movement in Jamaica.

'Maybe you'd like to continue this conversation down the nick then?'

He shrugged, looking completely unruffled. 'On what charge, my little piglet?'

'How about on suspicion of burglary?'

'Burglary where?'

40

'Moat House, next door, during the night.'

He shook his head. 'There can be no concept of burglary in our way of life. Ownership of property is itself theft and we do not believe in ownership of any kind. Our commune here acknowledges that everything is shared in the true spirit of peace and love.'

Kate ignored the spiel. She had heard it so many times before. 'Sadly, the rest of society doesn't share your generous philosophy. So, what were you doing in the barn at Moat House a week ago?'

He shrugged. 'Seemed like a good place for a kip. Nice soft blankets and some straw and that.'

'You don't deny you were there then?'

'Why should I deny it? I was committing no crime.'

'But do you deny breaking into the house last night? I don't think you said one way or the other just now.'

He held his hands out in front of him in an open gesture but said nothing.

Kate could feel the frustration building up inside her but controlled herself with an effort. 'Which is your vehicle?' she snapped.

He pointed at the VW.

'We need to search it.'

'Have you got a warrant?'

'We don't need one in these circumstances.'

'Oh, I think you do and I'm not giving you the keys anyway.'

Kate hesitated. She knew she might have grounds to search the car if it were on a public road and she had reasonable suspicion it contained illegal drugs or stolen property. But she knew that to use that power here on private land she would be stepping on very thin ice, even though he was actually trespassing. She had no evidence to suggest he was in possession of drugs and there was nothing to actually connect him to the break-in at the house. If she decided to take a chance and force the issue and he still refused to unlock the

41

car, what then? Would she be prepared to break a window to get into the vehicle? Obviously not.

'So, what have you got to hide?' Hayden cut in, anxious to lower the temperature.

Another shrug. 'That is for you to determine, old sport.'

Stalemate, and while Kate chewed her lip and Hayden fidgeted uneasily, her antagonist stood there with a broad grin on his face.

Hayden's sharp cough eventually broke the spell. Kate grimaced and climbed back into the CID car, staring the hippy out as she waited for Hayden to rejoin her. 'We'll be back,' she promised.

The other treated her to a half-bow. 'Always pleased to see the fuzz,' he said. 'Sorry we couldn't offer you any tea and biscuits.'

* * *

'We certainly sorted *him* out, didn't we?' Hayden commented sarcastically as they drove back to Moat House.

'There'll be other opportunities,' Kate replied, her face grim. 'Sooner or later the cocky little sod will overreach himself and then I'll be there to pull him down.'

'You believe he was responsible for the break-in, then?'

'It seems more than likely, don't you think? He freely admitted he was the man Matlock ejected from the barn, so it's a bit of a coincidence that he happened to be trespassing in the grounds just a week before. Also, the sort of stuff that was nicked last night — bread, milk, loose cash and so forth — was what someone sleeping rough would go for, isn't it? But unless SOCO can come up with something to positively tie him to the scene of the crime, that doesn't account for much, does it?'

'Maybe we should tackle things another way.'

'How so?'

'Well, instead of trying to link him to the burglary, con-centrate instead on finding out why he was in the barn in the first place. I mean, why would he need to doss there when he had a live-in motor less than a mile away? I think there's another dimension to this affair and don't forget Matlock's assertion that he was there for something much more personal than a doss and the knowing wink that accompanied his remark.'

'A woman. He was meeting a woman there. It had to be that.'

'*Was* meeting or had already met?'

There was an excited glint in Kate's eyes as she turned into the driveway of Moat House.

'Angela Dunbar?' she suggested, pulling up beside the SOCO van.

Hayden shrugged. 'Well, her father himself said she was neurotic, and you must admit, she did seem a bit flaky and rebellious when we spoke to her, showing contempt for him and reviling the rest of her family.'

'I think you've got something there. And she insisted on being called Cloud, didn't she? Which is a typical hippy name, like Autumn, Dawn and Leaf. You know, earth, wind and fire, Mother Nature and all that balls.'

'Exactly. Just the sort of anti-establishment type likely to be seduced by the alternative hippy culture—'

'And by one hippy in particular! Which means Matlock could have caught Adam and her, having it off in the barn?'

'*In flagrante delicto*,' he corrected pompously.

'What?'

He sighed and shook his head. 'Never mind. Just a nicer way of putting it.'

She tossed her head irritably at the implied rebuke. 'Can we just forget your stupid hang-ups about my language choices and concentrate instead on investigating a bloody burglary?'

He flushed, but before he could respond, a soft, slightly musical voice spoke almost at Kate's elbow. 'What's this? A detective domestic?'

Both of them had had their backs to the open front door and neither had heard the woman approach.

In her late forties to early fifties, tall and slim, with glossy black hair falling to her shoulders, she had the olive skin, dark-brown eyes and striking aquiline features of the Middle East. Dressed in a neat blue suit and high heels, she was clutching a set of ignition keys in her other hand, plainly on her way out somewhere.

'Yasmin Dunbar,' she said, betraying a faint American accent. A mocking smile hovered over her well-moulded lips, and she extended the hand with the keys towards Kate, briefly brushing her fingers.

'My husband told me you were here,' she went on, then released a soft, throaty chuckle. 'Not caught the dastardly felon yet, I presume?'

Kate shook her head. 'Not yet, ma'am. But we're working on it.'

'I am sure you are. And did Hubert introduce you to his hairy friends?'

Kate made a face. 'The spiders, you mean? Yes, he did. Creepy-crawlies are not my thing, though, I'm afraid.'

Another laugh. 'Mine neither and he's been obsessed with them ever since I've known him, travelling all over the world to find new specimens. But whatever turns you on, I suppose. The thing is, poor Hubert has spent so much time with creepy-crawlies, that I do believe he's actually turning into one himself. He certainly has all the right attributes of their kind too.'

She chuckled again, then flicking her wrist in a parting gesture, she crossed to the BMW car, and removed her shoes before climbing behind the wheel.

'Nice to meet you both,' she said through the open window. 'Maybe we'll chat again.'

Kate's eyes followed her as she drove off. 'Well, now,' she commented thoughtfully, 'that was a strange thing to say about your own husband.'

Hayden followed the direction of her gaze. 'Not if you're a member of this family,' he replied. 'And don't forget what the daughter said about him. Strikes me that there's no love lost between any of them.'

Kate nodded grimly. 'There are certainly dysfunctional relationships at play here,' she agreed. 'And I have the worrying suspicion that something is brewing within the undercurrent this has created that will ultimately lead to a lot more serious crime than a mere burglary.'

'What makes you say that?'

'Call it female intuition.'

He sighed. 'Ah, that remarkable gift you women have. Right.'

CHAPTER 5

The old shed was there at the end of the gravel path. Crouched among the gnarled apple trees. The patched wooden slats split and warped in places. The bitumen roof creased and torn.

It was happening all over again, and they would be waiting for her just like before. How they knew, she couldn't even begin to imagine, but she felt sure they were aware that she was coming, and the very thought terrified her.

There were always scores of them. Some so small you hardly knew they were there at all until they crept over your face or hands. Others a lot bigger and hairier, with bodies the size of five-penny pieces and long spindly legs that could move like lightning.

They lurked everywhere. Among the sacks of compost and leaking garden machinery. In the darkest corners. Out of reach of the weak strands of sunlight streaming in through the single skylight. Right up close to the vaulted roof in the thick, trailing webs that stretched between the wooden beams. Hiding. Watching. Waiting. Their multiple eyes probing the blackness. Their mandibles quivering in anticipation.

Over time, she had succeeded in squishing many of them. Shuddering as the still wriggling bodies were crushed to a slimy mess between her fingers. But there were always plenty more of them to come. In the end she'd been reduced to shrinking into a corner, screaming and sobbing in her panic-stricken hysteria.

Even as a ten-year-old, she had known that the spiders could not hurt her. There were no dangerous arachnids in Britain. But what got to her was the thought of all those hairy legs. The tiny glittering eyes reflected in the beam of the torch she had smuggled in with her. The grotesque way the creatures scuttled across the floor or dropped on to her head on the end of those long, sticky threads. Stoking her irrational, phobic dread of them that would be with her for the rest of her life.

Now the shed was in front of her once more. Its door shuddering open on rusty hinges. Its foul breath, a mix of rotting timber, creosote and stale engine oil, enveloping her in a noxious, invisible cloud as she was propelled inside. Then the door had slammed shut and the key turned in the lock behind her with a loud 'crack'. The glittering sequins materialised in the light of her torch almost immediately. Tiny, gimlet eyes that watched with a cold, calculating intensity. Something crawled across the back of her neck from her tangled mop of auburn hair and her left hand became enmeshed in a sticky cobweb. She could hear herself screaming. Choking and hyperventilating as she imagined she could feel other things crawling up her bare legs and under her short grey skirt. But there was no one to hear her. No one to care. Just the spiders that kept on coming . . .

'Kate! Kate!' the voice was literally bellowing in her ear, and she could feel a hand shaking her roughly by the arm.

She released her breath in a ragged, involuntary gasp and stared at the blazing light in her face. It looked at first sight like a powerful torch, but then, as her eyes accustomed themselves to the glare, she saw that it was a lamp on the coffee table beside her and just beyond it, Hayden's heavy-set figure, clad in a dressing gown, was bending over her, a concerned look on his chubby, good-natured face. She blinked hard several times to clear away the fug now clouding her brain. She remembered leaving the nick and later turning the key in the front door of their little cottage, but not much else, just a vision of the old shed and the spiders . . .

She hauled herself weakly up on the settee on which she had been lying, conscious of the perspiration trickling down her face and seeping through her thin blouse. The shade on the table lamp was skew-whiff, as if knocked sideways, and a broken wine glass lay in a pool of red beside the coffee table.

'Gordon Bennett!' Hayden exclaimed, straightening and stepping back from the settee, 'what on earth were you dreaming about?'

She took a deep breath and ran a hand through her long auburn hair. 'Bit of a nightmare, I think,' she said sheepishly. 'Too much red wine, probably. I must have dozed off when you went upstairs.'

'Dozed off?' he echoed, bending down to pick up the pieces of broken glass. 'Some doze. I was only in the shower for about twenty minutes, when I heard you screaming and ran down to find you throwing yourself about on the settee like someone in a fit. What was all that about?'

She sighed. 'Just a bad dream, Hayd. Nothing more. Forget it.' She gave a weak grin. 'Pity I spilled the wine, though. It was a rather expensive one.'

He grunted and deposited himself in the chair opposite. 'You were going on about something to do with spiders.'

'Just a bad dream, Hayd,' she repeated. 'Maybe it was a reaction after being shown Dunbar's creepy collection.'

He shook his head. 'There was more to it than that. Are you going to tell me about it?'

Her mouth tightened. 'There's nothing to tell,' she snapped. 'Just something that happened when I was a child. Forget it, will you?'

But he was not going to be put off that easily. 'It can help to talk about these things, you know. I remember an old pal of mine—'

'I said forget it, Hayd. *Capiche*?'

He frowned, met her gaze, then shrugged and capitulated. 'Your choice.'

'Exactly. Now, how about I make us both a nice cup of coffee before bed?'

Ostensibly the subject was closed, but even as she walked a little unsteadily across the room to the kitchen, the foul, cloying smell of the old shed came back to her, while other reawakened traumatic childhood memories started to gather on the edge of her tortured subconscious.

* * *

It had begun to rain in the early hours. Heavy bursts that rattled through the leaves of the trees and formed deep pools in the gravel hardstanding at the front of Moat House. The marshy land surrounding the property was soon a mire and the rhynes, already nearly full, were threatening to burst their banks. A small herd of Friesians stood dejectedly in the middle of an open-sided shed, making the most of its limited shelter. Twenty to thirty yards away a bedraggled, old fox, limped around the edge of the field after a recent encounter with a barbed wire fence. He braved the deluge and stopped to sniff the air for the scent of something that would provide him with his next meal. Other Levels denizens took full advantage of the sudden downpour. On a nearby riverbank, a pair of otters drawn excitedly from their holt by the rain, now pushed back through the miniature forest of reeds and bullrushes concealing the entrance to silently disappear beneath the choppy surface of the water, their coats gleaming in the shards of moonlight breaking through the heavy clouds.

The rain didn't bother the tall man in the waistcoat and jeans. He was already wet through. His shoulder-length hair was matted and hanging free of the bandana he usually wore, but his white teeth were bared in a wolfish grin as he trudged along the path from the ruined farm towards the tall chimneys of Moat House. It was well worth braving the rain for what he had lined up for himself.

He was confident that the naive young woman he had re-christened Cloud at the bogus hippy ceremony would turn up as usual. He had always been a draw for the ladies. A bit of rough for them to enjoy when they felt like breaking out of their boring, conventional lifestyles. She was easily his best conquest yet. What gave him even greater satisfaction was the fact that he was seducing the daughter of an upper-class establishment 'square'. One of the principal targets of the original hippy counterculture and therefore of the new naturalist or anarchist movement too. He would be moving on soon with the rest of his so-called commune. They never stayed that long in one place. The fact that he had no intention of taking her with him despite his promises did not trouble his conscience one iota. After all, free love without boundaries or responsibility was an integral part of the old hippy culture, wasn't it? A culture he was very much in favour of as a self-proclaimed naturalist. Or as Professor Dunbar would have described him, a spineless, work-shy waste of a skin.

Sadly, it wasn't as though he had not been given every opportunity to forge a first-class conventional life for himself. He was the well-educated son of a former police inspector and an ultra-religious grammar schoolteacher. Adam, real name Thomas Raymond Jackman, had been brought up in a strict Baptist regime and had won a scholarship to a prestigious university. But he had dropped out in his first 'freshers' year after getting involved with a disparate group of anti-establishment radicals preaching revolution and anarchy. He had been disowned by his own parents as a result.

Experimentation with illegal drugs had followed. Then, after resorting to selling crack cocaine and LSD on street corners to 'earn' enough money to survive in a succession of backstreet dives, he had ended up with a six-year prison sentence. On his release, he had returned to his old haunts, once again dealing in drugs, as well as shoplifting and breaking into houses. After picking up a further prison sentence of four years for burglary, he finally saw the red light and had thrown in his lot with a wandering group of hippies. They sang his song of a life of carefree idleness at the tax-payers' expense.

He had been with the same little group ever since, surviving on a mix of begging, state hand-outs, drug-pushing and the proceeds of theft and opportunist burglary. Now, at thirty-two, the irony was that he was just as trapped in his chosen way of life as the 'straights' he had once so despised. His parents were both dead, he had no family or friends apart from the commune and with his past history he was unemployable. Not that he would ever have considered taking up a job offer anyway.

On the face of it then, his long-term future could not have looked any bleaker. But fortunately for him, he was the sort of pseudo, opportunist hippy who refused to think long-term. He lived solely from day to day, and he fully agreed with the old maxim of letting the future take care of itself. To do that, though, he needed a decent meal ticket to keep him going and Angela Dunbar looked like being the best thing on offer for the time being. But he would have to be careful. That detective bitch would be looking for any excuse to feel his collar after their last contretemps and he had no desire to end up in stir yet again.

The double doors of the old barn were closed over when he arrived outside, but one opened with scarcely any effort. A paraffin lamp had been lit and it stood on an upturned beer barrel. Cloud, as she now called herself, emerged from a doorway to his right, wearing a denim shirt and jeans. Like him, she appeared to be soaked to the skin, her hair plastered over her forehead. She looked angry and he sensed it wasn't just because of the weather.

He grinned and gave her the peace sign. 'Cool night, eh, babe?'

She snorted. 'Don't give me that load of crap. Where the hell have you been? We agreed to meet here an hour ago. I thought you'd run out on me after the burglary at the house?'

He held both hands up against his chest in mock indignation. '*Qui moi?*'

'I'm serious.'

He stripped off his waistcoat, his bare chest wet and gleaming after his soaking. 'No way, babe. We need each other, you and me.'

Some of her anger faded. 'Daddy's furious about the break-in. The police have been to the house and the commune is now the number one suspect.'

He war-danced out of his jeans and kicked off his shoes, unashamedly standing naked in front of her. 'That figures. We get blamed for everything.'

She studied him, then shook her head. 'I'm not in the mood.'

He shrugged and wrung out his jeans. 'Your choice? Did you bring what you said you would?'

She fumbled in her pocket and pulled out a wad of sodden notes. 'This *is* for that woman's sick baby, isn't it?'

He took the wad with a smile, counted it and bent down to stuff the notes into a pocket of his jeans. 'Of course,' he lied. He knew full well there was no baby, just a convincing story for a gullible chick. 'As I told you, she is hiding from her abusive partner and dare not try to get proper medical help in case he manages to trace her. The child should recover quickly from the fever once she has the proper medicine. You have saved a life and you should feel very proud of what you've done.'

He could feel her eyes studying him hungrily.

'And you will take me with you when you move on?' she added, her fingers plucking uncertainly at the zip of her jacket.

'I promised, didn't I? Now, get out of those wet clothes.'

She shook her head. 'In a minute. First I've got something important to tell you.'

But as Jackman listened intently to what she had to say, unbeknown to either of them, there was a dark figure standing outside with one eye pressed against the lighted crack in the doors who saw and heard everything. Like the new-age hippy who called himself Adam, this particular eavesdropper was not bothered about the rain either. Getting a soaking was a small price to pay for what he had discovered by following the young woman out into the night. Allegedly, Sir Francis Bacon had once said that knowledge was power, and Julian Dunbar had every intention of using that power to the best possible advantage for himself.

CHAPTER 6

Kate felt her stomach lurch when she pushed through the doors of the CID office the following morning. Charlie Woo was sitting behind the desk in the DI's glass-panelled inner sanctum. He looked up as she crossed the room to her desk and set her briefcase down beside it. Then he gave her an extravagant wave, indicating that she should join him. She made a face and stopped by the coffee machine to pour herself a black coffee on the way.

'Kate,' he began as she stepped into his office and closed the door behind her. 'I need to talk to you.'

She faced her dapper colleague and leaned against the wall, sipping her coffee slowly to try and hide her nerves.

'I don't really know what to say,' he said. 'This should be your office. I feel like a usurper.'

She took a deep breath. 'Don't let it bother you, Charlie. All's fair in love and war, as they say. And I'm not the only one to be disappointed. Jamie Foster would've been acting DS in my place if I'd got the job. But congratulations anyway.'

'I hope we can still work together nevertheless.'

'Of course. For as long as I am still here anyway.'

He frowned. 'That sounds ominous. You're not going to walk away, are you? We were already light of another DS when DS Percival got the Acting DI position before me, and now he's been made up to substantive DI at HQ, it doesn't look like we're going to get a replacement for him any time soon. To lose you as well would be a total calamity.'

She took another sip of her coffee. 'We shall have to see what happens, Charlie. I haven't made my mind up yet.'

He nodded. 'Look, Kate, I know how disappointed you must be, but we've always been good friends, and I hope this won't scupper our friendship.'

Kate could sense his embarrassment and forced a brief smile, keen to dispel any suspicion of sour grapes. 'I don't blame you at all, Charlie. My argument isn't and never will be with you.'

He nodded, his relief showing through. 'I'm glad about that because I will need all the support you can give me.'

She gulped some more coffee, this time to disguise emerging tears. 'You've got it, one hundred per cent.'

He sighed. 'Thank you. I appreciate that, I really do. I'll, er, leave you to get yourself settled back in.'

He held out his hand and after a brief hesitation, she came off the wall and shook it. Then she left the awkward atmosphere in the office behind and returned to her desk, feeling the eyes of the office manager and the other detectives seated behind their own desks flicking furtively in her direction and looking away again.

Due to the fact that it was only her second day back from sick leave, her 'in' tray was not nearly as full as usual, and she did her best to hide behind the stack of trays that usually held bundles of files and other documents. She tried hard to concentrate on what paperwork there was, but only succeeded in spilling some of her coffee as her trembling hand raised the plastic cup to her lips.

In the end, after over an hour, she could stand the tension in the room no longer. Pushing back her chair, she tapped a paperweight sharply on the desktop.

'Listen up, you lot,' she said in a loud voice that had just the suggestion of a quaver. Bodies swivelled round in chairs and half a dozen faces stared back at her.

She cleared her throat. 'I just want to clear the air. You will all know that I was due to take over the department this week as Acting DI. Well, it ain't going to happen now. Charlie Woo will be leading us instead and I want to emphasise that he will get my full unequivocal support, which means yours too. That's all I want to say. Now, let's get on with the job we're paid to do.'

Her legs were shaking as she sat down again, but to her astonishment the whole office jumped to their feet, clapping enthusiastically and giving her a rousing cheer. She nodded her thanks. She had done it.

Hayden met her down in the canteen half an hour later with a broad, satisfied grin. 'I'm so proud of you, old girl,' he said, drawing up a chair. 'It must have taken a lot to do what you've just done.'

'Thanks. Yes, it did.'

He scratched his nose. 'Er, does that mean you have given up on this daft idea of resigning?'

She studied him levelly. 'You'll be the first to know, Hayd,' she replied. 'The very first.'

* * *

CID had a visitor when Kate and Hayden returned to the office. She could see him talking to Charlie Woo in the DI's inner sanctum and her eyes narrowed when she saw who the visitor was.

She had never liked Detective Chief Inspector Toby Ricketts, the head of the local CID and Charlie Woo's boss. In his early thirties with sharp blue eyes, blond hair and a matching moustache, he was always immaculately turned out, even down to his manicured fingernails and highly polished black shoes. Originally a graduate-entry candidate, he had been seen as a high-flyer, earmarked for accelerated promotion, and he had been fast-tracked to his present rank. But he was a company 'yes' man and Kate didn't trust him. A view shared by her previous, now deceased boss, DI Ted Roscoe, who had said he was about as reliable as a broken wristwatch.

It was unusual to see Ricketts outside his own office, which was now at Bridgwater police station. He usually stuck to the telephone or email. She was therefore immediately suspicious of his visit.

She soon found out why he had 'graced the department with his presence' when he stuck his head round the door and rapped, 'Sergeant. Come in here, please.'

Making a face at Hayden, who had returned to his desk on the far side of the room, she complied, automatically closing the door of the DI's office behind her.

'I gather you are investigating a burglary at Moat House,' Ricketts said, a sour expression on his face.

'Yes, sir. A very minor job. Looks like the work of a dosser.'

'So I believe. You will no doubt be aware that Professor Dunbar is carrying out extremely important research into the neurotoxins in spider venom.'

'Yes, sir. He gave me a grand tour of his lab.'

'Did he indeed? Well, he is a very eminent man whose work is being funded by the government in partnership with a number of other major institutions. It is imperative that nothing is allowed to interfere with this research. Especially not a break-in perpetrated by some long-haired hippy who thinks the world owes him a living.'

'We don't yet have enough evidence to prove that the hippy is actually the perp, sir. He's only sus at the moment.'

'Is that right? Well, I suggest you put a little more effort into things and get that proof. Professor Dunbar has been on the phone to me this morning, concerned that the same thing could happen again. He asked for a permanent police presence at the house. Of course, I told him that that was not possible, but I did say you would be redoubling your efforts and would be investigating the crime as an absolute priority. So I suggest you do just that, and make sure you get a result p.d.q. I'm quite sure the DI here will be able to supply you with any additional resource you might need. Right, Mr Woo?'

Woo coughed, looking distinctly uncomfortable, and nodded almost apologetically to Kate. 'Of course, sir. But I have to say that we are a bit short-handed at the moment and our caseload is very—'

'Every confidence in you, Mr Woo,' Ricketts cut in dismissively and opened the door. 'So, I'll leave it with you then. Keep me informed.'

On his way out, he half-turned and stared directly at Kate. 'Oh, incidentally, Sergeant, so sorry you missed out on the acting rank. Very disappointing for you.' But he was unable to completely hide his smirk of satisfaction as he left.

'Pillock!' Kate breathed at his disappearing back.

Woo sighed. 'Don't mind him, Kate,' he said. 'I worked with the man at Bridgwater nick long enough to know that he can't help it. I think he must have had a charisma bypass. Now, you'd better bring me up to speed on this Moat House break-in. But I warn you, there are no additional resources I can give you despite what the DCI promised. From what I've been able to see since I arrived, everyone in the department is well tucked up on a multitude of jobs. I can let you have Hayden and Jamie Foster for two or three days, but that's it.'

'No word on a new skipper being appointed then? It seems we've been riding light of a second DS like for ever.'

He shook his head. 'Not so much as a whisper.'

'You're certainly inherited a poisoned chalice as DI then.'

He shrugged and grinned. 'Could have been you, couldn't it?'

'Thanks for rubbing it in.'

'Just do your level best to crack this one early, will you, Kate. I need a result to satisfy Ricketts like yesterday.'

She nodded. 'No pressure then?' she said drily.

* * *

Hayden was sitting at his desk when Kate left Woo's office. 'What was all that about, then?' he asked, swivelling round to face her. 'Ricketts looked his usual charming self.'

'Moat House is apparently top of our agenda,' she replied, staring critically at what looked like a fresh coffee stain on his shirt. 'So we need to do a lot more rapid digging. First, I want you to check with our local intelligence officer. See what Dave Gort can find out about the so-called hippy commune and in particular that cocky arsehole, Adam. After that, do a PNC check on the beaten-up VW that was parked on the site. I happened to notice while we were sitting there that you scribbled down the registration number.'

He nodded. 'Ever the boy scout, that's me.'

'Dib, dib, bloody dob! Just make sure you've got all the SP for me when I get back.'

'Back? So, where are you going?'

'Moat House again. I think the break-in needs some more in-depth inquiries before the trail goes totally cold.' She threw a glance across the room at Jamie Foster, the only other detective left in the office.

'Fancy a trip out, Jamie?' she said. 'There's a nice puzzle to unravel.'

He grinned and stood up, stretching his slim, whippet-like frame. 'Always like puzzles, skipper.'

On the way to the door, she threw him a quizzical glance. 'Sorry you lost your acting DS job because they cancelled mine.'

He shrugged, the smile on his boyish face unchanged. 'No probs, Kate,' he said. 'We can commiserate together.'

* * *

'Father's out,' Julian Dunbar snapped when he answered the front door. 'Won't be back till later.'

Kate eased him aside and walked through into the hallway. 'We haven't come to see your father, Julian,' she replied.

'Then who?'

'Well, you'll do for a start. We need to interview everyone about the burglary.'

The sneer was back on his face. 'Why?'

'Just routine. To see if anyone might have spotted or heard anything that could help us with our investigation. This is my colleague, DC Jamie Foster. Is there anywhere we can chat?'

He shrugged. 'Might as well use the sitting room. No one else ever does.'

Seated on a large chintzy settee, with Foster to her left, Kate had the opportunity to study the young man more closely as he lounged in an armchair opposite. He was still dressed in his creased, fawn T-shirt and green combat style trousers, and his shoulder-length, black hair looked tangled and unkempt. It suggested that it had not seen any shampoo or even a comb for quite some time. His thin, pinched face was exceptionally pale with rashes of acne on both cheeks and neck, and his brown eyes blinked constantly behind the thick lenses of his horn-rimmed glasses.

'How old are you, Julian?' she asked with a smile.

'What's that got to do with anything? I'm twenty, if you must know.'

'And you live here permanently?'

'Pretty obvious, I would have thought, even for a copper.'

It was at this point that Kate decided she really didn't like Julian Dunbar at all.

'Well, obvious or not, I have to ask it,' she said, her smile disappearing and her gaze hardening. 'You see, I have a job to do, and I need your cooperation to do it. After all, it's for your benefit that we are here.'

He smirked. 'Not for my benefit. It's the old man's place that got screwed, not mine, so it's his lookout. I just have a room here.'

'And where is this room?'

'Right at the back of the house, just down the hall from dear old mater and pater. And before you ask me, no, I didn't see or hear anything on the night of the burglary. I was sparko.'

'You say you live here permanently. So you're not between terms at uni or anything?'

'Dropped out. All a load of Neanderthals and queers there.'

'And you don't work?'

He sneered at her. 'No, but I would hardly screw this place for a hundred quid if that's what you're implying. I'm not that hard up. Anyway, the old man gives us all a monthly living allowance.'

'And why would you think we were suggesting you had anything to do with the burglary?' Foster put in, having already been briefed by Kate on the way to the house about the circumstances of the case.

'No idea. But you said you needed to interview everyone here. Why else would you want to do that?'

'We always need to question people at the scene of a crime in case they witnessed anything,' Foster continued quietly, unfazed by Dunbar's aggressive response. 'It's standard police procedure.'

'Yes,' Kate added, 'and you seem like the sort of lad who notices things.'

Dunbar smirked again, his eyes lighting up at the compliment 'I know lots of things that are going on in this shithole. None of it escapes my notice.'

'What sort of things?' Kate encouraged.

He shrugged. 'You'd be surprised. Nothing is what it seems, and the old man is too wrapped up with his stupid spider collection to see what's going on under his very nose.'

'Oh? So, what *is* going on then?' Foster put in again.

'Not for me to say, but it's all up here.' He tapped his temple with one forefinger. 'Every little detail. All stored and ready to come out when the time comes.'

'Pity you don't seem to have a clue as to who broke into the house, if you know so much,' Foster goaded.

'Maybe I do. But I wouldn't tell you anyway. Dear Father had it coming, so tough titty.'

'You don't seem to like your father.'

'No one who knows him likes him. Ask anyone in the family what they think of him, and they'll tell you what an arsehole he is.'

'How come he's an arsehole? You said yourself that he gives you all a monthly allowance. That strikes me as quite generous.'

'It's got nothing to do with generosity. He does it because he has to. End of.'

'Why does he have to?'

'Look bad to the outside world if he didn't provide for his family, wouldn't it? And he doesn't like scandal. Would ruin his precious reputation.' He stood up suddenly. 'Now, if you've finished wasting my time with stupid questions, I've got some jobs to do.'

'One further thing,' Kate said suddenly. 'When I spoke to your sister, she asked me if anyone had told me about someone called Gillian George. Can you tell me what she meant by that?'

Just for a second, he seemed to freeze. But then his sneer was back with a vengeance. 'No idea,' he replied. 'Sis is a silly cow anyway. Says a lot of stupid things.'

Then without another word he simply stalked from the room.

'Nice beauty,' Foster commented, now also on his feet.

Kate grunted and followed him out of the room. 'From what I've seen of this dysfunctional family so far, I suspect there's not much to choose between any of them,' she replied.

'So what was all that about Gillian George?'

'I haven't the faintest. I just suddenly remembered Angela Dunbar asking me if anyone had mentioned her to me, but she didn't say why. Probably nothing at all to do with this case, but I don't like unanswered questions.'

'It all sounds pretty weird.'

'This whole house seems weird to me. Anyway, let's take a fresh look at the crime scene. See if anything comes to mind other than what we already know.'

There was a plump, grey-haired woman, dressed in an apron, in the kitchen who appeared to be stirring some sort of stew on the range. The pleasant, spicy smell filled the kitchen, reminding Kate's murmuring stomach that it was approaching dinner time. She noticed that the broken windowpane had been boarded up and the room completely restored to normal.

'You must be Mrs Matlock?' Kate said.

The woman's suspicious frown abruptly vanished when she produced her warrant card. 'That's me. And you must be the detectives what's here about the burglary.'

Kate nodded. 'I gather some money, food and wine was stolen?'

Matlock continued stirring the pot. 'Aye. Made a proper mess of my kitchen they done an' all. Thievin' buggers.'

'You have no idea who they could have been, I suppose?'

'Not the slightest and I wouldn't want to know neither.'

'Seen no strangers hanging about here at all, have you?'

'Wouldn't have noticed if they was. Too busy cleaning or doin' the cooking. I do all the meals for the professor and his family, see. Breakfast, lunch and dinner. The youngsters come down at the set times if they want to eat. More often than not they don't. Always out somewhere, they be, but that's up to them, o'course. Food's still there.'

'So how long have you been working here?'

'Here?' She wrinkled her freckled brow for a moment. 'Must be all of twenty years now. Colonel Buxton took me and Josh on when he inherited the place from his father. Then the colonel died about three years ago and Professor Dunbar bought the place but kept us on.'

Matlock pushed past her to pick up a shallow dish containing what smelled like strong spices from the worksurface and tipped it into the pot she was stirring.

'Does it bother you what Professor Dunbar does for a living?'

'What, all them spiders, you mean?' She made a face. 'Horrible things. But nowt to do with me. Long as he keeps them in his little room in the annexe and they don't come into the laboratory when I do me weekly clean, I'm happy.' She released a sudden shriek of laughter. 'I'd need a change of knickers if they ever scuttled through the door.'

Kate smiled. 'How do you get on with the family?'

Abruptly the woman stiffened. 'I does me work, and I leaves them to do whatever they likes,' she replied. 'Nothin' to do with me.'

From the woman's sudden change of demeanour, Kate sensed that it was not worth pursuing that particular avenue any further. But turning to leave, she added, 'Did you know Gillian George?'

Matlock turned quickly to stare at her and nodded. 'Tragic business that were.' She lowered her voice. 'But the professor don't like no one talking about it. Too painful for him, I reckons.'

'Who was she?'

There was a heavy sigh. 'Pretty little thing. Used to come in here sometimes to pinch me gingerbread.'

'She used to live here then?'

'Had a room upstairs. Only temporary, like, when she was workin'. Lived with her mum out at some place in the Cotswolds when she weren't, I think . . . Some place called Burford, yes, that was it. Used to go home weekends.'

'What happened?'

Matlock shook her head, her mouth tightening. 'You should ask the professor. Not my place to gossip about the family. Now, you'd best be off, miss. I've got to get on with the evenin' dinner. Unlike the rest of the family, the professor and his good lady will be there in the dining room dead on time as usual and as I said before, Mr Dunbar don't like meals to be late.'

Kate hesitated, another question forming on her lips, but a warning furrowing of brows from Foster persuaded her not to probe any further.

'Good luck with the dinner, Mrs Matlock,' she said instead, but there was no response as they left the room.

'This Gillian George thing has got you, skipper, hasn't it?' Foster commented.

'Well, you must admit it's strange how everyone clams up when you mention her name.'

Foster shrugged. 'Not really. Personal tragedy can sometimes have that effect on people, and I can't see something like that having any relevance to a dosser breaking into a house and raiding the kitchen.'

She gave a rueful smile. 'You're probably right. But it's a pity Angela Dunbar doesn't appear to be about just now. Then I could have asked her a couple more questions to clear up the mystery and satisfy my curiosity.'

He laughed. 'You know what they say. Curiosity killed the cat. It's something that's certainly caused you enough problems in the past.'

'Ain't that the truth,' she muttered bitterly to herself, thinking of how that had probably contributed to her loss of Acting DI rank. 'Nice of you to remind me.'

CHAPTER 7

Kate was still dwelling on her recent humiliation when they left the house and that was probably why she didn't hear the sports car approaching. Foster pulled her back out of the way just in time as the car skidded to a stop on the gravel hard-standing just in front of her, kicking up gravel.

'I say, steady on,' the man behind the wheel shouted. 'Nearly had you there.'

Kate raised a hand apologetically as Howard Dunbar drove on and pulled up just past the front door. She watched him climb out of the car and waited for him to walk over to her. He looked to be in his early thirties and was dressed in a cloth cap and tweeds, reminding her of one of the characters out of the old film, *Genevieve*.

'Sorry about that,' she said. 'I was miles away then.'

He laughed. 'Wouldn't do to run down one of our finest, would it? Might prove a tad difficult to explain to the coroner.'

Kate half-turned to indicate Foster with a wave of one hand. 'My colleague, DC Jamie Foster.'

He nodded, oozing boyish charm. 'And what brings you back here? Looks like you can't keep away from the place.'

'Just continuing inquiries into the burglary. In fact, you turned up at the most convenient moment. Mind having a quick chat with us?'

He shrugged. 'My pleasure.' He laughed again. 'Should I confess now? It was the red wine I was really after, Your Worship. Can't leave the stuff alone.'

Kate humoured him with another smile. 'We won't keep you long, Mr Dunbar.'

'Hey, Howard, please.'

Like Julian, he showed them both into the sitting room, and waved them to a couple of armchairs. There was a small cocktail cabinet in a corner, and he opened it and produced a bottle of brandy.

'Mind if I . . . ?' he began, holding it up for inspection. 'Always like a drink before dinner, which I can smell is already in the offing.'

'Please do,' Kate replied and shook her head when he held out a crystal glass. 'We're on duty, I'm afraid.'

He nodded, half-filled the glass and dropped on to the settee facing them. 'So, how can I help you?' he went on, taking a gulp.

'I gather you live on the premises?'

'We all do. Me, Angela — correction, Cloud — and Julian. I have a self-contained apartment on the far side of the house.'

'Did you see or hear anything unusual the night of the burglary?'

'Not a sausage. I tend to sleep heavily, and my apartment is nowhere near the kitchen anyway.'

'If you don't mind my asking, what is your line of work?'

'Helping the old man most of the time. I'm a qualified accountant, you see, so I do his books and usually accompany him on his travels overseas, arranging flights, accommodation, that sort of thing.'

'Hunting for spider specimens?'

'Not me. Hate the bloody things. I leave Sam, er, Dr Samantha Lawrence, to get up close and personal with them.'

'Your father's assistant?'

'Yes, she's as much in love with the hairy horrors as he is.'

'She doesn't live here, though?'

'No. Got a cottage down the road, though she seems to spend more time in this house than in her own home. It's Mrs Matlock's pastries, I reckon.'

Kate slipped one in quickly now that a natural opening had been created. 'Just like Gillian George with her gingerbread, I suppose.'

At once the grin left his face and he seemed to stiffen. 'Gillian? What do you know about her?'

'Your sister asked me if anyone had told me about her, but no one seems to want to do so.'

He looked annoyed. 'Well, she's no business to have said anything. What happened to Gillian is a delicate, private matter that has nothing whatsoever to do with the burglary.'

Kate was noted for her brass neck, and she refused to take the hint.

'Family, was she?'

'She worked for Father.'

'What happened to her?'

'She, er, died. It was tragic.'

'How did it happen?'

He dismissed the question with an angry shake of his head and jumped to his feet. 'Look, I've said it's private and anyway, it has nothing to do with the burglary. I suggest you confine your questions to that and leave other matters that do not concern you alone.'

Then he simply walked out of the room, his face ashen.

Foster emitted a chuckle. 'Well, you certainly touched a nerve there, Kate. If you don't mind my saying, though, it does seem a bit out of order quizzing members of the family about a personal tragedy that is plainly unconnected with the break-in.'

Kate frowned. 'So what made Angela Dunbar specifically refer to it in the first place? There has to be a reason.'

'To draw your attention away from the investigation perhaps.'

'And why would she do that unless she was the one who did the job?'

He shrugged. 'No idea, but if it was a diversionary tactic, it seems to have worked. You look to be hung up on Gillian George, and with respect, if that's the case, there's a real danger you could lose proper focus on the break-in.'

'Nonsense. I am just curious.'

'Curious about what?' A short laugh. 'Forgive me, Kate, but we seem to have discussed that trait of yours not long ago.'

'Bollocks.'

'Charmed, I'm sure.'

* * *

Charlie Woo was still sitting in his office when Kate and Jamie Foster returned to the police station, apparently poring over a thick file. But the general office was deserted. Clearly everyone else was still out on other inquiries. Hayden pushed through the main doors moments later, evidence of a recent trip to the canteen apparent from the crumbs still attached to his chin and the front of his shirt. He had a buff-coloured file in one hand and was beaming with self-satisfaction.

'Thomas Raymond Jackman, CRO,' he said, slapping the file triumphantly on Kate's desk.

'Who?'

'Alias our hippy, Adam.'

'Ah!' Kate opened it and carried out a brief scan. 'Thirty-two years old. Cons for supplying crack cocaine and LSD, burglary and shoplifting. Total of ten years inside—'

'Though overall, he only actually served half that term,' Hayden pointed out. 'Released under the automatic early release policy.'

'Nice to see good old British justice is still working then?' she said sarcastically. 'With his form, he has to be a key suspect for the burglary. How did you manage to ID him?'

'Through the LIO record of a stop-check on the A39 a month ago by Traffic. They pulled him over driving that VW Camper van of his. No offences found, but he had to give his real name and produce his docs. They were suspicious of him and sent LIO details for file. When I checked PNC, I found that the description of the driver matched our arrogant hippy to a T. Admittedly, he looks a lot younger in the photo held on his CRO record and he's shown as clean-shaven, but the date of birth he gave is the same as that of the VW driver and it's plainly him.'

'I'm not surprised he was stopped if he was driving that flowery wreck of his.'

Hayden chuckled. 'Yes, and the cheeky so and so gave Mason's Farm as his regular address.'

'Which suggests he has no intention of going anywhere else in the immediate future.'

'Exactly. I wonder what's keeping him here.'

'More than likely Moat House and possibly, as we discussed before, the right little madam who lives there. All the signs are pointing to the fact that he's seeing to her, but maybe there's more to it than that. He could be bleeding her of cash on one pretext or another as well as being behind the burglary. After all, the family appear to be loaded.'

'Not being in at the start of this inquiry,' Foster interjected, 'by "madam", I assume you are referring to the young woman you told me about. Hubert Dunbar's daughter, Angela?'

Kate nodded. 'Or Cloud as she calls herself now. The gardener, Josh Matlock, allegedly found Jackman asleep in a barn on the premises about a week ago and chased him off. We think there was more to it than that and Matlock was being discreet to protect Angela Dunbar. In short, our hippy wasn't just sleeping there but had been caught . . . what was that phrase you used, Hayden?'

'*In flagrante delicto.*'

Foster chuckled. 'Trust you to come up with a fancy expression like that.'

'Not me,' Hayden replied modestly. 'It's from the Latin.'

'Well, I get the meaning anyway. And presumably that is why you're thinking that if Jackman did the burglary, Angela may have helped him?'

'That's about the strength of it, yes, but we haven't any evidence to connect either of them to it. It just seems a plausible scenario in the circumstances.'

'But you haven't tackled Angela yet about her possible connections with Jackman?'

Kate shrugged. 'How could we? We haven't any real evidence and anyway, even if she was at it with him in the barn, so what? She's on her own turf and from the look of her, she's well over age, which means she can shag anyone she likes.'

'So we keep the info in our back pocket for the time being?'

'Until we have a use for it, yes.'

Foster pursed his lips in thought. 'If Jackman did screw the house, it's possible she didn't know anything about it.'

'Of course it is, but it's also possible that she actively helped him do the job as a way of getting back at a father whom she plainly detests.'

Foster grunted. 'There certainly seems to be a wealth of intrigue in this case.'

'You can say that again. The old man has a persona like Dracula and seems to be pretty unpopular with at least two of his offspring. Even his wife doesn't appear to be that enamoured with him. As for his youngest son, Julian, he is an arrogant little sod and a real weirdo who allegedly creeps about spying on everyone. I haven't made my mind up yet about the older son, Howard, but the daughter, Angela, is, as I said just now, a right little madam, and as flaky as you can get. Then there's this mystery over Hubert Dunbar's former assistant, Gillian George, who no one seems to want to talk about, but who apparently died tragically somehow—'

'All of which has nothing whatsoever to do with the burglary we are supposed to be investigating, of course,' Foster reminded her mildly.

Kate gave a rueful smile. 'As you keep telling me, Jamie, but despite all you've said, I am still nonplussed as to why Angela mentioned Dunbar's former assistant in the first place.'

Hayden coughed and glanced at his watch. 'Maybe it's something worth sleeping on. There's nothing more we can do tonight.'

Kate's gaze quickly swept the empty office, noting the greying light outside the window, and she reluctantly took the hint. 'Okay, point taken. Maybe we should have an early night.'

'Not before we all have a swift half down the Black Cock,' Charlie Woo said directly behind them. 'I'm sure some of the others will already be down there and I'm buying.'

Kate raised an eyebrow. 'If you put it like that, guv,' she said, 'how could we possibly refuse?'

CHAPTER 8

Nightmares again as old, bruised memories returned. Kate was back in the shed with the spiders and yet it wasn't a shed anymore, but a metal box and the creatures were crawling all over her. She twisted and turned, hammering in a panic on the lid of the box, trying in vain to force it open. There was someone in there with her, too. No, not someone, *something*. It was lying right beside her, cold and wet and there was a strong, unpleasant stench all around her. Then a crack of light as the metal lid opened a fraction. She saw she wasn't in a box at all, but the boot of a car and the thing beside her was a dead body. A wrinkled old man with staring eyes and a slack mouth from which the spiders were streaming in their hundreds. She tried to scream, but no sound came out and the boot lid slammed shut again. She heard the sound of an engine, and something seized the car in a vice-like grip, piercing the thin body with giant teeth and lifting it off the ground. She could feel it being swung to one side and then the terrifying truth dawned on her. It was the big crane she had seen before. It had picked up the car in its giant claw and was swinging it towards the crusher. The next instant the claw released its grip, and the car was falling, dropping into the crusher's open mouth, as the corpse beside her released a hideous baying laugh . . .

She awoke in a cold sweat, her whole body shaking and her heart pounding with a stressed rasping note. Moonlight stole into the room through a gap in the curtains. Beside her, Hayden snored on as usual, completely dead to the world. Nothing save an exploding pie factory would waken him once he was asleep, she thought cynically.

Rolling over on to her side, she peered at the luminous dial of the bedside clock. It registered 3 a.m. She swung her legs over the edge of the bed and ran a hand through her mass of auburn hair. She felt dizzy and sick.

The psychiatrist had warned her that her recovery would take time. 'You suffered concussion and a severe trauma on that last case of yours,' he'd said. 'There could be relapses.'

She gritted her teeth, remembering all too vividly that horrific episode in the scrapyard. Of being waylaid and dumped in the boot of the car earmarked for the crusher by the madman she had been pursuing. Shut in the claustrophobic darkness with the corpse of his last victim for company. She had never forgotten the smell of that boot. The stench of petrol mixed with that of leaking body fluids. It had been with her, day and night ever since. But she had thought she was coming to terms with it all. With the help of expert counselling and the tablets she had been prescribed by the 'trick cyclist', the nightmares she had experienced had begun to fade. But now it looked like she was regressing. The spiders in Dunbar's lab had reawakened her long-held arachnophobia. First, opening the doors of her subconscious to memories of her tortured childhood, then acting as a trigger for the release of the more recent horrors she thought the therapy had helped her to pack away for good.

She had to get a grip before she fell to pieces completely. Heading to the bathroom, she turned on the shower and stood for a long time under its hot jets, feeling her body relax and that simple physical act gradually restore her mind to some sense of rationality.

She was no longer in the boot of the car, facing that horrific end. It was in the past and could not be repeated.

Her would-be killer was dead and lying at the bottom of a well. As for the old shed, that had been years ago, when she was a child, and her stepfather was also dead. The shed was gone too. She remembered the night she had crept out of the house in her nightdress and gumboots to torch it, though no one had ever found out. She had actually been guilty of committing a crime then and now here she was, a police detective investigating crimes. The irony of the situation was not lost on her, and she couldn't help allowing herself a small humourless smile.

Drying herself with more vigour than was absolutely necessary, she spent some time combing out her long hair, then slipped on a robe and went downstairs to the kitchen. There was no point going back to bed as she knew she wouldn't sleep anymore. So instead, she made herself a coffee and sat at the breakfast bar, sipping it slowly and turning things over in her mind as she watched the dawn light strengthen outside the window.

She had to make up her mind what she wanted to do about the job. The nightmares had given her cause to refocus her attention on how she saw her future. Her near breakdown after the last case and then her rejection for the acting rank position had certainly shaken her confidence. She'd always felt she was strong enough to take on anything, but now she felt empty and lost, with the present case testing her resilience and motivation to the extreme. She had always wanted to be a police officer and had worked so hard to get where she was. But had it all been worth it? More importantly, did she want to go on anymore? That was a decision that only she could make.

Whatever her final decision was going to be, she was determined to at least see this case through to the end. Quitting in the middle of something was not her style. But staying with it meant resolving some key issues which she could not see her doing without treading on some very sensitive corns. That was until the strident voice of the telephone cut through her deliberations.

'Kate?' Jamie Foster's voice queried. 'Sorry to wake you, but there's been a development.'

'I wasn't asleep. What's the development?'

'Control called me out after some guy was nabbed by uniform breaking into a local pub and I thought you'd like to know.'

But Kate was already ahead of him. 'Not our hippy?'

'Spot on. Your old friend Adam, otherwise known as Thomas Raymond Jackman.'

'I'll be right over.'

'Thought you might.'

* * *

Kate left Hayden still sleeping. Even the ring of the telephone and her getting ready hadn't wakened him and she was out of the house and en route to Highbridge police station within minutes.

Foster was in the CID office, no longer his smart, dapper self, but dressed in a roll-neck sweater and black threadbare jeans. He was unshaven, his tousled hair only lightly combed and his eyes heavy-lidded. He had a plastic cup of black coffee in one hand.

Kate grinned. 'You shouldn't have had that scotch on top of the red wine last night,' she said. 'What is it they say, don't mix the grape and the grain?'

He made a face. 'Thanks for the advice,' he said. 'But it's a bit late for that now.'

'So, what about our friend Adam?' she said, plonking herself on the corner of a desk as usual.

He took a sip of the coffee. 'Starlight Arms down the road. Licensee, George Turner, lives above and heard one of the side windows go about two a.m. Used his common sense and rang us before going downstairs to investigate. Confronted Jackman in the public bar as he was emptying the till. Unfortunately for him, Turner is an ex-boxer, built like a brick shithouse, and he immediately clocked him one without so much as an introduction. Jackman has one of the best shiners I've ever seen.'

'Where is he now, in the pokey?'

Foster nodded. 'Bleating about making a complaint of assault. Bloody cheek. But there's more to tell you, too.'

'Go on.'

'Uniform found what appears to be Jackman's VW Camper parked in an alleyway behind the pub. They searched it and guess what? They found two bottles of vintage Châteauneuf-du-Pape in a locker inside. One was empty and the other just half full.'

Kate's eyes gleamed. 'Brilliant. Got him at last!'

She borrowed Jamie's cup for a moment and took a sip of his coffee before returning it to him.

'Interview Room 1, I think,' she said.

'I'll set it up and join you there.'

* * *

Thomas Jackman was wheeled into the interview room in handcuffs by a uniformed constable and motioned to a chair facing Kate and Jamie. He was pale and dishevelled, and sporting a swollen left eye which had already started turning mauve.

'Nice to see you again, Adam,' Kate said, enjoying the moment. 'You really don't look well.'

'Very funny!' he retorted, his voice no longer polished like before, but coarse and hostile.

'Come on now,' she said reprovingly, 'where's all that love and peace gone?'

'Just get this over with,' he snarled. 'I need a kip.'

Kate turned, switched on the tape-recording machine behind her and when the continuous high-pitched note died, she went through the usual formalities, naming herself, Foster and Jackman as present and warning Jackman that he was still under caution.

'Mr Jackman, you know why you have been arrested, don't you?'

He lurched forward in his chair. 'I want to make a complaint against that bastard landlord. He belted me in the face. Look at my eye.'

She remained impassive. 'I said, do you know why you have been arrested?'

'Yes, I know. Hands up, I screwed his pub and broke into the bar till. Okay? Can I go back to my cell now?'

'Not quite. We have a few more questions to ask you about another matter.'

He threw a one-eyed gaze at the ceiling. 'Not that bloody job at Moat House again?'

For the benefit of the tape, Kate gave precise details of the Moat House burglary, then studied him for a moment.

'So, Mr Jackman, you will recall that we spoke to you about the burglary two days ago at Mason's Farm and you denied committing the crime. Do you still deny being the person responsible?'

''Course I do. Had nothing to do with it.'

'Do you know Angela Dunbar, or Cloud as she now calls herself? The daughter of the householder.'

He shook his head. 'No.'

'Did you meet up with her in a barn on the property a week ago before you were ejected by the gardener, Josh Matlock?'

He stiffened in the plastic chair. 'Don't know what you're talking about.'

Kate chanced a bluff. 'We have reason to believe you were having sex with her when you were ejected. That's the truth, isn't it?'

'Load of rubbish.'

'Mr Matlock can easily identify you,' Foster said. 'Described you to a T, even down to what he called your "goatee beard".'

Jackman hesitated, then treated him to a sneering grin. 'So what? Not against the law to have it off with a good-looking chick, is it?'

'But it is to later break into her house.'

'I said, I had nothing to do with that.'

'Did Angela tell you how to get into the place?' Kate came back in. 'Or maybe she planned the whole thing?'

He emitted a short derisive laugh. 'Planned it? That silly, little cow couldn't plan a piss-up in a brewery. I only shafted her to keep her happy. She thought I was going to take her away with me when I moved on. Said she wanted to join the commune and live the life. Even agreed to change her name to Cloud so she could fit in. Bloody hilarious. She never realised I just wanted her for what I could get out of her.'

'Money, you mean?'

'What else? No law against that either, though, is there? Up to her if she wants to help me out.'

'But she didn't give you enough, did she? You were greedy and wanted more, so you broke into the house to get it.'

'Believe what you like. You've got nothing on me.'

'Is that right? Among the items stolen from Moat House were two bottles of Châteauneuf-du-Pape red wine.' Kate glanced down at the document in front of her and for the benefit of the tape, she read out the exhibit number.

'So what? As I didn't screw the place I wouldn't know anyway.'

'Wouldn't you, now? Do you own a VW Camper van?' She gave the registration number. 'Police found it parked in an alleyway behind the Starlight public house in the early hours of this morning.'

'It's my wagon, yes.' He grinned. 'Why, park it on double yellow lines, did I? Maybe I could have that TIC — you know, what you bluebottles call taken into consideration — with the pub burglary?'

'Very funny, Mr Jackman,' Foster replied. 'Officers have carried out a search of the vehicle and guess what they found inside? Two bottles of the exact same Châteauneuf-du-Pape, one empty and the other partially consumed. Bit of a coincidence that, don't you think?'

'Not really. Maybe I like Château whatever it is.'

'What at over forty pounds a bottle? I hardly think someone like you living on benefits could afford that.'

Jackman suddenly looked uneasy and moistened his lips with his tongue. 'That's all you know.'

'What do you think we'll find when we fingerprint the bottles, Mr Jackman?' Kate continued.

'My dabs probably, which you'd expect to find if the booze was in my wagon.'

'Yes, but we're not talking about *your* prints, Mr Jackman, but the prints left on the bottles by the person originally purchasing them. All we will have to do is cross-reference those prints with those of that person to prove where the wine came from.'

Jackman's face twisted into a heavy scowl, and he looked from one to the other of his interrogators, a trapped expression on his face as he obviously weighed up his options. Then, no doubt concluding that he hadn't any, he capitulated and sat back with another broad grin.

'Okay, you win.'

'What do you mean by that?'

He shrugged. 'Guilty.'

'So, you admit to breaking into Moat House in addition to the burglary at the Starlight public house?'

He released a loud snort. 'Want me to bloody well sing a confession to you? Yes, I did both jobs. Satisfied now?'

'What happened to the property you stole, apart from the wine?'

He grinned. 'I ate it in a massive blow-out with some of the brothers.'

'What, the cash as well?'

He looked puzzled.

'Cash? What cash?'

'The cash you stole from the kitchen drawer.'

'There wasn't any cash in any drawer, and I did a pretty good search.'

'The drawer was locked. You forced it.'

He shook his head definitively. 'There was one locked drawer, I remember, but I didn't force it. Would have made too much noise and I couldn't risk waking everyone up. Why do you think I taped up the window before smashing it in the first place?"

Kate frowned. 'It's alleged a hundred pounds was taken from it.'

'Nothing to do with me. Believe me, I would have remembered finding that amount.'

'But I don't believe you.'

'So, why would I lie? I've admitted everything else, haven't I?'

Kate thought about that but didn't comment further. 'Well, thank you for your cooperation anyway, Mr Jackman,' she said. Then remembering his parting shot at Mason's Farm, she gave a sudden smile and added, 'Oh by the way, sorry we couldn't offer you tea and biscuits.'

CHAPTER 9

'So, what do you think?' Kate said to Foster after a uniformed officer had taken Jackman back to his cell in the basement. 'Do you believe him about the missing money?'

Foster leaned back in his chair. 'Don't know what to think,' he said. 'But as he said, why would he lie? He's admitted the burglary of Moat House. Whether he stole the cash or not won't make any difference to his sentence.'

'So, could Dunbar be lying about the money being there in the first place? If so, he would have needed Dorothy Matlock to be in cahoots with him. Alternatively, could Matlock herself have opened the drawer with her key after discovering the burglary, then stole the money, locked the drawer again and forced it to make it look like the intruder was responsible?'

'Neither of those scenarios seem plausible to me. In the case of Dunbar, what would be his motive? He's plainly loaded, and I can't see him doing something like that as an insurance fiddle. As for Dorothy Matlock, she is the most unlikely thief I can think of.'

'Then the only other option we've got is that there's another tea leaf at Moat House. Someone who must have discovered the burglary before Mrs Matlock and chose to take advantage of it.'

'Which suggests we're looking at another member of the family and aside from Dunbar's wife, Yasmin, and his so far unseen assistant, Dr Samantha Lawrence, who has allegedly been off for the past two days, we're left with just the three siblings.'

Kate climbed to her feet and picked up the sheaf of documents they had been referring to during the interview. 'And I reckon as far as suspects go, we'd be spoiled for choice there.'

Foster sighed heavily. 'You know,' he said, 'when you think about all the serious crimes we have on our books, this whole business is beyond trivial. The burglary itself was minor enough, but now we're saddled with the job of trying to ID a petty thief who evidently stole a hundred pounds. How did we get ourselves into this?'

She shrugged. 'Ask the DCI,' she replied. 'He's calling the shots and frankly, having missed breakfast, my main focus at the moment is on a trip to the canteen for a mammoth fry-up.'

'I can't think of a better idea.'

In fact, they got as far as the canteen doors and were just in time to savour the smell of frying bacon before the blast of the tannoy brought with it a premonition that the smell was the nearest they were going to get to their cooked breakfast.

'Detective Sergeant Lewis contact the detective inspector urgently,' the gravel voice said.

There was an internal phone on the wall by the doors and Kate picked it up and wearily dialled the CID number.

Charlie Woo answered immediately. 'Sorry, Kate,' he said. (Why did people always apologise when they were about to lumber you with a shitty job?) 'I know you and Jamie were called out earlier, but I need you to get over to Moat House again pronto. Uniform are already there, and I'll join you in a bit.'

Kate made a despairing face at Foster. 'Why, has the place burned down, guv?' she asked hopefully.

'Not quite that,' came the terse reply. 'But something equally serious. Howard Dunbar has been found seriously

injured in the laboratory. Allegedly having suffered a poten-
tially lethal bite from a poisonous spider which had escaped
from captivity.'

* * *

Hayden's big red Jaguar Mk II drove into the police station
car park as Kate and Jamie Foster strode towards one of the
parked CID cars. Kate waited for her other half to get out of
the Jag, then beckoned him over.

'You came to work early,' he said, looking slightly miffed.
'I was quite surprised to find you gone when I got up.'

She looked at her watch and raised an eyebrow. 'And
this must be a first for you, up and at 'em before seven,' she
said, handing Foster the ignition keys. 'You'd better get in
the back. I'll fill you in on the way.'

'Bit of a flap on then, is there?' he said as he clambered
into the car.

Kate grimaced. 'You could say that,' she said. 'I hope
you've got your long socks on. You might need them.'

An ambulance pulled away with a shriek as they
approached Moat House and they found two marked police
patrol cars drawn up at the front. A uniformed constable was
manning the front door. He stepped back with a nod to allow
them through.

'Everyone's out back, skipper,' he said. 'Ambulance has
just left with the casualty.'

Pushing past Julian and Angela Dunbar who were standing white-faced to one side of the courtyard, Kate ignored
their blurted questions and went straight to the uniformed
policeman guarding the annexe door. She recognised the
burly, grey-haired man as Sergeant Tom Bartholomew, a
long-serving local officer with a wealth of experience and
common sense.

'Professor Dunbar is inside now, looking for the thing,
Kate,' he said. 'But watch yourself. We don't know where it's
gone and it's apparently deadly.'

Kate felt a familiar shivery sensation run down her spine as she gingerly opened the door and stepped inside, forcing back the feeling of panic that was rising inside her, but comforted by the fact that the other two were with her.

Staring slowly around the room, she saw that the single window at the far end of the room appeared to have been smashed, with a small amount of broken glass visible on top of a metal cabinet. She also saw that several drawers in the big corner desk, as well as in some of the other cabinets, had been pulled open in a clumsy, haphazard way that seemed to indicate someone had been frantically searching for something.

As Foster crossed the room to look at the window, Hubert Dunbar appeared through the internal door to the side room containing the terrariums, his face grey. He was wearing a pair of long, thick gloves, which Kate guessed were designed to provide him with protection when handling his collection of spiders.

'I can't find her anywhere,' he rasped. 'Bloody dreadful business.'

'Her?' Kate echoed, glancing around the room again as she spoke, watching for the slightest movement in the shadowy corners. 'Exactly what is it you are looking for?'

He cast her a quick glance. 'Martha,' he said, 'my Brazilian wandering spider. She's escaped. It's a catastrophe. Took me weeks to get hold of her on a special trip to the Amazon rainforest. Now I'll have to start all over again.'

Kate was completely taken aback by his attitude. He seemed more concerned about the loss of the spider than the fate of his own son, and his use of the name, Martha, for such a horrible creature sickened her.

'I understand Howard was bitten by the spider?' she said, partly to remind him of what his priorities should be. 'How is he?'

He ran one hand through his hair. 'Not good,' he said. 'Seems to have been bitten on the neck. Saw clear evidence of fang marks in the wound.'

'Where did this happen?'

He pointed to what looked suspiciously like a sizeable patch of vomit a short distance away. 'Found him lying there when I walked in half an hour ago. The bite was already badly swollen and inflamed. He was sweating heavily, almost certainly feverish and suffering cramps. He must have been here half the night. Normally takes a good few hours for symptoms to get to that stage, you see. But the wound was in his neck which is possibly the worst place to be bitten.'

'Well anyway, it's a good job you came in early this morning. At least you found him in time to get him to the hospital. It's up to the medics now.'

He scowled. 'I always come in early. I start work here every morning before seven. But Howard has a dicky heart, and he suffers from high blood pressure, so despite my early intervention, his chances of survival don't look good.'

'Didn't you try injecting him with the antivenom when you found him?'

He waved a hand towards the metal cabinet he had shown her before. 'I would have done if I'd been able to. Take a look.'

Even as Kate started across the room, she could see the remains of the glass tubes. They were lying on the tiled floor below the open cabinet door, glittering in the circular, semi-dry stain left by their contents. Some jagged shards still projected from the rack which had previously held them, and the shattered hypodermic syringe lay a short distance away.

'How on earth did that happen?' she asked, turning back towards him.

'You tell me. That's how I found it all. I can only assume Howard tried to inject himself after he was bitten and in his panic dropped the rack.'

'But how did he come to be bitten in the first place? What was he doing in here, especially in the middle of the night?'

'I haven't the faintest idea. He has nothing to do with my work in here. He does my books and tax returns, that's all, and I think he has only visited the lab a couple of times in the past to carry out stock checks for me.'

'And how come the window got broken?' Foster put in, returning from his cursory inspection.

'Perhaps he smashed it after being bitten in a desperate attempt to get out?'

'But why would he have needed to climb out of the window if he came in through the front door?'

'Sam and I are the only ones with keys, and we always lock that door when we leave here. It was still locked when I came in this morning.'

'Which suggests he must have broken the window getting *in*, not trying to get *out*?' Kate said.

Dunbar seemed unable to meet her stare and there was a long pause before he answered. 'That can be the only answer, yes.'

'I see that most of the other drawers in here have been left open. Is that usual?'

'No, I always shut them before leaving at night. I like a tidy ship.'

'So the obvious conclusion to draw from it is that Howard must have opened them and that he broke in here specifically looking for something?'

'Perhaps he opened the drawers when he was hunting for the antivenom. As my accountant, he would have known I had the stuff, but not necessarily where I kept it.'

Kate frowned, unconvinced by what sounded like a very lame answer, and she sensed that Dunbar was hiding something.

'But none of this makes any sense. Why would Howard have gone to all the trouble of breaking into the lab in the first place? As I've already said, he must have been looking for something he knew was here — something he desperately wanted.'

There was no answer, merely a tightening of Dunbar's facial muscles.

Kate's irritation began to show. 'Professor Dunbar,' she said, 'with respect, I think there is something you are not telling us, and I have to warn you that you are already in hot water over what has happened here. Lack of cooperation with our inquiry will only make things worse. So I will ask you again, what do you think Howard was looking for in your laboratory?'

He released a ragged sigh. 'Money,' he said simply.

'How so?'

More hesitation. 'I regularly keep a very substantial sum locked in the bottom drawer of my desk with my diary, project records and keys for the locks on the terrariums. Running a lab like this can be an expensive business and I need sufficient funds to hand for specialist equipment, travel and research purposes, some of which I prefer to pay for in cash.'

'No doubt to escape liability for VAT,' Hayden commented drily. 'Must reduce the cost of everything considerably.'

Dunbar glared at him but didn't respond.

'Again, as my *de facto* accountant,' he said instead, 'Howard would have known about the money.'

'And you believe he would have been prepared to steal from his own father?'

He snorted disparagingly. 'You've no doubt gathered by now that there is little affection or loyalty among the members of this family, Sergeant. I give my children a monthly allowance, more to keep them off my back and to keep Yasmin happy than anything else. But Howard also has an addictive gambling habit, and he is forever in debt with some quite unpleasant people. I suspect he is under notice to pay up or risk the consequences, hence his decision to break into my lab for the money.'

'So how much money are we talking about?'

'Around four thousand, give or take.'

Kate heard Hayden's sharp intake of breath.

'Is it still there?'

'It was when I first checked the drawer after Howard was, er, taken away in the ambulance, but I've since removed it for safe-keeping.'

'You kept four thousand quid in a . . . a drawer?'

'Well, I didn't expect anyone to force it open, did I? Or to break into the lab in the first place. It's not exactly somewhere a thief would expect to find a large sum of money.'

'So Howard didn't actually manage to get what he came for, then?'

'If that's what he *did* come for, no. I always keep the key to the drawer on my person and he would not have known that. He obviously looked hard enough, though. The drawer has obviously been forced.'

'But if you say the money was still there when you got in here this morning, how come Howard didn't find it after forcing the drawer? A sum as large as that, even in twenties or fifties, would have been difficult to miss.'

Dunbar was unable to meet her gaze and she got it immediately. 'He did find the money, didn't he, Professor?' she accused. 'He had it on him when you checked him out.'

'No, it . . . it wasn't like that. Most of the money was still in the drawer, but some of it was scattered about the floor in front of the desk. Martha obviously attacked him while he was in the process of taking it. I, er, just retrieved it, that's all.'

There was utter contempt on Kate's face now and her mouth tightened into a hard line. 'While Howard was lying on the floor seriously hurt? Unbelievable. Well, you'd better show us this drawer, hadn't you?'

Dunbar said nothing, but led the way to the corner desk, where Kate saw that the front of the bottom right-hand drawer was badly split and that the lock was hanging off. She also spotted a large screwdriver lying on the floor under the desk. A clear indication of what had almost certainly caused the damage.

'Is this the only drawer you lock?' she said. 'I see locks on some of the other drawers too.'

'Yes, it's the only drawer with anything of value in it and I can't lock any of the others anyway as the keys have been lost. It's a very old desk, you see. I don't believe in wasting money on what is after all only office furniture.'

'Certainly a rum business,' she said, 'and we are unlikely to get to the bottom of it until and if we can speak to Howard. But back to this missing spider, which is a lot more of a pressing issue. Do you think the thing could have got out through the broken window? I mean, is it capable of climbing up there?'

He frowned, still avoiding her gaze. 'Well, Martha is a low-level predator, used to ambushing her prey on the jungle floor, so her instincts would have been to look for somewhere at ground level where she could hide. A dark place, like a cupboard or a box. Somewhere like that.'

'But it's possible the spider could have got outside?'

'All spiders have their own web silk produced by spin-nerets and although Brazilian wandering spiders do not spin webs to catch their prey, but rely on ground ambush, they are able to use their own web silk to climb smooth walls. So, yes, it is possible she could have got outside, but it is more likely she is still in the lab somewhere.'

That wasn't something Kate wanted to hear, and she felt her skin crawl again as she threw another couple of keen glances around the room.

'So, how did you discover, er, Martha was missing in the first place?'

He sighed heavily. 'After finding Howard on the floor, then ringing for the ambulance, I examined all the terrariums and though all seemed secure, she was the only arachnid I couldn't account for. I banged on the sliding doors of her ter-rarium several times. She is very bad-tempered and aggressive and usually reacts violently to this, as you saw when Julian tapped on the glass, but this time there was no response. So I physically checked inside and found that she was gone. That's how I knew what had bitten Howard.'

'You took a chance going in there.'

'He held up his gloved hands and shook his head. I know how to handle spiders. I've been doing it for much of my adult life.'

Kate steeled herself. 'Okay, then we'd better take a look at the terrarium, hadn't we?'

Despite the seriousness of his situation and his apparent reprehensible behaviour, Dunbar couldn't resist a sneer. 'You sure you want to do that?'

She met his gaze with an icy stare of her own. 'No, Professor, I don't, but I don't seem to have much choice, do I?'

Kate fancied she could hear multiple rustlings when they entered the small side room, but she couldn't be sure if it was just the mice in their cages. Nevertheless, she sensed movement in some of the terrariums and caught a glimpse of a dark shape pressed up against the glass of the one containing the giant tarantula. She tried not to think about it as she followed Dunbar over to the terrarium at the other end. She saw that one of the sliding doors was wide open.

'Checked the inside thoroughly,' Dunbar said. 'She's definitely not in there.'

'So how did the thing get out if you're saying the terrarium was secure?'

'I just don't know. I am so careful about security. All the terrariums are fitted with the same specially made ratchet locks you see here, and those locks have never let me down before.' He quickly closed the open door and locked it, leaving her to test it afterwards.

She grunted. 'Seems okay to me.'

He shrugged. 'Exactly my point.'

She stared at him again. 'Of course, it's possible the doors weren't closed over as tightly as you thought when you last locked up.'

'I assure you, Sergeant, I always check that the terrariums are secure before leaving the lab every night.'

'Well then, either we're dealing with a Houdini spider or someone else has been in here and tampered with the lock after you.'

'I don't see who that could have been. Sam has been off for two days and is only due back later this morning. And Howard is almost as averse to spiders as you are, Sergeant. The last thing he would have done was to try and interfere with one.'

'So, we're back to square one.'

'Not quite.' Hayden said to one side of her. 'I don't think the beastie got out through the front at all.' Moving closer to the terrarium, he raised himself up on tiptoe to peer at the glass lid. 'See that?'

'See what?' Dunbar replied, joining him. The next second Kate heard the professor's sharp intake of breath. 'Good grief,' he breathed, 'the lid is not on properly. It's come out of one of the grooves.'

Kate pushed between the two of them and, standing on tiptoe as Hayden had done, she saw the two-centimetre gap between the edge of the glass panel and the right-hand corner of the terrarium.

'Good on you, Hayd,' she breathed. 'So now we know how the creature escaped. Don't you padlock the lids of the terrariums as well?'

'The way they are constructed would make that a very difficult thing to do and I hadn't considered it necessary anyway. Sam and I are the only ones who ever open them and the locks on the sliding doors are essentially there to stop the doors being inadvertently left open or tampered on visits we occasionally get from sponsors or other biologists.'

'That being said, how often *are* the lids of the terrariums opened, Professor?'

He returned her stare, looking blank for a moment. He was obviously shaken afresh by the discovery and had lost his usual arrogant self-assurance with the realisation of his own culpability. 'Well, er, when we need to feed the arachnids,' he replied, 'or . . . or to clean up any detritus left behind. It's . . . it's more convenient and less risky than trying to do this by unlocking the sliding doors.'

'Do you remember when this lid was last opened?'

'Of course. It was yesterday. I fed Martha in the evening before leaving the lab to have dinner.'

'And unfortunately it looks as though you didn't secure the lid properly afterwards.'

He glared at her. 'But . . . but I thought I had. It was just an innocent mistake.'

Kate nodded grimly. 'A mistake, Professor, which, sadly, may have cost your own son his life, and may also have put this whole household at risk.'

'So — so what happens now?'

'We seal off the lab to allow a full search to be carried out for the spider. If it's not found, then we may have to consider advising the media so that the public can be warned if it turns up somewhere else.'

'But my work . . . ?'

Kate felt like saying 'sod your work,' but said instead, 'That will have to wait and in the meantime, you may want to consider your position.'

'My position? What do you mean?'

'This is a very serious matter, Professor, aside from what happened to your son. You may well have committed an offence under the Wildlife and Countryside Act by allowing the spider to escape in the first place, and the full circumstances will have to be investigated.'

'But my whole *raison d'être* here has been to aid medical research.'

'I'm quite sure it has, Professor,' she said, unable to feel at all sorry for him under the circumstances. 'Sadly, however, it seems to have had the very opposite effect.'

CHAPTER 10

Charlie Woo arrived shortly after Kate had finished with Hubert Dunbar. Leaving Sergeant Bartholomew to continue guarding the scene, she and Foster adjourned to his car, out of hearing of anyone else.

'I've just rung the hospital,' he said. 'They told me Howard Dunbar didn't make it. Popped his clogs twenty minutes ago. The hospital thinks it may not have been entirely due to the venom, though that was obviously a contributory factor, but was probably down to a massive stroke.'

Kate winced. 'Bloody hell!' she said. 'The family will have to be told the news.'

'I gather he's on his way to the hospital at the moment. Anyway, I've instructed Control to have the coroner's officer informed of the death, so that he may advise the coroner. I've also arranged for a few more uniforms to be sent here from the nick to carry out a search of the lab for the spider, which I gather still hasn't been found. The wildlife crime officer, Dave Robbins, will be with them, though I'm not sure whether he will be of much use. Exotic arachnids are a bit outside his area of expertise.'

'Shouldn't we be calling out a specialist team to do that? From DEFRA or whatever? A bite from this spider is obviously lethal.'

He gave a short, unamused laugh. 'I'm afraid there isn't any such thing as a specialist team to search for escaped spiders. I did a quick check before I came here. We are evidently "it", like we are for every other hazardous search, except maybe one involving nuclear materials. In short, the buck stops with us and we need to get weaving if we're to have any chance of catching the thing. Now, I think you'd better fill me in on the details of this incident.'

When Kate had finished her brief, with occasional comment from Hayden and Jamie Foster, which she didn't always appreciate, he said, 'So, regardless of the spider issue, we have a burglary here anyway, despite the fact that the perpetrator is now dead. Plainly, Howard Dunbar smashed the window to get into the lab, then forced open his old man's desk with the screwdriver that was found lying on the floor, to filch the wad that was in there. We've got witness evidence from the professor to say that notes were scattered around him when he was found, so it's obvious what he broke into the lab for. A nice open-and-shut case to my mind.'

'But can you actually burgle your own house?' Hayden put in. 'If not, then we are wasting our time here. Dunbar's death is tragic, but it's plainly an accident and hardly a CID matter.'

Kate gave him an old-fashioned look, guessing he was thinking about his stomach again.

Woo pursed his lips reflectively. 'Good point, Hayden, but in this case I suppose technically you *can* screw your own place. Don't forget, the break-in was committed in a so-called annexe separate from the main house, so Howard Dunbar wasn't breaking into his own place, but into a separate building where he had no right to be. And if not burglary, there's a case of criminal damage, I would have thought.'

Hayden looked disappointed, but didn't pursue the matter and Woo continued, with a knowing smile.

'Anyway, it'll take someone well above my paygrade to make the decision on how this business is going to be finally recorded and as far as we are concerned, it doesn't let us off the hook regarding the current investigation. A man is still dead and there's bound to be an inquest. At the very least, the coroner will want a full report on the circumstances. So, let's get SOCO down here pronto to go over the scene.'

Kate nodded. 'But they'll have to hang fire until your search team have given the lab a clean bill of health,' she said. 'We don't want Martha popping up to say "hello".'

'Martha?'

'Dunbar gave all his spiders names.'

'What? That really is sick.'

'Takes all types, I suppose . . .'

Woo didn't appear to be listening. 'Who's that there?' he said, pointing.

But Kate had seen the tall, slim figure in the neat blue trouser suit too. The woman had driven up in a smart silver BMW coupé and was now walking slowly towards the front door of the house, twice turning in mid-step to glance around her at the parked police cars as she did so. She had only just reached the door when Angela Dunbar came flying out to throw her arms around her neck, visibly sobbing.

'I've got a pretty good idea who it might be, guv,' Kate replied as the two women disappeared back inside the house. 'Dr Samantha Lawrence, I would think. The professor's absent assistant. I need to have a word with her.'

Woo nodded. 'Go ahead,' he said. 'I don't want to interfere with your investigation. But it doesn't need three of you, does it? Take Jamie with you. Hayden and I will coordinate the search of the lab once we've got the team out here. We can liaise with SOCO afterwards.'

The detectives found Samantha Lawrence and Angela Dunbar in the sitting room. Dunbar, who was sitting on the settee, was talking excitedly to the venomologist, her words punctuated by more sobs. But Kate saw through the tears to the 'crocodile' lurking beneath, noting that her cheeks were hardly wet and remembering the young woman's recent derogatory comment about her brother.

The conversation ceased as soon as they walked in and the hostility in Dunbar's stare was unmistakable. Before Kate could say anything, she jumped to her feet and stalked out of the room, tossing her curls like a recalcitrant schoolgirl.

'Dr Lawrence, isn't it?' Kate asked, not giving Angela Dunbar a second glance, and producing her warrant card. 'Detective Sergeant Kate Lewis and this is Detective Constable Jamie Foster.'

Penetrating grey eyes fastened on her from behind what looked like designer cat-eye spectacles, and the pale, porcelain like face, with its prominent high cheekbones, remained impassive as Lawrence raised delicate manicured hands to smooth back her shoulder-length black hair.

'Sam, please, Detective Sergeant,' she said. 'Angela — er Cloud — has just told me about poor Howard. How on earth did that happen?'

Kate indicated a chair, but Lawrence chose to sit on the edge of the settee Dunbar had been occupying. She and Foster dropped into the two armchairs opposite.

'That's what we are investigating,' Kate went on. 'Do you mind if we ask you a few questions?'

Lawrence shook her head a little uncertainly. 'Of course not, but I'm not sure how I can help. I've been off for the past couple of days.'

'So I gather. Visiting your aunt, Professor Dunbar told me.'

She nodded and waited patiently for Kate to continue.

'How long have you worked for the professor?'

'Oh, about six months now. He needed a qualified biologist to assist him with his work.'

'A venomologist.'

She smiled. 'Not a description I choose to recognise. I prefer to regard myself as an invertebrate biologist, with a particular specialism in the study of the physiology and anatomy of arachnids and the toxicity of their venom.'

'I think we'll stick to the term venomologist, if you don't mind.'

'Whatever you wish.'

'How did you know to apply for the job?'

'The vacancy was advertised in one of our journals. I had worked on arachnid research in a number of countries overseas and I had only just completed a fact-finding visit to Costa Rica on behalf of a medical research facility, so I was looking for a new challenge. This project sounded particularly interesting and so far it has certainly fulfilled my expectations.'

'Why was there a vacancy in the first place? Do you know?'

Kate sensed Foster tense in the adjacent chair, and she could feel his critical gaze on her for returning to what he saw as her personal fixation.

Lawrence frowned, obviously unsure where the questions were going. 'I understand the previous incumbent suffered a fatal accident on a trip overseas.'

'Oh, how tragic. Who was she?'

'I don't know. I never met her.'

'Do you know what happened?'

'Not exactly, only that she died after some sort of accident in Brazil. Why do you ask?'

Kate didn't answer and quickly changed tack. 'Enjoy your job here, do you?'

'Very much so.'

'The professor is a good man to work for, then?'

'He is very dedicated and meticulous, and I ask for nothing more.'

'Yet it was during his watch that a poisonous spider escaped from his laboratory and caused serious harm to his son, Howard.'

'So Cloud has just told me. She is obviously extremely upset over it all. But you must understand that accidents can and do happen in laboratories of all sorts, Sergeant, however much care is taken. It could equally have happened during my watch. Do you know which arachnid was responsible?'

'The Brazilian wandering spider, we believe.'

'Ah. Not good. Arachnida of the genus *Phoneutria* are very aggressive, and their venom contains powerful neurotoxins which can adversely affect the chemical receptors of the neuromuscular system. This is what makes them so dangerous to human beings, although I have to say that the number of people who have actually died from their bite is only small.'

'Tell that to Howard Dunbar,' Foster said drily.

She frowned at the remark and studied him for a moment. 'Obviously I have every sympathy for Howard, officer, but I would have to ask what he was doing in the laboratory at all *and* how he got in.'

'We're looking into that at present,' Kate replied.

Lawrence nodded. 'The thing is, Professor Dunbar and myself are the only ones with keys and the professor is very strict about ensuring the place is locked up when we leave at night. Martha' (that name again, Kate thought savagely) 'would only have bitten someone if she'd felt threatened, so he must have done something to warrant this. Did Howard tamper with the lock on the sliding doors of the terrarium, do you think?'

'No,' Kate replied. 'It seems that the lid on the terrarium had not been replaced properly. That's how the spider escaped.'

Lawrence closed her eyes tightly for a second. 'Oh, I see,' she said in a much more subdued tone, no doubt now appreciating the possible legal implications for the professor. 'How is Howard now?'

'Not good,' Kate replied, deciding against passing on the bad news at this stage to someone who was not a member of the family. 'The problem is, your spider hasn't been found, and I can't allow anyone into the laboratory until the place has been thoroughly searched.'

'But we have a duty of care to the remaining arachnids, not to mention the other animals and invertebrates we are responsible for. You know, feeding and so forth.'

Kate thought of the mice and the fate that awaited them and shuddered yet again.

'We shouldn't be too long.'

'Maybe I can help? I am well experienced in handling spiders and know the sort of places in which Martha might be hiding. It could be dangerous if your search team were to suddenly come upon her. She can move extremely fast, and her first instinct would be to attack. I'm sure you wouldn't want one of your police officers to be bitten, too.'

Kate's eyes narrowed, sensing the inference of 'on your head be it if you refuse' in the ostensibly innocent remark.

'I'm sure our team would be only too pleased to have your expert assistance when they arrive,' she replied, adding in a heavily loaded reply, 'after all, the only other option would be to fumigate the laboratory and destroy the spider, which I'm sure you wouldn't want to happen . . .'

Foster couldn't resist having a dig of his own after Lawrence had left them. 'Still hung up on Gillian George then, are you, skipper?' he said mildly.

Kate rounded on him. 'If that's a problem for you, Jamie,' she grated, 'you can always go back to pushing paper at the nick.'

He held both hands up in front of him in a fake defensive gesture. 'Okay, okay, don't get so touchy. Just taking the mick, that's all.'

She grunted, only partially satisfied. 'Well, don't. I'm not in a particularly jocular mood. My gut tells me there is something about this Gillian George business that has led to the strange behaviour of people in this house, and I intend getting to the bottom of it.'

He sighed. 'Fine. It's your call. What did you think of Dr Lawrence?'

'Seemed a genuine sort of woman. Obviously very sharp and I think, like everyone else, she knows all about her predecessor, but doesn't want to get involved. Wants to keep her distance.'

'My feelings too. After all, she's only been here six months, so she wouldn't want to queer her pitch with the professor.'

'Speaking of the devil,' Kate murmured and stopped just inside the hallway as Dunbar strode through the front door, glancing briefly at the half-dozen uniformed police officers in protective clothing who were climbing out of a Ford Transit, which had just drawn up outside.

'Sorry for your loss, Professor,' Kate said to him as he made to walk past.

'Has Martha been found yet?' he snapped, without commenting on the death of his son.

'I'm afraid not, sir,' Kate replied. 'But our police team have just arrived to carry out a search, and Doctor Lawrence has agreed to help us.'

'Sam is here?' he said. 'Excellent. I'll speak to her when she's finished doing that, but first I have to pop upstairs to see my wife and, er, break the awful news to her.'

'I understand perfectly, Professor. We'll catch up later.'

'Obviously a sensitive, caring man,' Foster murmured sarcastically as they both watched Dunbar mount the staircase two steps at a time.

Kate nodded. 'Certainly a real loving father,' she agreed drily. 'Maybe his wife was a lot nearer the truth than she realised when she told me he has all the attributes of one of his own creepy-crawlies.'

CHAPTER 11

'The "plod" team have been briefed and they're carrying out their search of the lab as I speak,' Charlie Woo declared when he and Hayden met up with Kate and Jamie Foster in the sitting room of Moat House a couple of hours later.

'I don't reckon they'll find the spider,' Kate said. 'It's more than likely that it got out through the broken window.'

'Which means it could be anywhere in the grounds by now,' Woo said dismally, 'just waiting to sink its fangs into anyone that happens to stumble on it.'

'That's not very likely, though, is it, Foster commented. 'This place could not be more isolated. There are no other properties close by and the nearest village is several miles away. Unless our spider is into long-distance hiking, I can't see it straying outside the grounds.' Then he added wickedly. 'Except maybe to the hippie camp at Mason's Farm.'

'Also, don't forget it's a tropical spider, used to a warm, moist rainforest environment,' Hayden put in helpfully, 'and with autumn now here and the colder weather approaching, I can't see it surviving long outside.'

'Great. Then all we have to do is to pray for early snow so that it catches flu,' Woo finished sarcastically. He glanced at his watch. 'Now I've got to head back to the nick. Just had a call from Indrani Purewal that she's just nicked one of our target villains, Toby Moffatt. He's in the frame for several local arsons, and I want to be in on the interview.'

Kate nodded. 'No problem, guv. You might as well take Jamie back with you. He's been on since the early hours and needs a break. Hayden and I will liaise with SOCO when they arrive and call it a day after a couple more inquiries.'

Woo turned for the door. 'Right then, I'll leave you with it.' He grinned. 'But if Martha isn't found, don't go wandering into any long grass, will you?'

Hayden expressed his concerns about the situation even before the sound of the CID car had faded down the drive.

'I just don't understand why we are getting so involved in all this,' he complained. 'I mean, as I've said before, we're dealing with little more than a tragic accident. It's hardly the crime of the century.'

Kate sighed. 'What's up, Hayd?' she said. 'The old empty belly syndrome again, is it?'

He snorted. 'Well, it *is* lunchtime, and I am beginning to feel quite faint. We could have gone back to the station for a bite to eat, *then* come back to wrap things up.'

She nodded. 'So you need some sustenance, do you?'

'Well, er, very much so. It's to do with my metabolism.'

'Then I may have just what you need.'

'You have?'

'Of course.'

As he stared at her curiously, she reached into her pocket and produced something wrapped in silver foil.

'My last Polo Mint,' she said. 'Make it last, won't you?'

* * *

As it turned out, Kate's misgivings about the missing spider proved to be accurate. After an exhaustive search, even with the help of Dr Lawrence, the police team found no trace of so-called Martha. After briefing the SOCO manager, a rather sour-faced woman named Andrea James, she and

Hayden left them to their designated task and headed back to the house.

They ran into Angela Dunbar on the way. She was coming out of the kitchen with a mug of coffee in one hand.

'Just the person,' Kate said, blocking the passageway. 'Can I have a word?'

Dunbar scowled at her. 'I'm not talking to you,' she replied. 'You've caused enough trouble here already.'

'Oh? What trouble is that? Maybe we should have a chat about it.'

'You locked up Adam for no reason.'

'Not me personally, but he did break into a local pub.'

'That's a load of balls. You coppers are all the same, setting people up.'

'Well, he was found actually in the public bar in the early hours of the morning trying to force the till.'

'I don't believe you. Adam is a kind, thoughtful person and the fuzz never leave him alone.'

'Sorry, love, but Adam is a crook with a record nearly as long as your arm.'

There were real tears in her eyes now and she pushed against Kate, slopping coffee on to the hall carpet. 'Out of my way. You're nothing more than a vicious, lying bitch.'

Kate bit hard. 'And you are a silly, little girl who needs to grow up.'

'You can't talk to me like that.'

'I can talk to you in any way I believe to be necessary to make you see the truth.'

Kate was aware of Hayden twitching uneasily behind her. She knew he would not be comfortable with the confrontation, but she firmly stood her ground. For a second Dunbar continued to push against her. Then quite suddenly, and to the surprise of both detectives, she lost her grip on the mug of coffee completely. As it slipped from her grasp, she collapsed in a heap on the floor, sobbing hysterically.

Kate's reaction was immediate. Dropping to her knees beside her, she gently put an arm around her shoulders, allowing the young woman to bury her face in her chest, while Hayden simply stood there gaping.

'How far gone are you?' Kate said softly, sensing intuitively the real reason for her distress.

Dunbar confirmed her suspicions. 'About six weeks,' she choked.

'You were hiding in the barn when Josh Matlock ejected him, weren't you?'

Dunbar nodded. 'We . . . we'd been seeing each other for some time, and we used to meet there at night. He — Adam — said he would take me away with him, but deep down I knew it was all a lie.'

Kate sighed. The same old story, she thought bitterly, remembering in a sudden painful flashback the first love in her own life before Hayden, who had promised her the earth, but had then been caught by her in bed with a couple of call girls.

'Let's have that little chat,' she said as she helped Dunbar to her feet. She threw Hayden a hard, meaningful look. 'Just you and me, okay?'

Hayden took the hint, relief written into his expression. He stepped back out of the way to allow Kate to lead Dunbar down the hallway to the sitting room, before disappearing at a commendable rate of knots through the kitchen doorway.

'Did you tell Adam you were pregnant?' Kate asked shortly afterwards as she settled on to the settee beside the still crying, sniffing young woman.

She had no real interest in Dunbar's predicament, and while she had every sympathy for her and what she was going through, the brutal truth was that her main objective was to gain her confidence sufficiently to be able to extract the information she needed to assist her investigation.

Dunbar wiped her eyes on the cuff of the pullover she was wearing. 'He just laughed,' she said. 'The bastard just laughed in my face and said he hoped the two of us would be very happy.'

Kate grimaced. 'You need help, young lady. What about your father? Does he know?'

'My father?' Dunbar's face registered a kind of cynical incredulity. 'He's the last person I would tell. All he thinks about is his work with his spiders and his glowing professional reputation as an arachnologist. He lives in constant fear of the slightest hint of scandal. This . . . this awful business with Howard has already hit him hard. He knows it could end in disgrace for him and the loss of his revered status in the scientific community. If he knew about me being in the club as well, I don't know what he'd do to stop it getting out. At the very least I would find myself dumped on the street.'

Kate saw the opening and went for it. 'Was Gillian George's death a scandal too? Is that why the professor doesn't like anyone talking about it?'

Angela stood up quickly. 'I shouldn't have mentioned her to you,' she said, staring nervously at the open door, as if she feared someone could be listening. 'Sometimes when I'm in a bad mood I say things I shouldn't. It's the devil in me.'

'Well, seeing as you *have* mentioned her, you might as well finish the story. I gather she died. How did it happen?'

She shook. her head. 'I'm sorry, I can't help you.'

'She was the professor's previous assistant, wasn't she?'

Angela nodded and for a moment Kate thought she was going to bolt for the door.

'I understand she died in Brazil. Is that right?'

The young woman started, seemingly surprised Kate knew that much. 'Yes, last year. She and Father were on an expedition to the Amazon rainforest to collect specimens. She . . . she got bitten by a spider and . . . and died. It was awful.'

'Like Howard, you mean?'

Her eyes widened. 'Howard's *dead*?' she whispered.

Kate bit her lip, cursing herself for the inadvertent slip. 'Your father hasn't told you?'

'Father never tells us anything. He's a brute. The only reason we all stay with him is because of the money he gives us.' She paused briefly. 'When did Howard die?'

'About an hour ago now.'

'Which spider attacked him?'

'The Brazilian wandering spider, we believe.'

She closed her eyes tightly, trying to control her emotions. 'The worst of them, Father once told us, and it's still on the loose?'

'Well, we haven't found it yet.'

'Do . . . do you know why Howard was in the lab?'

'I'm sorry, we're not sure about that yet.'

For a few seconds there was silence. It seemed to Kate that Angela wanted to say something else but was unsure whether to or not. Then suddenly she blurted, 'The spider that bit Gillian was also a Brazilian wandering spider. You should remember that.'

Then she was gone again, avoiding any further questions and running out into the hallway. Moments later Kate heard her thumping up the stairs.

Kate was left in a partial daze by Angela's parting shot, and she was still struggling to work out what she could have meant by it when there was a discreet knock on the open door and Hayden stepped inside.

'Safe to return now, is it?' he quipped. Then his grin changed to a frown. 'What's up, old girl? Didn't make a pass at you, did she?'

Kate stared through him, her thoughts in chaos. 'Remember when you and I first met her at the beginning of this inquiry, she asked us if anyone had told us about someone called Gillian George?' she said. 'Well, it seems the lady in question died in Brazil from the bite of a wandering spider.'

'Good lord. That's a bit of a coincidence. She actually told you that, did she?'

Kate nodded slowly. 'She also said I should remember it. Now, why would she say that?'

'Maybe she thought it was a coincidence, too.'

'Or maybe she meant something more.'

He groaned. 'Oh come on, don't start reading something sinister into that like you do everything else.'

'Well, it was a strange thing to say.'

'People say a lot of funny things, don't they? And Andrea James, our "happy smiling" SOCO manager has texted me. She apparently has something strange to tell you too. She's waiting in the courtyard of the annexe.'

'Then we'd better see what she wants.'

The SOCO manager was leaning against the courtyard wall when Kate and Hayden arrived. Kate nodded to Sergeant Bartholomew who was still patiently guarding the door to the annexe and went over to her.

'Thought you might be interested in something we found,' she said, coming off the wall. 'Care to take a walk?'

Opening the side gate, she led the way along the wall of the annexe and turned sharp left at the end until all three of them stood under the broken window. Kate saw that there was an old rain butt, maybe from the original building, standing beneath the window on equally ancient flagstones. Glittering shards of broken glass lay on top of the lid of the rain butt which appeared to be broken in half. They were also scattered across the flagstones, together with splintered wooden fragments from the window frame.

'So?' Kate queried.

'So,' James repeated, 'what does this tell you?'

'That the window was smashed with some force . . .' Then she broke off and stared at her as the answer dawned on her. 'Hell's Bells, but from the inside!'

'Exactly. Most of the broken glass is lying out here and only a very small amount is actually in the lab itself. Furthermore, close examination of the window frame has revealed that the main impact damage was to the exterior trim, with most of the wood splinters lying on the slabs out here as well. If the window had been smashed from the outside, you would have expected the opposite. Whoever did this job, broke the window from inside to make it look as though it was done externally. Not a very clever attempt at subterfuge, though. Surprised you ace detectives didn't tumble to it originally. And if you want more evidence, the rain butt could not have assisted an offender to climb up to reach the pane. One of my lads hopped up there to check and the lid caved in under him. He's still moaning about his wet socks.'

'Didn't see a spider floating in the rain butt, did you?' Kate said hopefully.

'No such luck, but you're welcome to take a look, if you like?'

To the SOCO manager's surprise, Kate nodded to Hayden, and they did just that, overturning the rain butt before she could get out of the way and splattering her with foul-smelling dirty water.

'Empty,' Kate said with a grin, adding in response to her own dig, 'but even so, I'm surprised you ace SOCOs didn't think of looking in it just in case.'

'That was a bit mean,' Hayden commented as they returned to the house.

Kate chuckled. 'There's an old saying, Hayd,' she replied. 'If you can't take it, don't give it. But on a more serious note, we have a further issue to address.'

'Which is?'

'If Howard didn't climb into the lab via the window, but smashed the glass from the inside and the professor and his assistant are the only ones with keys to the front door, how the hell did he get into the place to start with?'

'He must have had a key.'

'Exactly, and if he did, it must still be in his pocket. So, that needs to be checked out at the hospital p.d.q.'

'Perhaps the professor collected his personal effects when he visited the hospital earlier.'

'He wasn't carrying anything when he got back, so it looks like they must still be there. It's worth the chance and anyway, I will have to have a chat with the staff who dealt with him and view the body before any post-mortem.'

He frowned. 'But it's not a murder inquiry and as his death was accidental and occurred in hospital while he was under their care, surely there's more likely to be a hospital autopsy rather than an external post-mortem?'

'Not sure about that. Depends on the coroner. But you never know how things will sometimes turn out and it's best to be thorough. We'll leave Tom Bartholomew here to ensure SOCO can work undisturbed while we nip over to the hospital now.'

She noted his pained expression. 'Don't forget, the hospital will have a canteen. You might even be able to get a sandwich or a cream bun there.'

He was immediately converted to the idea.

CHAPTER 12

Howard Dunbar was already in the hospital mortuary and Jane Morgan, the APT, or Anatomical Pathology Technologist as she was officially known, rolled his corpse out of the refrigerator for them to inspect.

There appeared to be three bite wounds on his pale body. These were visible as ugly lesions, one on the palm of his right hand, the second on his arm just above the elbow and the third, as the professor had described, on the side of his neck. Each wound was discoloured and presenting as a large red-dish-brown swelling. The tell-tale twin puncture marks were clearly visible in the neck wound. Kate hadn't seen the lesions before and was quite shocked at the state of them.

'Looks like it ran up his hand and arm, to his neck, inflicting the bites on the way,' Hayden said.

'I don't know a great deal about this particular case,' the technician commented, 'but I hear it was a venomous spider bite. I used to be in the army. Served as a medic all over the Middle East and Asia. Saw a lot of spider bites. Do you know what spider was responsible here?'

'Brazilian wandering spider, we believe,' Kate replied.

Morgan shook her head. 'Don't know that one, but I do know that the venom of a lot of tropical spiders can cause necrosis and gangrene after just a few days when the lesions develop into open sores as the flesh dies or rots. The venom in other spider bites carries a neurotoxin which attacks the central nervous system. Not a nice way to go in either case. Maybe this feller was lucky to die so quickly. I know of cases where—'

'Yes, yes,' Kate interjected hastily, not wishing to dwell on the subject. 'When will the autopsy take place?'

The other shrugged. 'Too early to say yet. Only just brought in. Should be within two to three days. I will know by tomorrow morning when I have all the schedules. Should be an interesting one for the pathologist. Sort of unusual.'

'What happened to the deceased's clothes and personal effects?'

'Still have 'em. In my office. Just about to bag 'em up.'

'Can we take a look?'

Morgan shrugged. 'Probably be all right.'

She led the way through another door into a small office. The room contained a desk and swivel chair in the far corner and a long table alongside the right-hand wall. There were some large empty plastic bags lying at one end of the long table, with some plastic seals beside them. Next to the bags was a neat pile of clothing, plus a filing tray containing a number of small items, including a watch a handkerchief, and a pair of spectacles.

'Did you find a key anywhere on him?' Kate asked, her disappointment showing.

Morgan stepped forward and flicked the handkerchief to one side. The dull yellow Yale key gleamed at Kate in the office strip light.

Kate seized it. 'We'll have to take this,' she said.

Morgan frowned uncertainly. 'Don't know about that. It's a patient's personal property. My responsibility.'

'It could be evidence in a criminal investigation,' Kate said firmly.

'This is most irregular.'

'I'll sign for it.'

Morgan thought a little longer, then shrugged. 'Don't suppose it would matter. Deceased's father was in earlier and carried out a formal ID. Signed a disclaimer for the stuff. Said to send it to the dump or burn it in our incinerator, whatever was most appropriate.' She shook her head. 'Strange man, he was.'

Kate nodded in agreement. 'Strange is an understatement,' she replied drily, wondering whether the professor had even had an inkling about the key. 'Did he go through the property?'

'Nope. Just signed the form and left. Never even shed a tear. He was more interested in the bite wounds than anything else. Studied them for several minutes. Even took some pictures on his mobile. Now that is creepy.'

'Professional interest, do you think?' Hayden said as he followed Kate across a small courtyard to the hospital's main entrance.

Kate stopped for a moment and turned towards him. 'Maybe it was,' she replied, 'but you wouldn't think he'd be doing something like that when the corpse is that of his own son. The man's a cold-hearted moron.'

'Quite agree. A right bounder. Now, didn't you say we'd stop off at the hospital canteen before going back? I believe you said something about a sandwich and a cream bun . . .'

* * *

The laboratory was shut up when Kate and Hayden got back. SOCO had obviously completed their task and had left. Only a very bored looking Sergeant Bartholomew remained at his post by the door. Kate felt guilty when she saw him.

'Sorry, Tom,' she said. 'You should have left when SOCO went.'

He grunted, plainly not too impressed. 'Wasn't sure I should before you returned, Kate,' he replied. 'But now you have, I'll head back to the nick.'

'Well, thanks for all your help anyway. Any developments while we've been gone?'

He shook his head. 'Only that I did use my judgement and let Dr Lawrence in after SOCO had finished. She said she had to attend to the other spiders, some of which needed to be fed. Professor Dunbar stopped by too, but they're both gone now, and the place is securely locked up.'

'Who actually did the locking up?'

'Dr Lawrence. She apparently had her own key to the door here.'

'How do you know it was her key?'

'She asked if we were finished in the lab and could she lock up. I saw her do the honours myself.'

'Thanks, Tom. Now you'd better get off. I'll buy you a pint when you're next in the club.'

He grinned. 'That'll be a novel experience, Kate, and I'll certainly hold you to it. Hayden can be my witness.'

She watched the uniformed man walk briskly across the courtyard to the rear door of the house and only when he had gone through, closing the door behind him, did she do what she had come to do.

The key she had retrieved from Howard Dunbar's personal effects was stiff at first, but after a bit of pressure it turned in the lock and she was able to pull the door open.

'Bingo!' Hayden breathed. 'You were right. Dunbar obviously got in via the front door, locking it after him, then smashed the window to make it look like the place had been burgled.'

She nodded. 'I think he may have got the idea from Jackman after our born-again hippy screwed the kitchen. No doubt he stumbled on to the break-in quite by accident before Dorothy Matlock turned up for work. Then, knowing the housekeeping wad was in the kitchen drawer, he seized the opportunity to nick it, leaving the burglar to take the blame for that as well.'

'Which means Jackman *was* telling the truth when he said he didn't steal the money?'

'Exactly, and it was shortly after this that Howard came up with the idea of screwing the lab, assuming we would suspect that both jobs were carried out by the same perp. But unfortunately for him, his plan went horribly awry. While he was searching for the key to the drawer, he encountered Martha.'

'Who proved to be a lot better guard dog than a Rottweiler,' another voice said.

Turning quickly, Kate faced a smirking Julian Dunbar, who was standing there with his hands in the pockets of a grey hoodie. He was wearing soft trainers and she had been so engrossed in checking out the door lock that she hadn't heard him enter the courtyard from the side gate which she now saw to be wide open. What was it Angela Dunbar had said about her brother? *A psycho, who creeps around all the time spying on people.* Going by his sudden appearance almost at her elbow, that certainly seemed to be a pretty accurate description

'What are you doing here?' she snapped.

'I happen to live at Moat House,' he sneered. 'What's your excuse?'

'You have no right of access to the annexe. It's out of bounds to everyone save the professor and Dr Lawrence.'

'So what? I'm not in the annexe, am I? Wouldn't want to be, with that spider knocking about in there either.'

Kate's eyes narrowed. 'Why are you creeping about out here?'

'Been for a walk, haven't I? Not against the law to walk around the grounds of your own house, is it?'

'You were snooping.'

He turned away from them. 'Just got a healthy interest in things, that's all. As I told you before, I know everything that's going on in this house.'

Then he strode nonchalantly across the courtyard and disappeared through the door into the house, still with one hand in his pocket.

'Do you think he sussed what we were doing here?' Hayden asked.

Kate grimaced. 'More than likely. But there's nothing we can do about it now and I don't think he'll say anything to anyone. He's a secretive little sod and I suspect he gets a kick out of being the font of all knowledge on matters involving Moat House. Gives him a sense of superiority.'

'If he's that clever, perhaps he'll find Martha for us.'

She gave a short humourless laugh. 'Or maybe she'll find him.'

* * *

The autumn light was fast fading when they got back to the police station and Charlie Woo was waiting for them. He waved them towards a couple of plastic chairs in front of his desk before closing the door and dropping into the swivel behind his desk.

'So, what else have you got?' he asked.

Kate quickly brought him up to speed on all the afternoon's inquiries, excluding only the information she had extracted from Angela Dunbar in relation to Gillian George, which she suspected would not earn her any brownie points at a time when her focus should have been solely on the death of Howard Dunbar.

'So, our man had his own key, did he? Any idea how he might have come by it?'

'Not yet. But he must have managed to get hold of either the professor's or the one allocated to Dr Lawrence, then had a duplicate cut. My money is on Dr Lawrence when she was off on her couple of days' leave. I doubt that she would have taken her key with her in view of the professor's tight controls on access to the lab, and once Howard had found out where it was kept in the house, getting the job done would have been easy. There are any number of local businesses that provide a key-cutting service, and they never ask questions.'

'A good hypothesis, Kate, but that's all it can be at the moment.'

'Agreed, but we'll check things out tomorrow with both Lawrence and the professor.'

He made a face. 'DCI is concerned about how much time we're spending on what is after all nothing more than an accidental death.'

Kate raised an eyebrow. 'With respect, guv, he was the one who designated this as a priority and you yourself indicated that we needed to do a thorough job for the benefit of the coroner.'

'I know,' he replied ruefully. 'But we have to satisfy two competing demands here, I'm afraid, and one is about justifying the cost of the time spent on the investigation.'

'Are you suggesting we just walk away from it?'

'No, but I *am* saying that you need to ensure you can account for every hour you spend on it. No time for excursions into other non-relevant areas, like someone called Gillian George.'

Kate shook her head bitterly. 'Jamie told you?'

'He's concerned that you might be losing your focus.'

She stood up, scowling at Hayden who was nodding in agreement beside her. 'I'll thank him for his concern when I see him again,' she said sarcastically, but turned at the sound of a knock on the door. Andrea James was standing there, a disconcerting gleam in her eyes.

Woo beckoned her inside. She was carrying a sealed plastic bag in one hand and without a word, she stepped past Kate and laid it carefully on Woo's desk. Both Woo and Kate bent over it curiously.

The object inside the bag was about an inch and a half long and less than the thickness of a thin straw. Light brown in colour, but bearing black bands, at first sight it looked like the hairy stalk from a plant, but that it wasn't was evinced by the fact that it appeared to be jointed.

'What the hell is that?' Woo exclaimed.

James smiled her satisfaction. 'What do you think it is?' she asked, enjoying the moment.

'A spider's leg,' Hayden said simply.

She nodded. 'But not any old spider's leg. According to Dr Lawrence who I showed it to, it is part of a rear leg from a Brazilian wandering spider.'

Woo whistled. 'But how did the thing lose part of its leg?'

'It looks like it got caught up among a bunch of keys and in its panic to get away, it left one of its legs behind.'

Kate, who had been silently studying the leg, looked up. 'A bunch of keys. And where were these keys?'

'In the damaged drawer of Professor Dunbar's desk. One of my team was checking the drawer for any forensic traces and found it wedged in the back projecting from the keyring which was trapped behind some ledgers. It looks very much like your deceased burglar forced the drawer, stuck his hand inside, maybe reaching for the bunch of keys, and the spider went for him.'

Woo frowned. 'But I don't understand. If the drawer needed to be forced because it was locked, how the hell did the spider get in there in the first place?'

'My thoughts entirely, so I thoroughly checked around it for any other openings. I did find a hole in the bottom right-hand corner at the back. It had been badly patched, but had come away again, leaving an irregular one-and-a-half-inch diameter hole. It looked like old damage and the desk was certainly antiquated, with evidence of other damage in places seeming to bear this out. Furthermore, there were no traces of any matching slivers of wood in the drawer or on the floor underneath it. Nothing to suggest it could have jammed, then split when the lock itself was forced and the drawer was suddenly yanked open. But whether a large spider could have got into the drawer through an aperture that size, it is difficult to say without seeking an expert opinion.'

Woo looked worried. 'That issue aside, are you suggesting that the thing might have been put in the drawer *before* it was locked?'

'I'm not suggesting anything. I am merely presenting you with the preliminary findings of my team from the forensic examination of the scene. How you wish to interpret those findings is a matter for you.'

'But they nevertheless raise a whole load of new questions about the death of Howard Dunbar,' Kate pointed out grimly, 'and they could very well mean we are looking at something a lot more serious than an unfortunate accident.'

'Something more serious?' Woo echoed. 'Surely you don't suspect Dunbar was murdered?'

'I don't honestly know. But it's a bit farcical to think that this bloody spider could have escaped accidentally in the way it's supposed to have done, then just happened to crawl through a small hole in the back of the very desk drawer that our victim decided to force open. A spider's leg *was* found inside the drawer, which Dr Lawrence has identified as belonging to a spider of the same genus as the one we're looking for, so the creature was obviously inside the drawer when it was forced open. Though we have nothing yet to positively indicate foul play, the whole episode seems mighty suspicious to me.'

Woo waved a hand dismissively. 'Be that as it may, at the moment all we can determine beyond reasonable doubt is that Howard Dunbar was fatally bitten in the lab by a poisonous spider. The rest has to be conjecture until and if we can prove otherwise. The DCI is unlikely to launch a major crime investigation on what we've got so far. There are too many ifs and buts. He'll want more certainty.'

Kate made a face. 'Then you'd better warn him that certainty is a bit like perfection, guv. It tends to take a lot longer to establish. The only saving grace is that, with the injury the spider sustained from losing its leg, it is unlikely to survive long, and it might already be dead.'

Not necessarily,' James cut in. 'If you look at the leg again, you'll see that it has come apart at one of the joints. According to Dr Lawrence, most spiders can shed a leg without suffering serious harm, provided the separation is at a joint or breakpoint, like this, which would enable the muscles to clamp shut around the wound, preventing excess blood loss.'

Woo released his breath with a loud hiss. 'So, instead of an eight-legged monstrosity to deal with, we could have a seven-legged one instead?' he said drily. 'Somehow I don't see that as much of a reassurance.'

'Well, at least it won't be able to run after you as fast,' Hayden put in with his usual flippancy. But no one laughed.

CHAPTER 13

The atmosphere in the sitting room was tense. Hubert Dunbar had to sit down, and he was shaking even more than before.

'Why on earth would I deliberately take a deadly spider from its terrarium and lock it in my desk drawer, if that's what you are suggesting?' he said. 'For what possible purpose would I do that?'

Propped on the arm of the settee, Kate shook her head. 'You tell me, Professor.'

'Of course,' Hayden drawled from the other armchair, not entirely in agreement with Kate's emerging suspicions, but happy to act as devil's advocate, 'if you had got an inkling of Howard's intention to break into your lab, you would have known that he was bound to make a beeline for the one drawer in your desk which happened to be locked. That held the greatest promise of being the drawer containing the money he was looking for—'

'What?' Dunbar rose in his chair, his face completely bloodless now. 'How dare you! You're not seriously suggesting that I put Martha in there to attack him when he broke into the drawer? That's an abominable thing to say.'

Hayden was unruffled by his angry reaction. 'Maybe it is, Professor, but in our experience, people are prone to doing abominable things. No one would even have suspected that the spider was put in the drawer if Martha had not left one of her legs behind.'

Dunbar slumped back in his chair, looking drained from his sudden outburst. 'These slurs are absolutely disgraceful,' he rasped. 'I shall be on to your chief constable about this first thing in the morning.'

'Your prerogative, Professor,' Kate said. 'But before you do, can you tell me where you keep the key to the front door of the lab and your desk drawer when you are not working there?'

Dunbar dug into his pocket and produced a fob holding a brass Yale key and several small, silver-coloured keys. 'They are always with me on this ring when I am working.'

'Yes, yes, as you told us before. But what about when you are not working? Do you take them to bed with you, for instance?'

'Of course not. They are kept in a wall safe in my bedroom, and before you ask, the same applies to Dr Lawrence's keys when she goes home at night or is not at work. As was the case this week. But if you're thinking Howard could have gone into my bedroom in the middle of the night and taken one of the keys from the safe, you can think again. It could never have happened. He would have needed to know the safe combination, which I don't share with anyone.'

'Okay, but just for the sake of argument, what if by some fluke he had managed to sus the access code?'

'He would still have had to get in and out of my bedroom without disturbing me, which would have been next to impossible. The safe is in the wall just above the headboard where I sleep.'

'Do you sleep alone?'

'That is none of your damned business, Sergeant.'

'I'm afraid it is very much my business, Professor. I am conducting a very serious police inquiry here and nothing is off limits. Now, I'll ask you again, do you sleep alone?'

Dunbar took a deep breath and nodded. 'My wife and I have separate bedrooms linked by a small sitting-room-cum-study which was converted from another bedroom. Yasmin suffers from acute migraine and anxiety problems and needs her own space to, er, cope with the attacks that can come on at any time.'

'You say your bedroom safe has a combination lock?'

'Absolutely.'

'And what sort of access code do you use?'

'You of all people shouldn't be asking me that.'

'Ordinarily I would agree with you, but the damage is done now. It is very likely that that access code has already been breached and if the security of the safe has been compromised, you will have to change it now anyway. Presumably, you didn't use your date of birth for the code?'

He gaped. 'How on earth did you know that?'

Kate's fears were confirmed, and she winced. A clever intellectual, she thought, with a complete absence of common sense. 'Because a lot of people do exactly the same thing as it is an easily remembered number. But most criminals know that too and frequently use it to their advantage.'

'It is easy to be wise after the event, Sergeant,' he said acidly. 'But aside from my evident naivety, do you really think that Howard must have somehow got into my room and accessed the safe?'

'It's very possible if he knew your date of birth and decided to make an educated guess at the combination. But then, either you would have been left without a key for a while, giving him time to have a fresh one cut, or he would have had to make an impression of the key in something like a soap block and have someone in the criminal fraternity make a new one up from that.' She looked doubtful. 'An almost impossible thing to do, except in fiction writing, and also it would have meant he was moving in some very shady circles to start with.'

She treated him to a hard stare. 'I want you to level with me, Professor. There must have been times over the past few weeks that necessitated you being away from home, at a meeting or a conference, for example? This could have resulted in your key being left locked in the safe for a protracted period.'

He seemed to be ahead of her now and he closed his eyes briefly in resignation, running a hand through his hair. 'The Bristol conference,' he said. 'It was two weeks ago. I had to address a meeting of biologists and was away for the best part of the day.'

'Which would have given Howard ample time to "borrow" your key and get another one cut.'

Dunbar shook his head desperately. 'But . . . but I had specifically locked the key away in the safe. I had genuinely thought it was secure.'

'No one is apportioning blame in this respect, Professor. I am merely trying to work out how Howard could have got hold of it.'

'So if your suspicions are accurate, why didn't he get the drawer key cut as well? Then he wouldn't have needed to force the lock.'

'Because he needed to make the theft look like a genuine burglary to throw the police off the scent. A screwdriver was found on the floor under your desk which is currently being forensically examined. He obviously brought that along to use on the drawer in lieu of the key. Despite what you told me, I think we can safely assume that, as your accountant, Howard would have known precisely where your money was stashed before he broke into the lab and that the drawer would be easy to force. He obviously pulled open all the other drawers and cupboards in the room solely to suggest that the burglar had carried out an untidy search before forcing the locked desk drawer. We have also established that the window of the lab was smashed from the inside, which is further evidence of his attempt to conceal the fact that the break-in was an inside job. I can also now tell you that we have found the extra key that enabled Howard to access the lab in the first place. It was with his other personal effects at the mortuary. So it would seem that your wall safe was not quite as secure as you believed.'

He shook his head in resignation. 'The scheming little swine,' he said bitterly. 'I never dreamed he had it in him.'

Kate sighed. 'I'm afraid it does rather seem that the son you regarded as nothing more than a feckless wastrel had hidden depths. He might well have got away with his audacious plan too if Martha had not intervened. It was at that point that any gambler's luck he might have been relying on failed him in spectacular fashion.'

She rose from the arm of the settee and smoothed imaginary creases out of her trousers.

'Now, if you don't mind, Professor, I would like to move things on by taking a look at the rooms upstairs, particularly yours and Howard's, and it would be most helpful if we could then have a chat with your wife. Purely routine, of course.'

His indignation resurfaced in a rush. 'I don't see the point in that,' he blustered, 'and anyway, can you do that without a warrant?'

Kate evaded the question, knowing full well that she had insufficient grounds to apply for one.

'I am trying to get to the bottom of a serious incident that cost your son his life, Professor,' she said instead. 'I'm sure you wouldn't want the coroner to think you were being obstructive.'

For a moment he hesitated, his jaw thrust out stubbornly. Then abruptly, he seemed to sag in the middle. 'Oh very well,' he replied, wearily caving in. 'Whatever you wish. But I'll have to check with Yasmin that she is well enough to see you first. The death of Howard has shaken her up quite badly.'

Kate was tempted to raise the subject of Gillian George with him then but thought better of it. There would be time enough for that later. After she had managed to gain a bit more information on the tragedy. Furthermore, probing such a sensitive issue when he was already in a state of high dudgeon could be counterproductive if, as she suspected, it was likely to wind him up still more. At that precise moment she needed his full cooperation if she was to continue to get the access to the bedrooms she needed to check.

'I understand perfectly,' she said instead. 'It's been a bad business all round.'

'There goes a very worried man,' Hayden murmured as Dunbar's feet could be heard clumping up the stairs.

Kate's mouth tightened. 'He has every reason to be. Someone put that deadly spider in the lab drawer, and I am pretty sure it wasn't Howard. Until the creature is found, everyone in this house is at risk from the thing, and that includes us.'

* * *

The professor's bedroom opened off a narrow, thinly carpeted corridor at the top of the stairs which creaked a lot under their feet. There wasn't much to see, just a neat, medium-sized room, plainly decorated and containing just a big double bed, a wardrobe and a chest of drawers. The safe was as Dunbar had described. It was set in the wall above the headboard of the bed. To get to it would have required kneeling on the edge of the bed to reach the combination dial in the centre.

There was a white painted door to the left of the bed. Kate guessed it was the connecting door to the sitting room the professor had mentioned, but she could not see anything of the other room as the door was closed. Perhaps Yasmin was preparing herself for her forthcoming interview, Kate thought wryly. From their previous brief meeting, she had struck Kate as the sort of woman who put great store by her appearance and the way she came across to others. Time would tell if she was right.

Howard had occupied an apartment at the end of the corridor and there were two more doors opening off a short passageway just before it on the right. 'Angela and Julian's bedrooms,' the professor explained in passing. 'Both a waste of space, I'm afraid.'

Nice to see that fatherly affection is still alive and kicking, Kate thought as Dunbar unlocked the door to the apartment and they followed him inside.

Howard's accommodation turned out to consist of a single bedroom, a small lounge and an en suite bathroom and toilet. The whole place was smartly appointed with expensive looking ultra-modern furniture, deep, brightly coloured carpets and modern spotlights suspended from the ceiling which provided quite a subtle, restful illumination. The walls were tastefully painted in pale pastel shades and were graced with several erotic photographs of nude female models.

'Sorry about that,' Dunbar said, plainly embarrassed. 'Howard had a quirky taste.'

'So I see,' Kate replied, admiring the artistry in the photographs. 'Looks like he had expensive tastes too.'

She picked up an ornate, gold-coloured carriage clock framed by naked nymphs blowing long, slender trumpets and nodded her appreciation.

'That was always his trouble,' Dunbar said. 'Lived well beyond his means, despite the allowance I gave him. Fancy furnishings, flashy cars and designer clothes he couldn't afford. Drank like a damned fish too. Not your cheap Tesco wine either, but the best vintages, plus top-class spirits. He was always entertaining some damned woman or other up here as well.'

He pointed to a smoky black glass cabinet in the corner of the lounge beside a massive television. 'You'll find everything in there, plus crystal glasses from Venice, Paris and Vienna that were way out of his league. This is the result.'

He jerked open the top drawer of a sideboard and, thrusting his hand inside, produced a wad of paper which he dumped on to a small table. Kate leafed through the documents and found that they were betting slips, demands for payment. In one case there was a letter from a London casino carrying a thinly veiled threat if a five-hundred-pound bill was not paid by the end of the previous month.

'I'll leave you to look around,' he said. 'Yasmin said she'd be happy to see you when you're finished.'

Hayden gently closed the door behind him and turned expectantly towards Kate. 'So, what now, Oh Great Medusa.'

'Shut it, Hayd,' Kate breathed. 'Just get on with the search, will you.'

'And what are we searching for exactly?'

'Anything that might tell us who hated Howard enough to want him dead.'

* * *

The search of Howard's room at first yielded very little, apart from scores more betting slips and bookmakers' payment demands stuffed in different drawers, indicating that the deceased gambler had an even bigger problem than they had been made aware of.

But that was before Hayden made his discovery. 'Gordon Bennett, look what I've just found,' he called out to Kate from the lounge as she was in the process of opening up a laptop computer on a small table in the bedroom.

'Bloody computer is password protected,' she muttered, breaking off from her task and returning to the lounge. 'We'll need technical support if we want to open it—'

Then her voice trailed off as she saw the slim, black mobile telephone he was holding up in his hand.

'Found it down the side of the armchair,' he said. 'Thing is, it's one of the latest smartphones, yet it's not even protected by a passcode or facial ID.'

'Brilliant,' she exclaimed. 'I wonder what's on it.'

But she wasn't given the opportunity of finding out. The voice that spoke from the doorway was sharp and angry.

'What are you doing in here?'

Angela Dunbar was standing there, barefoot and dressed in a short, white bathrobe. Her hair was a tangled, wet mess and her legs and feet glistened in the lounge lights. It was obvious that she had just got out of the bath or shower, and that there was a complete change in her personality from the last time Kate had spoken to her. She was no longer the vulnerable little girl facing an unwanted pregnancy who had needed a comforting arm and had cried on Kate's shoulder.

She had reverted to her former anti-social persona and radiated hostility and aggression.

Hayden had the good sense to slip the phone up his sleeve before she could see it, throwing her a guilty schoolboy smile at the same time. But Kate's reaction was cool and dismissive.

'We're here on police business,' she said. 'Now, will you close the door and let us get on with it.'

Angela was not intimidated and stood her ground. 'Have you got a search warrant?' she demanded, her face white and her eyes blazing. 'You have no right to be in Howard's room.'

Kate manufactured a weary sigh. 'We don't need a warrant,' she said glibly. 'And your father is fully aware of the fact that we are here. Now, I must ask you to leave.'

'Ask *me* to leave? I live here.'

'Not in this room, you don't.'

The other stared at her incredulously for a moment, then quite suddenly, her attitude changed, and she emitted a hard disbelieving laugh.

'You've got some balls,' she said.

Kate returned her smile. 'I do hope not.'

'You won't find anything in here.'

'Oh, then you must know what we're looking for.'

'No, I don't. I just know you're wasting your time and that whatever you may be thinking, you've got it all wrong. There isn't anything to find. Howard was my brother, but he was a useless prat. That's why he cocked up trying to burgle my father's laboratory and got himself killed.'

'How do you know that's what he was doing in the laboratory? I never told you.'

She laughed again. 'You don't have to be Sherlock Holmes to work that one out. There's no great conspiracy here, just a tragic misadventure and the sooner you lot accept that and get back to chasing real criminals, the better.'

'So why after I told you earlier that Howard had died from the bite of a Brazilian wandering spider and you said that Gillian George had died the same way, did you use the words "you should remember that"? Were you suggesting the two cases are linked?'

'I haven't the faintest idea what you are talking about. Now, I have to dry myself.'

Then she turned on her heel and left them to it.

Kate looked at Hayden curiously after she had gone. 'Why did she deny saying that to me about Gillian George?' she echoed. 'And why on earth would she come up with a word like conspiracy?'

He flicked his eyebrows in the semblance of a shrug. 'Maybe because she thinks you are looking for something that isn't there.'

'Or maybe because she knows there *is* a conspiracy,' she said.

CHAPTER 14

Yasmin Dunbar was all smiles when she admitted Kate and Hayden to her upstairs sitting room.

'Ah, Sergeant,' she said, rising from an armchair in response to their knock. 'Hubert tells me you wanted to scrutinise my little hideaway.'

She was dressed in a green silk kimono and wore little gold sandals on her feet. Kate noticed that the room, which was quite small, was beautifully decorated in a rich arabesque style, with a thick Persian rug covering the floor. One corner was obscured by a screen with an ornate design made up of intertwining plants, and a lacquer cabinet stood in another. The room was furnished with a single armchair and a chaise longue with gold-coloured leopard's feet. There was a white painted door on each side obviously connecting to both bedrooms and a third door which was open slightly to reveal an en suite bathroom. The opulence of the room was so out of character with the rest of the house that for a moment both detectives simply stood there staring around them in astonishment.

'You like my little pad, then?' Yasmin Dunbar said. Kate noticed once again just a faint American accent. Dunbar gave a soft laugh, but it lacked any real warmth and there was a haunted look in her eyes that was quite noticeable. 'It makes me feel at home, you see.'

'And where *is* home?' Kate asked.

She waved them to the chaise longue. 'I was actually born in Persia, now Iran. My mother was of Persian nobility, and my father was a diplomat. But I have lived in England for much of my life and was educated at a private school in Surrey.'

'So how long have you been married?'

'To Hubert? Oh, only about ten years. We were both married before, you see. My first husband was also a diplomat, but he was killed in a road accident in America where we were living at the time.'

'I'm sorry. How on earth did you and the professor get to meet?'

'Need you ask?' she said, her eyes gently mocking. 'Spiders! He was lecturing to biology students at a university facility in Texas while visiting the state in search of Brown Recluse spider specimens for his research. I was working in the library at the university, following the death of my husband, and he came in, seeking local geographical information. I helped him with his research, and we agreed to keep in touch. Shortly after this he lost his own wife, Madelaine, to suicide and we sort of got together. On the rebound, I suppose you'd say.'

'So Howard, Julian and Angela are not your children?'

'No, I inherited them unfortunately.'

'Why unfortunately?'

'Because at least two of them have resented me ever since Hubert and I got married, especially Julian who was only a child of about ten at the time. He has quite a nasty, sly nature and I'm always afraid he might do something horrible to me.'

'Like putting a spider in your bed?' Hayden said with a typical tactless attempt at humour.

Kate winced and threw him a scathing glance, but Dunbar didn't bat an eyelid. She simply nodded and said, 'Hopefully not, but it wouldn't surprise me if he did.'

'What about Angela?' Kate asked, anxious to move on.

'Ah, Angela, or Cloud as she likes to be called now. A rather deep, mixed-up, young woman with demons of her own to deal with, I would think.'

'Why do you say that?'

'Just a feeling I get with her. She seems to be perpetually anti-everything. Men, the Christian church, the government, bankers. You name it and she is against it. But beneath all the hostility I sense there is a fragile little girl lost. Someone who can't make up her mind who she is or what she wants out of life. Hubert's first wife, Madelaine, committed suicide and I fear Angela could end up the same way.'

Kate frowned, thinking of Angela's erratic behaviour and her unwanted pregnancy, and finding herself very much in agreement with Yasmin Dunbar's potted assessment.

'Let's hope not,' she said. 'But what about Howard? What was he like?'

Dunbar's expression saddened. 'Howard was just Howard,' she said. 'Man about town. One of the lads. Lived for the moment. Never a bad word to say about anyone. Very likeable, but with shallow aspirations. Unable to commit to anything and with the worst judgement I have ever seen in anyone.'

It was Kate's turn to laugh. 'You seem to be a bit of a psychologist.'

She nodded. 'Used to be once. I majored in psychology at university and had my own small partnership in Manchester before I met John, my late husband. But the business folded, and I moved to the States with him soon after we met.'

'No children of your own then? Oh, sorry, I am poking my nose.'

'It's fine. But no, I don't have any children and I fear I am too old for that now even if I wanted them, which I don't.' The dark eyes sparkled mischievously. 'Anyway, poor Hubert is far too busy with his spiders to think about starting another family and he's so obsessed with the little horrors that he has probably forgotten how to start one anyway.'

Kate laughed with her, but then broke off with a more serious question. 'Did you know Howard was in debt?'

'Everyone knew that. He didn't exactly try to conceal it and I know he pleaded with Hubert just a week ago to advance him a very large loan.'

'How much was it for?'

'Ten thousand pounds.'

'Heavens, that *was* a tidy sum. I take it the professor refused?'

She shrugged. 'Of course. He knew Howard was a compulsive gambler and would never be able to pay it back. Even Howard's flashy car is in imminent danger of being repossessed because he has defaulted on the payments.'

'You seem to know a lot about Howard's personal problems. Did he talk to you a lot then?'

'Well, he could hardly talk to Hubert, could he?' There was a trace of anger in her expression. 'My husband has a heart of stone. So he unloaded on me.'

'Did you help him?'

'I tried. I gave him a couple of thousand without Hubert knowing, but Howard promptly put it on the nose of "a dead cert" at Cheltenham and, of course, lost the lot.'

'I gather you already know he was attacked by an escaped spider in your husband's laboratory and didn't recover from the toxin?'

'Hubert told me straight after he had found him there. I understand he was after a large sum of money Hubert had locked in his desk drawer.'

'We don't know that for certain, but it seems to be the most plausible explanation, yes.'

Kate hesitated, then took the plunge. 'From some of the comments you have made to me on the now two occasions we have met, you don't seem to get on that well with your husband.'

For a second Kate thought she had gone too far, but after a noticeable narrowing of her eyes, Dunbar smiled again. But the smile was one of irony. 'I think that could be described as an understatement, Sergeant,' she said. 'Hubert and I live in the same house, we often eat together in the same dining room, we even talk to each other occasionally, but we are two entirely different people. We haven't slept in the same bed for I can't remember how long, and we live totally separate lives.'

'Yet you have stayed together for ten years?'

'I have no choice. You see, Hubert is very well off and I am accustomed to the lifestyle I have enjoyed for so long.' She sighed. 'So I stay and he . . . he goes off on his trips abroad and shacks up with whatever little tramp takes his fancy.'

'So he's been having affairs?'

To Kate's surprise, Yasmin threw back her head and burst into a fit of laughter. 'Having affairs?' she chortled. 'How quaint.' She leaned forward. 'My dear, that man is a serial seducer of any girl out of school uniform.'

Somehow Kate just couldn't see that. 'He doesn't exactly strike me as the Don Juan type.'

'Don't you believe it. He can put on a sort of dark charm when it suits him, and that makes him irresistible to adventurous young women. I'm waiting to see how long it takes before he beds Sam, his new assistant, like he did the last one, though I suspect she will be a tougher nut to crack.'

Kate could feel her stomach muscles tighten after what Dunbar had said, but she tried not to let it show. 'Was that Gillian George?'

Dunbar's laughter abruptly ceased. 'Yes, that was her. Pretty little thing and young enough to be taken for his daughter. Exactly his type. Took her with him to the Amazon rainforest, ostensibly on a field trip. Then along came the spider, just like in the nursery rhyme, and "Ouch!", poor little Miss Muffet was no more.'

The vindictive bitterness in the woman's tone had surfaced in a rush, and for the first time Kate saw the hate and the hurt that lurked behind the beautiful 'mask' she had cultivated.

'How did the accident happen?' she went on.

Yasmin sat back in her chair and reached for a gold-coloured cigarette holder lying on a glass-topped table next to her chair. Then she selected a cigarette from a packet that had been lying beside it and inserted it carefully in the end. Kate waited patiently for her reply as she lit up, filling the room with clouds of aromatic smoke.

'How?' she said. 'I don't know all the details, but I believe the thing got into her room somehow and bit her while she was lying in bed. At least, according to Hubert. I am only surprised he wasn't in bed with her at the same time. I mean, that really would have been poetic justice, wouldn't it?'

'Was the occurrence investigated by the police?'

'Oh yes, and Hubert said it was in all the local papers. Even made it back here too, but it was just a paragraph I saw in a couple of the nationals. You know the sort of thing: "Young British scientist dies of a poison spider bite while on a field trip to the Amazon. Police say it was a tragic accident." There then followed a whole dramatic piece about how many deadly spiders there are in the Amazon rainforest and how long their bite would take to kill you. Usual rubbish.'

'Do you believe it *was* an accident?'

Dunbar seemed to consider the question carefully, then she nodded. 'No reason to think otherwise, Sergeant. Hubert may be a lying, disloyal letch, but I can't see him murdering someone. And why would he anyway? He was having a whale of a time with his bit on the side and was well away from prying eyes too. So, quite safe from the scandal of being caught *in flagrante.*'

That phrase again, Kate mused. It kept coming up in this investigation.

'And what about Howard?' she asked. 'Do you think that was an accident too?'

'Again, I don't know all the details, though from what I've been told, I can't see it being anything else. But if you're suspecting my husband of being behind it, I'd have to ask myself why would he want to kill his own son over such a thing and why would he go to such extraordinary lengths to

135

do it? A simple punishment would have sufficed. Don't you agree?'

But Kate chose not to answer, for another chilling thought had occurred to her. What if Howard's death *had* been an accident and he had simply been in the wrong place at the wrong time? What if the target had not been Howard at all, but Professor Hubert Dunbar?

* * *

It was well into the evening before Kate and Hayden got back to Highbridge police station from Moat House and not surprisingly, the canteen was already closed. But despite Hayden's protestations, she showed no intention of signing off for the day. Instead, she sent her truculent husband out for a Chinese takeaway while she turned her attention to Howard Dunbar's mobile phone they had brought back with them after issuing a disinterested Professor Dunbar with an official receipt.

She was still going through this when Hayden got back with two large foil containers of chicken chop suey and a couple of cans of Coca Cola, dumping them on her desk in the empty CID office and grabbing a chair.

'Anything?' he asked, ripping the lid off one of the containers and tucking into his meal with gusto.

She peeled the lid off her own meal and sat back, shaking her head.

'Nothing so far. There're only a load of rubbish emails on it from irate bookmaker creditors demanding payment, similar to the corres we found in his apartment.'

'Might as well go home after we've eaten this, then,' he said. 'I know I could do with an early night.'

She grimaced over her foil container and dipped into her meal with the plastic fork that had been supplied, ignoring his suggestion.

'I should have grabbed the bloody computer too,' she said. 'But as it was password protected, it would have had to be sent off to the techies and I don't think the DCI would have been very happy about me doing that without a cast-iron reason. Let me just check his call logs.'

As she ate with one hand, she worked the phone with the thumb of her other hand and seconds later stiffened.

'Now, what's this?' she breathed.

Hayden looked up with his laden fork halfway to its destination. 'What's what?' he asked through a mouthful of chicken and rice.

'Seems our Howard received a mobile phone call at 1.10 a.m. on the very night he died,' she said. 'It's recorded in his missed calls log.'

'Funny time to ring someone.'

Her eyes gleamed triumphantly. 'You miss the point. It suggests that the caller must have actually expected Howard to be in a position to answer, otherwise why ring him in the first place at such an hour? They obviously didn't realise he had left his phone behind.'

He frowned. 'Bit odd, I must admit.'

'It's a lot more than that, mister.' She slid the mobile across to him. 'Look at the ID of the caller.'

He picked the phone up, then abruptly froze in mid-chew. 'Good lord. Yasmin.'

'That's what it says. His "loving" stepmom. It would be just too much of a coincidence for it to have been someone else with the same name.'

'But why on earth would Yasmin Dunbar be ringing him in the middle of the night?'

'Exactly my thoughts, especially on the very night Howard had chosen to stage his burglary at the lab. There's something else too.'

'Go on.'

'It's occurred to me since our chat with Yasmin that although the facts that have so far come to light would suggest Howard's death *was* suspicious, it is possible that the professor actually had nothing to with it but was himself the intended target. Maybe Howard just got in the way.'

She saw him frown. 'We've got absolute zilch to support that theory, but if you're right, it would certainly add a whole new dimension to this investigation.'

She flicked open the tab of her can of coke and took a long, hard pull before setting it down again. 'Well, it's something worth thinking about, isn't it? But in any event with what we've got, I reckon our Yasmin has some difficult questions to answer, don't you?'

He looked at his watch, then stared at her suspiciously. 'Hopefully not tonight, though,' he said.

CHAPTER 15

The inquiry team's meeting with the DCI first thing in the morning was short and anything but sweet.

'I am minded to pull the plug on this thing,' he warned after he had been fully updated on the investigation. 'It's already tied up our resources for far too long. In this area alone, we currently have three rape investigations on the go, a series of high-value burglaries, a post office robbery and only yesterday, a serious assault on a care worker on her way to work.

'As you will know only too well, we have been travelling light of a second DS and two DCs on this department for over a year and a half now. Previously, Detective Sergeant Percival was supposed to have been sent to fill the DS vacancy. But what happened? He was later appointed Acting DI with the unfortunate death of Detective Inspector Roscoe and then promptly promoted to substantive DI at Headquarters. As a result, we have now ended up back where we started, with just DS Lewis here remaining on the department and yet another Acting DI appointed instead of a substantive one.' He added hastily, 'Oh, Mr Woo, no offence.' Then he frowned at the grins the remark elicited.

He was no doubt totally unaware, Kate thought, of the lyrics in the old George Formby song about a Chinese laundryman, but no one bothered to enlighten him, and he coughed and carried on with his analysis.

'I am reluctant to countenance the expenditure of any more time or resources on something that is plainly nothing more than a tragic accident. Especially as it appears that this deceased man, Howard Dunbar, was carrying out a burglary at the time of his death anyway.'

Kate fidgeted in her plastic chair and darted a glance at Hayden, then at Charlie Woo seated to one side of his desk which he had vacated in deference to Ricketts's rank.

Woo issued a discreet cough. 'Kate, er, DS Lewis is convinced that Dunbar's death was suspicious, guv, and that it requires further investigation.'

Ricketts made an irritable clicking sound with his tongue and concentrated his cold gaze on her.

'Nonsense,' he said. 'We have established that Howard Dunbar was bitten by a poisonous spider that apparently escaped from its confinement because of Professor Dunbar's carelessness. Dr Lawrence and Professor Dunbar himself, both experts in their field, have said its instincts would have been to look for somewhere dark in which to hide. We know there was a hole in the back of the desk drawer where it allegedly ended up and it seems logical to me that this, er, thing would have made use of that hole to crawl into the drawer. I have made a point of ringing another eminent arachnologist, a Professor Stapleton who works for the government in the same field as Professor Dunbar. I sent him an email attachment with one of the SOCO photographs of this drawer, including the measurements of the hole. He has already responded and is satisfied that the hole was big enough for the creature to have got through and he agrees with Professor Dunbar that it would have been looking for somewhere like that in which to hide.'

He smirked his satisfaction at his own bit of detective work. 'So as far as I can see, the case is cut and dried. Your man got into the laboratory with the key he had in his pocket, forced open the drawer looking for the large sum of money that had been deposited in it and was attacked and bitten, fatally as it transpires, by the creature hiding there. Simple as that. All this talk of foul play is just noise, and I won't have a perfectly obvious accident turned into something it is not. We have all the information the coroner will require to consider the matter, including photographs and forensic material gathered by SOCO, and I feel we should leave it at that.'

'I have reason to believe that Howard Dunbar was unlawfully killed, sir,' Kate cut in quietly as she saw which way things were going. 'We have uncovered some suspicious aspects to the case which suggest that the spider might have been deliberately put in that drawer. But I believe that Howard Dunbar was not the target. I think he just happened to be where he shouldn't have been and that the fate he suffered may have originally been intended for Professor Dunbar.'

Ricketts stared at her as if she had suddenly claimed the earth was flat. 'And where is the evidence for all this?' he said. 'For heaven's sake, Sergeant, stay in the real world, will you. In none of the briefings I have received to date is there the slightest hint of a threat towards the professor, and why should there be? He may not be the most popular man in the world, but I can't see why anyone would have chosen to go to such elaborate lengths to murder him when other much simpler methods are available. No, I am a lot more concerned about the present whereabouts of the missing spider than anything else, so I suggest you return to Moat House and make damned sure it isn't still lurking somewhere on the premises. Then wrap this inquiry up and get back to some proper detective work. Understood? You have twenty-four hours.'

Then without another word and waving Kate to silence as she opened her mouth to protest further, he swept from the room and marched back across the general office to exit the department through the double doors.

'So, how are we supposed to find this spider?' Hayden said wryly from his spot in the corner. 'Leave some milk out for it?'

Woo returned to the chair behind his desk and sat down with an explosive sigh. 'Sorry, guys,' he said, 'but you heard the man. Twenty-four hours and that's it.'

Kate's face was like thunder. 'I *know* this job is sus,' she grated. 'And I'm also convinced that Howard wasn't the target. He was just in the wrong place at the wrong time. The professor was meant to be the one to open that drawer. Someone went into the lab before Howard arrived, took the spider from the terrarium and locked it in that drawer. They knew somehow that the first thing the professor always did when he got into work each morning was to unlock that particular drawer because all his lab keys were kept in it, along with his diary and project book.'

Woo sucked his teeth. 'I've every sympathy for what you're saying, Kate,' he said, 'but as Mr Ricketts pointed out, you've not got an ounce of proof of this. If your assumption is right, the most likely culprit would be Dr Lawrence, as she looks to be the only other person in Moat House who knows how to handle spiders.'

Kate shook her head. 'She was off for two days over the period when all this happened.'

'Then who else are we looking at?'

'I don't know. The professor was loaded, and he was disliked intensely by every member of his family. His wife appears to regard him with contempt and intimated that he was a serial adulterer. His daughter, Angela, described him as cold and calculating. His son, Julian, was far more blunt, and said he was an arsehole. None of them seemed to have a good word to say about him and I suspect that they are all very keen to inherit his money.'

Woo tutted impatiently. 'Hypothesis and conjecture, Kate. All you've got is a vague suspicion. Absolutely nothing else.'

Kate snorted her desperation. 'I just can't understand why Ricketts has changed his tune so suddenly. Right at the start of this thing, when the first break-in occurred, he said the investigation was a priority. Now when we have an even more serious case on our hands, he wants to bury it. Where exactly is he at?'

Woo nodded. 'I can see where you're coming from, but you have to understand that Professor Dunbar is very well connected, and our esteemed DCI is under a lot of pressure from the top to prevent waves. At the start, it was a clear-cut case of burglary, which in order to satisfy the powers that be, required the rapid detection we actually got. But Howard Dunbar's death is an entirely different proposition. It already has the potential for attracting keen press interest, particularly if the professor is later found to be culpable through negligence, and I'm surprised we don't already have reporters sniffing around.'

'By rights, guv, shouldn't we have alerted the media to the spider's escape anyway,' Foster interjected. 'In the interests of public safety.'

Woo shrugged. 'If Moat House was in a residential area maybe,' he agreed. 'But as the place is miles off the beaten track, the risk to the public is negligible, and in any event, the super himself has apparently ruled this out to avoid causing a press feeding frenzy and creating unnecessary local panic.'

Kate snorted. 'And also to protect the DCI's arse and give him time to produce a successful result in a nicely wrapped up parcel ahead of any criticism.'

The DI smirked. 'You may be right, Kate, which means that the last thing the DCI needs on top of it all is the merest hint of a police investigation into possible foul play. That would almost certainly explode into a major scandal, scotch the work the professor is engaged in, and have quite a career-limiting effect on his future prospects as a consequence.'

'So he wants to see the whole thing cuffed?'

'Wouldn't you in his position?'

'No, I wouldn't. I'm not a bloody weathervane, so I don't swing with the wind.'

'That's probably why you're a DS and not a DCI. In any event, I'm afraid you've got just twenty-four hours to come up with something definite or it's *finito*.'

'I thought you were on my side in this. When we discussed it previously, you seemed to share my feelings about the case being sus. Now you appear to have suddenly changed your mind. Trying to be a weathervane too, are you?'

His expression hardened. 'I'll pretend I didn't hear that, Kate. Now, I suggest you just get on with what you have to do. You're already running out of time.'

She stood up sharply. 'And if the professor ends up the same way as his son. What then?'

'We'll just have to hope it doesn't come to that,' he said.

* * *

'So what now?' Hayden asked when Kate steered him away from the department and into one of the vacant interview rooms downstairs.

'Research,' Kate replied. 'First another trip to the LIO, Dave Gort, to see if he can look into the background of the Dunbar family for us and in particular, to find out all he can about Gillian George. I think she is the key to this whole business.'

'And then?'

'A nice little chat with Yasmin Dunbar to find out why she chose to ring Howard at past one o'clock in the morning on the exact same night that he was attacked by Martha.'

'You're using the name the professor gave to that spider quite a lot now.'

'I know and it's sick. But at least it's easier than constantly referring to the creature as "the spider".'

He grinned. 'Actually, I think that deep down you're getting quite fond of the little thing.'

'I can't wait to meet her,' she said sarcastically.

'Hm, as they say, be careful what you wish for!'

Kate once more thought of the shed from her childhood and felt her skin prickle.

* * *

Moat House seemed like a mausoleum. There wasn't a sign of anyone when Kate and Hayden pulled up outside. But both the BMW and Howard's Triumph Spitfire were still parked to one side of the front door which was ajar.

Kate rang the bell and called through the gap. 'Hello, anyone in?'

Her greeting went unanswered, and she cast Hayden a frown.

She was on the point of pushing the door wide and stepping inside when Angela Dunbar appeared in the doorway.

'Still snooping around, then?' she sneered. 'You would think the police had something better to do.' She pushed between them. 'If you want to see dear pater, he is out again.'

'No,' Kate replied, 'we have come to see your mother actually.'

Dunbar spun round in the driveway. 'Mother?' she exclaimed. 'She's not my bloody mother. She's just the cow my father was shagging when my real mother committed suicide.'

Then she turned her back on them and strode quickly to the Spitfire and climbed inside. Moments later she disappeared in a flurry of loose gravel.

'Well, well, well,' Kate said. 'I certainly touched a nerve there.'

But Hayden was not listening. His gaze was fixed on the disappearing sports car with a look of total adoration.

'Now poor old Howard is gone,' he murmured, 'do you think his creditors might be prepared to sell me that little beauty?'

She dug him viciously in the ribs, making him gasp. 'To hell with the bloody car,' she snapped. 'Twenty-four hours, that's all we've got, remember? Now, let's find the lovely Yasmin.'

In fact, the professor's attractive other half was not far away. They heard her voice first and realised she was in the dining room, apparently talking to Dorothy Matlock. Kate threw an arm across Hayden's chest to stop him in his tracks and paused a moment to listen.

'So, do we understand each other, Mrs Matlock?' they heard the lady of the house purr. 'Mum is the word, eh? You've not seen or heard anything.'

'Yes, ma'am,' Matlock replied. 'You can count on me.'

'Excellent,' Dunbar said, but the next instant she froze in the doorway as she clapped eyes on the two detectives in the hallway.

'Why, Sergeant Lewis,' she said, nodding to Hayden, 'what a surprise.'

'I'm sure,' Kate replied, meeting the now narrowed gaze and sensing the animosity directed towards them.

Dunbar quickly recovered her composure and managed a smile. 'I was, er, just speaking to Mrs Matlock about a special dinner she is preparing for Julian's twenty-first birthday. All a big secret actually.'

'Of course,' Kate replied sweetly, glimpsing Dorothy Matlock fussing nervously around the table with an armful of dirty breakfast plates. 'You can't do enough for a loving son, can you?'

The barbs were out, and Kate could feel Hayden fidgeting awkwardly just behind her.

'So what is it we can do for you this time?' Dunbar went on.

'We'd like a few words with you if you don't mind.'

'Of course. Shall we adjourn to the sitting room?'

Kate carefully closed the door behind them and waited while Dunbar settled into an armchair. Then she propped herself on the edge of the settee beside Hayden as in previous interviews.

'I get the impression that you were pretty close to Howard. Rather more in fact than Julian or Angela.'

'Yes, I suppose I was. He was a very likeable young man. If I had ever had a son, I'd have hoped he would have been like him.'

'Even though he was unable to control his gambling obsession and was in debt up to the eyeballs.'

She shrugged. 'These things happen, Sergeant. None of us is perfect.'

'No, but from our inquiries, it would seem he had planned to steal a large sum of money from your husband's drawer in the laboratory.'

'So I believe.'

'Were you aware that this was his intention?'

'Sorry? Me aware? Of course not. How could I be?'

Kate jumped in at the deep end. 'Didn't you have another key to the laboratory cut, so that he could get in?'

Dunbar's gaze hardened and there was a gleam in her eyes that Kate had not seen before. But she showed no obvious sign of emotion at the blatant accusation.

'Not at all, Sergeant. I rather think you have let your imagination run away with you. Now, after that, I think you ought to leave my house.'

Kate didn't budge. 'Were you in regular contact with Howard?'

'Sergeant, we lived in the same house. I would think it's pretty obvious that we would have had regular contact with each other. As I still do with Julian and Angela.'

'Do you use a mobile phone?'

'Er, sometimes, yes.'

'Can you give me the number?'

'Of course.' She produced a phone from the pocket of her jeans and read it out.

'Did you ever ring Howard on his mobile?'

'Why would I need to do that when he was living just along the corridor? I don't think I even knew his number.'

'If that's the case, how is it that you were able to telephone him at just after one a.m. the night he died?'

'You must be mistaken.'

Kate shook her head. 'We carried out a search of Howard's apartment yesterday and recovered his mobile phone from a chair. The name Yasmin was recorded in his missed calls log. How do you explain that?'

She affected a laugh but didn't answer the question. 'Am I being accused of something, Sergeant?'

'We would just like to know why you rang him, Mrs Dunbar,' Hayden put in. 'It's a rather unusual time to be ringing someone, wouldn't you agree?'

'Especially as it was on the very night he died,' Kate added.

Dunbar shrugged but hung on to her cool. 'Well, I can't explain it. The only thing I can think of is that I fell asleep with it in bed with me and laid on the phone and it somehow dialled Howard automatically from my list of contacts.'

'Then you do know his number? Just now, you said you didn't.'

'That's right. I said I didn't know his number and I still don't. But I must have added it to my list of contacts at some time in the past.'

'I'm sure you can see how unlikely it is you could have accidentally dialled his number in the way you have just said.'

'Well, I can't think how else it could have happened. If it did.'

'I'm sorry, Mrs Dunbar, but I don't believe you.'

'That's your prerogative, Sergeant. Now, I would be grateful if you would leave my house. I find your manner offensive.'

'I'm sure you will appreciate that it is our job to get to the truth, Mrs Dunbar, and that this sometimes involves asking uncomfortable questions.'

'Of course, but don't you think you are making a mountain out of a molehill on this inquiry? Howard's death was an accident after all.'

'We're not entirely convinced on that score, I'm afraid.'

Her eyes widened and she sat forward in her chair. 'Not an accident? Surely you're not suggesting Howard was murdered?'

'We're investigating all possibilities.'

'But . . . but he was bitten by a poisonous spider. How could that be murder?'

'It is something we are looking into, but there are a number of anomalies associated with his death that need to be resolved.'

Kate knew she was on shaky ground, and she tried not to think about the DCI's likely reaction if he were to hear about her blatant disobedience to his instructions to wrap things up. But it was too late for misgivings now and she pressed on, ignoring more uneasy twitching from Hayden beside her.

'So you can see the reason for my rather blunt questions.'

'But surely you don't think that I . . . ? Good heavens, I wouldn't go anywhere near those beastly things, and I am the last person who would want Howard . . .'

Her voice trailed off and Kate raised an inquiring eyebrow. 'Dead?' she finished for her.

A marked change came over Dunbar and she slumped back in her chair, her confidence gone and the same haunted look that Kate had noticed before returning to her eyes.

The next moment her hand was fumbling in the pocket of the cardigan she was wearing, withdrawing a packet of cigarettes and lighting up with trembling fingers, this time without her cigarette holder.

Kate waited patiently, sensing she was on the verge of saying something else.

'I was in love with him,' she said finally, her eyes filling up with tears.

It was the last thing Kate had expected her to say and for a second she simply stared at her in stunned silence. Hayden was unable to contain himself, however.

'Love?' he exclaimed. 'With your own son?'

She shook her head wearily and exhaled a stream of smoke. 'He *wasn't* my son, that's the whole point,' she said. 'He was just a nice, warm man I could relate to, after the cold, unfeeling relationship I had endured for so long with a husband who had lost interest in me and persistently played away. Consequently, I fell for him completely. He was, of course, a lot younger than me, but it didn't seem to make a difference and we just seemed to gel.'

'And did the professor know about the relationship?' Kate asked, recovering from her shock.

'No, he hadn't a clue. We used to visit each other late at night when he was fast asleep.' Her face darkened. 'But Julian is likely to enlighten him very soon.'

'Julian?'

'Yes, the slimy, little toad is always creeping about the house at night, watching and listening. He found out about Howard and me and I've been paying him two-hundred pounds a month ever since just to keep him quiet. Now poor Howard's gone, he wants more money and I'm going to refuse, which means he will almost certainly tell Hubert all about my disreputable behaviour. Then I shall have to leave.'

'Blackmail,' Hayden breathed. 'What a family!'

Dunbar laughed. 'Yes, a lovely lot, aren't we?'

'So,' Kate said, keen to get things back on track, 'you did ring Howard that night, didn't you?'

She nodded. 'I desperately wanted to see him, but he didn't answer his phone.'

'No, he left it behind in his apartment when he went down to the lab. Which brings me to my earlier question. Did you arrange to have another key to the lab cut for him?'

She frowned in thought for a moment.

'No, I didn't.'

'I believe you did. I think you knew the combination of your husband's safe, that you got into it when he was away on his recent conference and had the duplicate key made by one of the local key-cutting services. Probably paying in cash so the purchase couldn't be tied to you at a later date.'

'I suppose that is plausible. But please go on.'

'I think you and Howard hatched the plot between you. As your husband's accountant, Howard knew about the money the professor had in his desk drawer and saw the "break-in" as a golden opportunity to secure the means to pay off his creditors. So he staged the whole thing, assuming we, the police, would conclude that the same person who burgled the kitchen before was responsible for this crime as well.'

'A very good hypothetical scenario, Sergeant, but hypothetical nevertheless.'

Dunbar met Kate's intense stare and smiled as her unspoken admission of guilt passed between them.

'Of course,' she said, 'had I done all this, I would be guilty of aiding and abetting a crime, but since I didn't, I have nothing to answer for, have I?'

Kate made a wry grimace. 'Not unless we happen to turn up something else in the future, no. But luck is a fickle creature, so you never know.'

Dunbar stood up, wiped the tears from her eyes and forced another smile. 'Point taken, Sergeant,' she said. 'Now, I really must get on. I have a lot to do today.'

'Not to mention the preparations for Julian's twenty-first,' Kate commented drily.

'Well, you're only twenty-one once, aren't you?' Dunbar replied and stubbed out her cigarette before heading for the door.

CHAPTER 16

'So, we've sort of got to the bottom of things, then,' Charlie Woo commented when Kate returned to the station. After leaving Hayden to wander off to the canteen for lunch, Kate had headed straight for the DI's office to brief him on the morning's developments, and it seemed he was well pleased with the way things had gone. A sentiment she didn't share.

She took a sip of the coffee he had poured for her and shook her head. 'Hardly. It's pretty obvious Yasmin Dunbar borrowed the lab key from the professor's safe while he was away and that she had the extra one cut so that Howard could get into the place, which means she's an accessory to the break-in. But she hasn't actually confessed to it, and we can't prove anything against her yet. In fact she was just playing with us when we interviewed her.'

'Can't we check around local key-cutting services to try to find out the one she used?'

She shook her head. 'That would be horrendously labour intensive, bearing in mind the number of small shops providing that sort of service throughout the area. Also, we have no idea how far we would have to extend such checks. She could have gone to Cheddar, one of the local villages, or even into Bristol or Taunton. On top of that, she probably paid in cash. How likely is it that an individual shopkeeper would be able to remember a particular customer from the hundreds that pass through their doors?'

He grunted. 'See your point.' Then he shrugged and shifted into a more comfortable position in his chair. 'Ah well, *c'est la vie*. I don't think the DCI will be too worried about the niceties here. The main offender is dead, the money has been recovered and at least we have managed to tie up most of the loose ends. Even if we haven't been able to get an out and out confession from her ladyship, at least from a police investigatory perspective we can join up the dots sufficiently to file the case as a "detected". As for the coroner, what we have should be enough to satisfy him that the death of Howard Dunbar was as a result of an accident.'

'And you are happy with that?'

'It isn't a question of being happy with anything. Sometimes you have to be pragmatic about things and accept a particular outcome as the only feasible option.'

'So we just drop everything, is that what you're saying? Bury the whole thing?'

'You heard Mr Ricketts earlier. I don't see that we've got much choice.'

'And the possibility that Howard Dunbar was the victim of a premeditated murder? We just bury that?'

He groaned and raised his eyes to the ceiling. 'For goodness' sake, Kate. We have no evidence to suggest foul play is involved here. It was just a tragic accident, a burglary that went fatally wrong. Can't you just accept that and move on?'

'No, I can't. Not when I know in my gut that we're dealing with a crime and—'

'Sod it!' Woo practically yelled in exasperation. 'Just stop right there!' He took a deep breath and paused a second before continuing with barely suppressed emotion. 'Listen to yourself. You're ploughing the same bloody furrow that you've always ploughed with your stubborn, off-the-wall notions. Have you learned nothing from what's happened to you in the last few days? You should have been sitting here where I'm sitting and the only reason you're not, is because you're seen as too flaky and unreliable.'

He threw a pencil at her across the desk in a gesture of frustration and slammed back in his chair, refusing to look at her and focused on the window with his face set in a tight mask.

Kate simply stared back at him in stunned silence. Tears were forming in her eyes again as she tried to come to terms with the fact that someone she had always counted a friend could issue such a vitriolic condemnation of her as a person. Then abruptly she stood up and turned for the door. 'Thanks for the coffee,' she said and walked out.

* * *

'Want one of these?' Jamie Foster found Kate in the police station yard sitting in her car and slipped into the passenger seat beside her.

She stared at the packet of cigarettes he thrust towards her, then took one with a heavy, trembling sigh. 'I don't smoke,' she said, accepting the lighted match and sucking in the bitter smoke gratefully.

He waited patiently while she coughed up her insides for a few seconds, then said, 'Don't judge Charlie too harshly. He's under a colossal amount of pressure from above.'

She cast him a sideways glance through the smoke and shook her head in resignation. 'How the hell did you know what happened just now?' she said. 'There was no one in the general office.'

'He told me when I came back in,' he said.

'Told you what?'

'That he'd been a prat and he was sorry.'

'Couldn't he have said that himself?'

'He will do, I'm sure, but he sent me out to find you in case you did anything . . .'

'Stupid?'

'Something like that.'

'Let me ask you something else. Do you think I'm flaky?'

He grinned. 'Totally. With respect, of course.'

'And what about the rest of the team?'

'They think you're flaky too.'

'Then maybe it's best I *do* put my ticket in. Everything's gone to rat-shit anyway.'

'Flaky can mean different things to different people. In your case it means offbeat, unconventional, unorthodox and impulsive — traits that madden the hell out of our rules-based hierarchy. But your detection record is second to none and that should speak for itself.'

She stared at him suspiciously. 'Buttering me up now with warm words and compliments doesn't alter the fact that I seem to be regarded by many as a pain in the arse. So maybe I should just Foxtrot Oscar and make everyone's day.'

He shrugged. 'That's up to you. Yes, you are a pain in the arse, but having someone like that on a team can have its advantages. Up until now, though, no one has seen you as a quitter and a lot of people will be very disappointed if you decide to throw in the towel just because things got a bit rough.'

'Thanks, I'll bear that in mind. But it's a pity those at the top don't seem to think the same.'

'They will if you pull this latest job off.'

'How can I in less than twenty-four hours?'

'Follow your nose like you always do and turn over a few stones to see what's underneath. And these should help.' He handed her a small collection of documents. 'Dave Gort, the LIO, brought these up to your office for you after you'd gone off in your huff.'

She made a face at the dig and took the documents from him.

'I'll leave you to digest the contents,' he said and threw open the car door. 'Oh yes, and did you realise you were on fire?'

The cigarette! In a panic Kate jumped out of the car, sweeping the still smouldering filter-tip from her lap and beating furiously at her smoking jeans with both hands.

'They do say that smoking costs lives,' Foster chuckled over his shoulder as he headed back into the police station through the rear door. 'You should give it up.'

* * *

Kate found Hayden in the canteen, wiping his mouth on his sleeve as he belched over an empty plate bearing traces of gravy. He grinned happily when he saw her.

'Okay, old girl?' he said, then winced as he noted the grinning faces on an adjacent table. 'Er . . . Sergeant.'

Kate drew up a chair facing him and slid the papers she had just received across the table to him. In the space of ten minutes since her conversation with Foster her mood had changed from one of bitter negativity to that of upbeat excitement.

'Read and inwardly digest,' she said, then left him briefly to buy a sandwich and a coffee.

When she got back to the table, he was just finishing his perusal of the documents. He looked up, nodding soberly.

'Dave Gort did a brilliant job, then,' he said. 'It must have taken him most of the morning to dig this lot up.'

Kate took a bite out of her sandwich. 'Press office at HQ helped him a lot,' she said, 'but we certainly owe him one. What do you make of it all?'

He took a deep breath and frowned. 'Press reports are seldom one hundred per cent accurate,' he said, 'but these, from two of our respected nationals, do give us a clearer picture of what allegedly happened to Gillian George.'

'So what have you learned?'

'That Gillian George was on a field trip to the Amazon with Professor Dunbar. Had been there about a week, staying in a compound on the edge of the rainforest. Apparently seen going for a walk on her own one afternoon. Then the following morning she was found dead in her room. A mangled Brazilian wandering spider was stuck to the sheets of her bed. Autopsy later revealed that death was due to the spider's bite.' He frowned. 'Well, we already knew that she died from a spider bite—'

'Yes, but did you read the last para in *The Times*?'

He looked back at one of the sheets of paper. 'Yes, police couldn't understand why she hadn't gone for help as soon as she was bitten, since she would have known that Professor Dunbar had a stock of antivenom with him. Also, her key was still on the inside of the unlocked door of the rondavel type hut in which she was sleeping, and the compound's main building was only a couple of hundred yards away. Some unanswered questions there, I would say. Local police seem to have been more than a little negligent.'

'I agree there. The whole thing stinks. But that aside, you seem to have missed the most important bit. It says here that, according to Gillian George's friends back home in some village near Burford, she was single and unattached. Yet the autopsy revealed that she was eight weeks pregnant.'

'Meaning?'

'Come on, Hayd. Meaning that someone put the baby there. Yet she seems to have had no known boyfriend and had been living at Moat House for several months before she went to the Amazon with a man said by members of his own family to be a womaniser.'

She produced her pocketbook, flicked through some pages and referred to a specific entry. 'In the notes I made straight after our first interview of Yasmin Dunbar she described her husband as, and I quote, "a serial seducer" and she said, "I'm just waiting to see how long it takes before he beds Sam, his new assistant, *like he did the last one*". Don't you see? The randy professor screws Gillian, puts her in the family way, then gets rid of her when he finds out, by introducing a poisonous spider into her room while they are on their field trip to the Amazon. An "accident" like that is the perfect cover for a murder. Does that MO sound a little familiar vis-à-vis Howard Dunbar?'

'Gordon Bennett, your brain really has been working overtime!' Hayden leaned back in his chair, staring at her with an incredulous expression on his face. 'But I thought you had the professor down as the potential target of someone with an axe to grind against him. Now you're back to suggesting he is the murderer.'

'I'm looking at all possible scenarios. But the very similar pattern in the two deaths is a bit of a coincidence, you have to agree."

'I see what you're getting at, but honestly, don't you think it's a bit of a stretch to try and link these two jobs? The professor is an intelligent man. He's unlikely to have used the same MO in two different murders. That would have invited immediate suspicion.'

'Yes, but don't forget that the death of Gillian George occurred thousands of miles away in Brazil. Ordinarily, who would be likely to connect the two cases? Think about it. Everything adds up. No wonder the professor doesn't want anyone talking about it. He killed her to save himself from a subsequent scandal. If he was capable of doing that to his ex-lover, he could easily have been of a mind to murder Howard after he discovered somehow that his wayward son was planning to burgle his precious lab. The man's obviously a bloody psycho, Hayd.'

Hayden was still dubious. 'Perhaps he is, but you haven't one shred of evidence, not even of the most circumstantial kind, to suggest he could have been responsible for either death. Everything you've come up with so far is based on supposition, with one strand inevitably leading to another due to your own preconceived ideas. It could be that Ricketts is right. Howard Dunbar's death was an accident, pure and simple, and the same could also apply to the demise of Gillian George.'

Kate thought for a moment, gnawing at her bottom lip, then shook her head. 'I can't accept that,' she said. 'The link between these two cases is too starkly obvious. My gut instinct tells me that both victims were murdered.'

He stood up and raised his hands in capitulation. 'Okay, okay,' he said, 'so all you have to do is find the evidence.' Then he lumbered back to the counter to get his sweet.

CHAPTER 17

Charlie Woo buttonholed Kate in the corridor as she headed for the stairs leading back to her office. He nodded towards one of the interview rooms and she followed him inside.

'I wanted to apologise,' he said. 'I behaved like a cretin upstairs and I shouldn't have said some of the things I said to you.'

Kate studied him coldly. 'You still said them, so you must have meant what you said,' she replied.

He took a deep breath, then exhaled with just as much force. 'I was angry,' he said. 'We all say things sometimes in the heat of the moment.'

'You told me I was flaky and unreliable with stubborn, off-the-wall notions and that's why you had got the job instead of me,' she reminded him.

He winced. 'I know and it was an outburst that was well out of order. If it's any consolation to you, I didn't mean any of it. I was just mad at you because, deep down, I knew you were right, and the DCI was trying to cuff something that needed to be fully investigated.'

She raised an eyebrow. 'Maybe you should tell him that.'
'I already have.'
'What?'

'I rang him shortly after you left.'

'And what did he say?'

'His reply was unrepeatable.'

'So, what do we do now?'

'You carry on with the investigation as necessary. No time limit. My decision.'

'Which could mean another vacancy for a DI in this department.'

'That would be a decision for Headquarters, not the DCI.'

'You could even end up back on the streets in uniform wearing a funny hat.'

'I'll take my chances.'

She nodded and for the first time treated him to a wry smile. 'Well, we shall have to avoid that at all costs, won't we, Charlie? For a start, everyone knows you're afraid of the dark.'

Feeling a lot happier with her situation now that the air had been cleared, Kate headed back to the office, only to be waylaid on the stairs by Dave Gort, the LIO, carrying yet another piece of paper.

'Ah, Kate,' he said. 'Got something else for you on your Munster family. Got a minute?'

Curious, she followed him back along the corridor to his office where he offered her his swivel chair and dropped some papers on to his computer desk in front of her before propping himself on a corner.

'You probably won't be able to read most of that as they're just scribbled notes.' he said. 'I had to take it down over the phone in longhand from the LIO in Maidenhead.'

Kate scanned the notes, then frowned and shook her head. 'I think you'd better tell me,' she said.

He grinned. 'Professor Dunbar and his family originally came from just outside Maidenhead. They evidently had a big house near the village of Cookham,' he explained. 'Kids were born and grew up there and went to a local private school. The youngsters were not popular, however, and their headmaster described them all as a bit odd, particularly the youngest lad, Julian, who was always in trouble at the school.'

'What sort of trouble?'

'Oh, unpleasant pranks on other pupils who fell out with him. Like destroying their artwork and slipping dog faeces in the pockets of their school uniforms when they were playing sport. Then on one occasion, when he was about eight, he was accused of torturing and killing the school cat.'

'Oh, *nice*.'

'Apparently it scratched him when he twisted one of its ears and later that day the cat was found hanging from a tree in the grounds. It had been doused in petrol and set alight.'

'Good grief.'

'Julian denied doing this, of course, but he had been seen by a couple of the other pupils who reported it. The police were called and as he was below the age of criminal responsibility, he was let off with a caution and a severe reprimand from the school.'

'Your LIO seems have a very detailed knowledge of the incident.'

'He should have. He was the one who gave the caution when he was the ABO or beat officer for that area long before he became LIO. I was lucky to get hold of him as he is retiring next week. And from what he told me, Julian's misdemeanours didn't stop at the cat.'

'I'm all ears.'

'Only a few months afterwards he was ticked off in front of the class for insolence. A day later he was caught red-handed trashing the headmaster's study after breaking in after dark. Again he got a caution because of his age. But Professor Dunbar managed to get the whole thing hushed up by agreeing to remove him from the school to avoid official expulsion and making a substantial donation to their sports fund.'

Kate grunted. 'Money and influence certainly talk.'

'You're damned right there. Predictably, the lad earned an unenviable reputation as a troublemaker at his new school and each time he was castigated by one of the staff, something happened to the staff member's car or their property. Damage, graffiti, that sort of thing, though nothing could be proved against young Julian.

'Finally, just after his tenth birthday, following the suicide of his mother, he was caught shoplifting in a local store and slashed a shop assistant with a Stanley knife as he fled. By this time, at ten, he had reached the age of criminal responsibility and because of the seriousness of the offence, he could have been given a youth custody sentence. But once more he was lucky. His father interceded on his behalf, and both the store and the shop assistant refused to press charges or support a prosecution, allegedly because of Julian's "tender" age and the trauma he had suffered over his mother's death. John Craddock, the LIO, suspected that there was a financial incentive behind it all, too, but he couldn't do anything about it. Anyway, the case was dropped, and no reference was ever made to it in the media. So the matter was effectively buried.'

Kate gnawed at her lip. 'Typical. Anything more on the family?'

'Nothing that I can find out, no.'

'What about the mother's suicide?'

'Seemingly all above board. She had had a history of treatment for psychosis and one day she just threw herself off a bridge in front of a train. The family then moved to somewhere in Kent and Craddock lost trace of them until I rang him to tell him they were now living in our neck of the woods. He, er, wished us the best of luck.'

Kate issued another grunt. 'From what I've seen of the weird, dysfunctional tribe living at Moat House, I think we'll need it.'

She stood up and folded the notes he had made neatly in half before climbing to her feet.

'But a big thank you for all the research you've carried out for us, Dave. At least it has given us a lot more food for thought.'

He made an apologetic face. 'Pity I couldn't have given you a nice "collar" to go with it.'

'Hopefully, that will come in due course.'

* * *

'So now you reckon Julian Dunbar is likely to have been responsible for his brother's death, do you?' Hayden said when she returned to the empty CID office and told him what Gort had uncovered. 'Are you suggesting he stiffed him deliberately or are you sticking to your previous theory that the professor may have actually been the target, not the killer, and that Howard's death was a mistake? You seem to keep changing your mind.'

There was more than a trace of weary cynicism in his tone. Kate hesitated before answering.

'I think the jury is out on all of it,' she said warily. 'But from what I have seen and heard of young Julian, I think he would be capable of doing anything to anybody if they ruffled his feathers enough over something. He certainly hated his father and it's possible he had it in for his brother over some real or imagined slight too. Even as a child, he seemed to have been a particularly unpleasant character with a hang-up about getting his own back on people who crossed him.'

He sighed. 'Most people get satisfaction out of avenging wrongs perpetrated against them. You could say it's the darker side of human nature.'

'Yes, but it appears to have been a sort of compulsion with him. A vicious desire for vengeance that has probably become permanently embedded in his psyche. I read somewhere not so long ago that there is a view among psychologists that an uncontrollable urge for revenge can be attributed to something called OCD, or obsessive-compulsive disorder, stemming from the need to satisfy unresolved anger.'

He emitted a low whistle. 'Well, get you! I never realised you had majored in psychoanalysis.'

She tutted impatiently. 'Never mind the sarcasm, Hayd. The fact remains that if he had a mental condition like that as a child, without therapy he is unlikely to have moderated his attitude now that he has become an adolescent. If Howard *had* upset him enough over some slight, imagined or otherwise, maybe this was his way of getting his own back.'

'Bit of a drastic response, though, don't you think?' he said, with a patronising smile. 'I mean, you annoy me sometimes, but I wouldn't set a poisonous spider on you.'

Her lip curled slightly. 'Well, thanks for that reassurance. At least I won't have to check under the bed tonight.'

'So what about Gillian George? Have you now ditched your theory that the deaths of both she and the Dunbar lad were linked and down to the same person?'

'No, I still think they are linked. I just can't put my finger on how at the moment.'

'So where does George's death come into things if Julian murdered Howard Dunbar? Was he in the Amazon with the professor when she died? Was he having the affair with her and then killed her? Or when he heard what had happened, did he perhaps think, "Ooh, that's a good idea, I'll kill Howard the same way"?'

There was more than a suggestion of derision in his tone which was most unusual for Hayden and her expression changed. 'What's ailing you, Hayd? I'm not stupid. I can sense when you've got something on your mind.'

This time the sigh was more of an explosive exhale. 'Kate, I'm just worried about your state of mind. You haven't been the same since you came back from the clinic. I also hear that Charlie Woo had a go at you earlier.'

'He has since apologised and agreed to remove the time constraints on the investigation, which is what I wanted.'

'Okay, okay, but I gather he lost it at one point.'

'How do you know that? Did he tell you?'

'Never mind who told me. But the fact remains that for Charlie to lose his cool is pretty unusual. He's one of the most even-tempered chaps I know.'

'Meaning?' Her voice was hard now.

'It's just that you seem to be right back to your old ways and in some sort of fantasy land. I've said it before. You've got this stupid bee in your bonnet about a murder, and you can't see sense. In fact, I think you're losing the plot, like some neurotic schoolgirl. First the culprit is the professor and now you've latched on to Julian. Who else will it be next? Mrs Matlock, the cook? It's as if you're indulging in some sort of real-life board game, like Cluedo, only there's no Colonel Mustard on your list of suspects. I've gone along with you on everything up until now, even making suggestions to humour your fantasies, but I can't do it anymore. You have to wise up and realise that this case is going nowhere. Howard Dunbar's death was an accident, pure and simple, and the sooner you accept that the better for all of us.'

She nodded, but her gaze was icy. 'The better for you, you mean?' she rasped, her hurt dissolving into rage. 'Then you can slum around doing nothing like the weak, lazy bum you are. Well, be my guest. I don't need a patronising hypocrite like you trailing along behind me.'

'That's not fair,' he blustered.

'Not fair, is it? After all that you've just said to me? At the very least I should be able to expect loyalty and support from my own husband. But clearly you see me as some kind of neurotic screwball. So maybe it's time for us to think about going our separate ways.'

'Now you're being silly.'

'Am I?' Wrenching her wedding ring off her finger, she threw it at him. 'Well, once this case is over, I shall be getting out of your life altogether, and until then, when we're off duty I don't want you anywhere near me.'

Then she left him there gaping and stuttering and not for the first time that day, stormed out of the office without a backward glance.

Where she intended going was not clear. She just had a desperate need to get as far away as possible from the police station and everyone in it. But as she barged through the back door into the yard, the shrill activation of her mobile stopped her in her tracks.

'What?' she snarled, expecting to hear Hayden's voice.

'Is that Defective Lewis?' a drawling voice mocked.

She stopped dead and scowled. 'Who is this?' she snapped back.

'Why, it's Julian Dunbar,' came the reply. 'You left me your card, so I thought I'd ring you to ask you if you're up for something.'

Kate's teeth snapped together in a grimace. 'What are you talking about?'

'I have some information for you. If you're interested, of course.'

'What sort of information?'

'Ah, now that would be telling, wouldn't it? And it will cost you.'

'Don't play games with me, Julian. I'm not in the mood.'

'Oh, there are no games involved. I know all about the police informants' fund and I want some of it in exchange for hot off the press info.'

She emitted a hard laugh. 'You're living in fairyland. We won't be paying you anything. But if you're withholding evidence, you could find yourself in deep trouble.'

Dunbar gave a theatrical sigh. 'Oh dear, I don't think you quite get the picture. You see, I know who killed my brother, Howard, and why. I told you I know everything that goes on in Moat House. But if you're not interested, maybe I should approach one of the national newspapers. I suspect they'd be very interested, especially if I told them that the local police have been carrying out a totally incompetent investigation.'

'You slimy little toad.'

'Now, that's rude. I could be offended. But never mind, here's the deal. I'm prepared to hand over my information to you on payment of one thousand pounds cash.'

'You're dreaming. It doesn't work like that.'

'Well, I'm happy to negotiate if you are. Do you know the old bird hide by the lake at Moat House?'

'What if I do?'

'Meet me there tonight at one a.m. and I'm sure we can come to a mutual agreement.'

'You have to be joking.'

'No, I'm quite serious actually. Anyway, I shall be there waiting for you. But if you don't turn up, I suggest you prepare yourself for a sudden influx of reporters with questions to ask . . . Oh and come alone or I won't show. Toodle-pip.'

The phone went dead.

CHAPTER 18

Julian Dunbar had spent most of his late adolescence prying into other people's lives. Watching, listening, snooping. It had provided a lucrative return for him too over the past couple of years. He had learned very early on that most people had secrets. Had done things that they weren't proud of and were keen to ensure no one else found out about their misdemeanours. Yes, and they were almost always prepared to pay up to keep their secrets from getting out.

Sweet, little sister, Angela, was one of them. He had learned a lot about her that night outside the barn when he had listened in on the conversation between her and that hippy scrounger, Adam. She had already handed over the first of the blackmail instalments her darling brother had demanded and there would be a lot more to come. Then there was his loving stepmum. She'd had a lot more to hide than Angela, and she had been paying the price for quite a while now. There were others too, like poor Howard who was now no more, and good, old respectable pater who had even more to hide and was terrified at the thought of any kind of scandal.

As a result, Julian, who was by no means unblemished himself, had managed to tuck a tidy little sum away in his room, and the payments still kept on coming. But now he had the opportunity of earning the biggest pay-off of all with the information he was planning to give to that stupid detective bitch. He had read all about the police informants' fund and he was hopeful that she would be able to twist arms to get him what he wanted. If not, and he mentally shrugged, he would carry out his threat and see what sort of offer one of the national newspapers or maybe even the BBC would make him. Then Miss High and Mighty Lewis could go whistle for the info.

If he was honest with himself, he was not entirely at ease with what he had planned to do this time. It stimulated his ego to know that he had single-handedly managed to 'unmask' Howard's killer when the police couldn't do that themselves, but he had no illusions as to what would happen to him if the person he was about to finger somehow found out that he had uncovered their guilty secret. He had no desire to end up like Howard. Yet the thought not only of the money but of the opportunity to rub Detective Sergeant Kate Lewis's nose in it swept aside any misgivings he might have had.

Slipping on a thick anorak, he grabbed a torch and carefully opened his bedroom door. The house was deathly still, and he could hear the grandfather clock ticking in the gloom of the hallway below.

Gritting his teeth, he crept out into the corridor, closing the door quietly after him. Then avoiding the loose floorboard by Angela's room, he joined the main hallway outside Howard's apartment and turned left towards the stairs. His father and stepmother's bedroom doors were both closed, and he smirked when he heard someone inside one of the rooms snoring loudly. So far so good.

He made the downstairs hallway without a problem and slipped out into the night moments later, wincing as the front door groaned shut behind him.

The moon greeted him with a cold ambivalent stare, the blue veins across its blazing white face forming into a sneer.

He could feel the night chill on his skin, and he saw that the two cars parked close by were already exhibiting faint signs of frost. His feet crunched in the loose gravel as he headed across the hardstanding towards the footpath running down the side of the house. It was then that he got the uneasy feeling that someone was watching him. He turned quickly to look behind, but there was no one in sight.

Shortly afterwards he reached the old barn where he had eavesdropped on the conversation between Angela and the hippy, and he found herself casting repeated glances at the patched timbers and holed roof as he passed by, half expecting to see someone lurking there. There was no one. An owl hooted as he crossed the yard towards the footpath, making him start involuntarily, but otherwise the night remained perfectly still and he felt himself relax. Think of the money, Julian, the voice in his head told him, think of all that lovely money.

Then the dark mouth of the footpath to Mason's Farm was there, and for some reason he found himself hesitating before it. What was the matter with him? He was big and ugly enough to take care of himself and if the copper didn't turn up, so what? He'd just head back again, with no one being any the wiser. That was why he had chosen 1 a.m. for the meet. Everyone would be in bed fast asleep. Yeah, and by the time they woke up in the morning he could be all the richer.

With a grin he plunged into the tunnel.

* * *

Kate stood by the patio doors and stared out into the night. The stars were presented in a glittering panoply, crowding a full moon, and the first signs of early frost had touched the over-long back lawn with a ghostly, bluish fire. She couldn't help shivering, not just from the coldness of the room either, and she felt a stab of excitement mixed with apprehension slice deep into her belly as she thought about her nocturnal meeting with Julian Dunbar.

She had spent the first few hours of the night on the sofa. That left the big double bed upstairs to Hayden after their monumental bust-up in the CID office that afternoon which had continued even when they'd got home from work. Hayden had done his best to rescue the situation, but it hadn't cut any ice with her. Unreasoning bitterness over the way she felt the job and the people she had trusted so much had treated her in the last few days had resurfaced with a vengeance. She now felt more betrayed and alone than ever before. Her relationship with Hayden over the years had always been a tempestuous one, but this was by far the worst row of all, and she was determined to make him see that.

Of course, her decision to meet Julian Dunbar alone without telling him or any of her colleagues in advance was foolhardy and exactly the sort of thing that she had been criticised for by the hierarchy in the past. But she didn't see it like that and didn't care anyway. She had the bit between her teeth and was determined to go through with it whatever risks were involved.

In a way the argument with Hayden had helped her, too. Insisting on sleeping on the settee downstairs, she was out of sight and earshot of her husband. That meant she could leave the house without him being any the wiser. He always slept like the dead and certainly wouldn't hear her close the front door or drive away. By the time he woke up she expected to be back home again, armed with all the information she needed to make the collar of her career. That would show them all, she mused. Then maybe they would have to eat humble pie before she finally left the job for good.

She was already fully dressed. She had made a point of sleeping in her clothes on the settee to be ready for her nocturnal meeting. So it was simply a question of grabbing a torch, mobile and her anorak and heading out to her car in the driveway. Once clear of the house, having closed the front door very quietly behind her, she made her way across the patch of lawn instead of using the shingle drive just in case there was the remotest chance that Hayden might stir in his sleep.

A badger crossed the road hurriedly as she pulled out and shortly afterwards the white ghost of a barn owl swept past the windscreen, making for a spinney on the far side of a marshy field. It had something gripped between its talons. You'll feed well tonight, old girl, Kate mused, then grimaced as she remembered that 'old girl' was what Hayden liked to call her when they were on speaking terms.

She saw very little traffic, apart from the occasional blaze of headlights on a distant main road, as she negotiated a succession of droves to the other side of the marsh, and she found herself approaching the entrance to Moat House before she realised it. Pulling over on to a grass verge and parking up, she strode quickly across the road and slipped through a hole in the hedge, striking diagonally through the neglected woodland towards the house. She emerged on the deserted hardstanding and within minutes was on the edge of the rubbish-strewn yard in front of the old barn.

Nothing moved. Unsurprisingly the barn was shut up and in darkness. There wasn't even the faintest rustle among the tangle of upright and partially uprooted trees thrusting out of the rough scrub like diseased fingers. Once again, visions of the garden shed of her childhood flashed through her mind, and she shook her head irritably to dislodge the memories.

Then she saw the tunnel-like hole in the undergrowth to her left which Josh Matlock had pointed out to her. 'Path goes all the way through the woods past the old bird hide on the edge of the lake,' he'd told her. She remembered fragments of what Julian Dunbar had said. 'The old bird hide by the lake . . . ? Tonight. One a.m. Come alone.'

'Come alone.' Why alone and why in a place like this in the middle of the night? The risks attached to such a meeting had been obvious to her from the start. She already saw Julian as mentally unstable and a possible suspect in Howard Dunbar's 'murder'. Furthermore, he looked to be fit and strong and had the benefit of youth on his side. She could be in deadly peril. Especially if he thought that she might have evidence linking him to Howard's death. Why had she decided to come at all?

Then suddenly she thought of the lethal spider that could be loose somewhere in the grounds. This only added to her trepidation. She directed the torch into the tangled vegetation in which her long boots were partially buried. What if . . . ? Tugging her feet free, she stepped hurriedly out into the moonlight where she could see the ground around her more clearly.

A vixen screeched like a child in agony somewhere in the distance and a branch broke with a loud 'crack' much closer to her. She spun round and glimpsed the shadow of what had to be a muntjac deer merging back into the scrub.

Gripping the torch more firmly, she took a deep breath and plunged into the tunnel to the left of the shed and into pitch blackness.

As her eyes adjusted to the gloom, she saw that the path curled around to the right and the beam of her torch almost immediately picked out the gleam of water among the trees. Moments later she found herself standing beside a rotting log pile two to three yards from a small reed-fringed lake. Silver moonlight touched the still, dark water and the gaunt skeleton of a wooden building on piles close to the edge stood out in stark relief against the face of the moon. A short landing stage thrust out from beside it towards a tiny scrub-covered island. 'Just what the doctor ordered,' Kate breathed, thinking of the horror film, *Friday The Thirteenth*, she had watched in her teens.

There was no sign of anyone in the vicinity and the bird hide was in total darkness. Not so much as a torch glimmered in the single window facing her and she assumed the hatches that would be fronting the lake were likely to be tightly closed.

'Julian,' she called softly. There was no reply and still no sign of any movement in response.

'Julian,' she called again. Then glancing about her nervously, she moved closer to the hide.

A duck erupted from the reeds just as she reached the flight of three steps below the door, flapping away in noisy panic, making her jump.

'Julian!' Kate snapped, losing her patience.

Still nothing. Kate glanced at her watch. 1.15 a.m. She'd arrived a few minutes late. Damn it! Had Dunbar got tired of waiting and left?

Something moved in the undergrowth behind her, and she swung round again, directing her torch at the spot. The sounds were not repeated. Probably another muntjac or a wandering fox.

Climbing the steps to the door of the hide, Kate tried the door. It was unlocked and opened with a tired groan. Musty, damp air rushed out to meet her, and she stood there for a moment, shining the torch around the inside. It was empty.

Cursing, she shut the door and took the steps back down to the bank. What a waste of bloody time, she mused. Maybe Julian had simply got tired of waiting and returned home. Or more likely, he had set this whole thing up as some kind of unfunny prank to teach the interfering copper a lesson. The little jerk!

She was on the point of retracing her steps completely when something made her decide to check out the landing stage. She immediately regretted it. Some of the wooden planks were rotten and loose with a few gaps in places, and there was no handrail of any sort on either side. She had to pick her way very carefully along it to avoid plunging through or going over the edge, conscious of the whole thing shaking almost with every step. There was a half-sunken rowing boat at the end, still moored to a post by a tatty rope and with just its bow above the surface of the water, but there was nothing else of interest.

It wasn't until she began retracing her steps that she noticed the thing seemingly trapped half under the landing stage up against one of the supporting piles near the bank. At first she thought it was a sack of something or a large cushion someone had dumped in the lake. She got down on her hands and knees for a closer look, feeling the planks under her sway alarmingly as she did so. She couldn't have been more wrong. It wasn't a sack or a cushion at all, but in a sudden heart-stopping moment she realised that she had finally found Julian Dunbar.

* * *

The log Kate was sitting on, with her hands clasped tightly around the plastic cup of hot, black coffee Charlie Woo had given her on his arrival, was wet and she could feel it soaking through the thighs of her jeans, adding to the sodden feel of her legs and feet inside the high boots. The moon and panorama of glittering stars that had graced the night earlier had since given way to a grey, misty first light. But visibility was still poor and in the gloom the SOCO team in their white nylon overalls moving backwards and forwards along the bank of the lake looked strangely disembodied and wraith-like in the smoky yellow eyes of the spotlights that had been set up.

The police surgeon had been and gone and following the concerns he had expressed after carrying out his preliminary examination, the DI had called for the forensic pathologist to attend. A small tent had been erected over Julian Dunbar's lifeless body in the meantime, concealing it from view, and uniformed officers had been stationed on the other side of the tapes that had been erected along the perimeter of the encircling woodland well back from the lake shore, to prevent unauthorised access.

'You okay there?' Charlie Woo asked, materialising at her elbow.

Kate nodded, then eyed him quizzically. 'Did Hayden say anything to you about us?'

He looked baffled. 'Say anything about what?'

'We had a bit of a row last night.'

He grinned. 'Situation normal, I would say.'

'Bit more than that this time.'

'Oh.' He looked concerned. 'Look, I don't know what it was all about, and I don't want to know, but I hope it is not going to get in the way of you two working together. I can't have personal issues being brought into the department to the detriment of our overall operational effectiveness.'

She nodded slowly, thinking of the wedding ring she had hurled at her other half in her rage. She felt sick now she had the time to think about it.

'So, anything I should know?'

She bit her lip. 'No, it's nothing, honestly. It won't affect the job.'

'Good. Now, about our drowning. You okay with it? Can't have been pleasant.'

'Rather a nasty shock to find him lying in the water, that's all.' She made a rueful grimace. 'Got a bit wet pulling him out. Good job I had my knee-high boots on, but at least the lake was not that deep there. Er, thanks for the coffee.'

Woo nodded. 'You must be soaked through. Do you want to leave things to me while you go home and change into some fresh clothes?'

She shook her head. 'No thanks. I want to stay here. I'll soon dry off.'

'Your decision. Doc has said death was obviously due to drowning. But he's not happy about the circumstances surrounding it or the fact that the youngster appears to have sustained a wound to the side of his head which he doesn't believe could have been caused by a fall from the landing stage.'

'Well, Julian certainly didn't drown himself. As I told you just now, he set up this meet in the first place claiming he knew who had killed his brother and offering to part with the info for a grand. Why then chuck himself in the drink before he even saw me?'

'Could he perhaps have lost his footing on that pretty dodgy landing stage and hit his head on something on the way down?'

'An accident, you mean? Hardly likely, is it? A fit young-ster like that knocking himself out and drowning in relatively shallow water so close to the bank? I don't buy that, and you obviously don't either. Otherwise you wouldn't have author-ised the call-out of the forensic pathologist.'

Woo thought about that for a moment, but it was apparent that his mind was on something else and after a moment's hesitation, he came out with it.

'You shouldn't have come here on your own without telling someone, you know that, don't you?' he said. 'The DCI won't be very happy about you doing another solo job after everything that's been said.'

Kate emptied the cup and handed it back to him to replace on his flask. 'Ricketts is never happy about anything,' she replied, 'and anyway, what was I supposed to do? As I've already explained, Julian told me on the phone that he knew who had killed Howard Dunbar and why, and that if I turned up at the meet with anyone else he wouldn't show. I couldn't risk missing the chance of nailing his brother's killer.'

'You could have approached him later.'

'And he would then have denied ringing me at all. I was faced with a *fait accompli*.'

Woo poured some coffee from his flask for himself. 'Well, there'll be time enough to chat about the rights and wrongs of it all later. Right now, we're left with a lot of ques-tions, no answers and another body to sort out.'

He glanced back at the footpath to the lake which was now bisected by police tape with a uniformed policeman standing there.

'Surprised none of the family, especially the professor, have come down here yet to see what's going on,' he said. 'It's as if they're in denial.'

Kate shrugged. 'Well, I sent the sergeant who arrived with the uniformed contingent back up to the house as soon as they all arrived to break the news to the family. I gather he told the professor himself, but they must all know by now.'

He made a face. 'Well, one of them will have to face things in due course to provide formal ID of the body. Be interesting to see who bites the bullet and—'

He broke off, emptying his cup of coffee in the bushes behind the log. 'Ah, here comes our pathologist if I'm not very much mistaken.'

He wasn't and Kate breathed a sigh of relief when she glimpsed the blonde-haired woman walking towards them carrying a large black bag. She quit her uncomfortable seat and stepped forward to meet her, recognising her immediately even in the uncertain light. Dr Lydia Summers had worked with Kate on a number of cases and a mutual sense of trust and respect, as well as a measure of friendship, had developed between them over the years.

'Morning, Kate,' she said. 'What juicy cadaver have you got for me this time?'

Kate introduced Charlie Woo, then detailed the circumstances of the case as Summers unzipped her bag and started pulling on her protective clothing.

The pathologist sniffed and glanced around her critically. 'Not the best of nights for a moonlit dip, I must admit,' she said with her usual cynicism, 'and that water looks as though it could do with a public health warning.'

Kate grimaced. 'You can say that again, Doctor. My boots are still saturated from it and will probably have to be dumped.'

'Stiff whisky, Kate, that's what you need,' Summers chuckled and left them to duck inside the tent.

It was fully light by the time she reappeared, and her face was grim.

'Death occurred about six hours ago, I would suggest,' she announced. 'Normally, my professional opinion would be based entirely on a clinical assessment which adheres to established scientific protocols. That is to say, present rectal temperature coupled with the effects of *algor mortis*, or changes in body temperature after death, including such external factors as fluctuations in the ambient temperature of the immediate environment, the thermal conductivity of the ground on which the deceased is lying at the time and the effect of thermal insulation provided by clothing. But since we have Kate's supportive evidence of this prearranged meeting for one a.m., I don't think my calculations will be far off the mark.'

'And the actual cause of death is definitely drowning?' the DI said.

Summers nodded. 'From the known circumstances and the condition of the body, I would say that that is a foregone conclusion, Detective Inspector, but I should be able to provide you with a more detailed report after the post-mortem.'

'The police surgeon was concerned about a head injury and some superficial injuries he found,' Kate put in.

'I'm not surprised,' Summers replied. 'The head wound which is to the left side of the skull seems to have been made with some degree of force and I wouldn't be surprised if the skull itself had not sustained a hairline fracture.'

'Any idea of a weapon?' the DI asked.

Summers threw him an irritable glance. She didn't like being interrupted. 'A blunt instrument of some sort,' she said. 'Something like a metal bar or a heavy walking stick. It is difficult to tell in this poor visibility, even with the spot-lamps and my torch, but there does not appear to be any foreign matter, apart from strands of his long hair, trapped in the rather nasty four-to-five-centimetre wound inflicted by the blow. His assailant obviously meant business.'

'But it didn't kill him?'

'Not in my opinion, but it was none the less significant and a lot more noticeable now than when the good doctor would have carried out his own examination. You see, the thing about violent death is that post-mortem, it is an evolving as well as a degenerative process. What is apparent in an initial examination does not always tell the whole story. More physical signs, such as cuts, bruises and abrasions, can manifest themselves to a greater extent with the passage of time, as is the case here. Your so-called marks form a peculiar pattern of deep cuts and pockmarks to the forehead and one side of the face. These would have become more pronounced in the six hours since his demise.

'The most plausible scenario is that the deceased was struck quite forcefully with the weapon and pitched into the water from the landing stage. His head was then forced under the water so that his face was in contact with pebbles and other debris at the bottom of the lake and held there until he was asphyxiated by a combination of the water and other detritus that he plainly ingested. This tends to be supported by the fact that two of his upper front teeth have been loosened and pushed inwards and his airways left partially blocked by a quantity of mud. Your killer certainly made sure that if, due to the coldness of the water, Mr Dunbar did manage to regain his senses sufficiently to prevent himself from drowning, he wouldn't survive his involuntary moonlit dip for long afterwards.'

'Not a very nice end, for a young man just starting out,' Woo commented after the pathologist had left.

Kate shrugged, conscious of the sort of nasty, vicious person Julian had been in life, finding herself unable to feel anything but indifference towards his untimely death. 'Well, he always boasted that he knew everything about what was going on at Moat House,' she said grimly, ignoring the DI's look of surprise at her apparent lack of sympathy for the victim, 'but there are clearly occasions when you can know a little too much.'

Woo grunted. 'Pity he didn't get the chance of sharing any of it with us before he copped it, though,' he said. 'It leaves us right back at the starting block.'

Kate nodded. 'And that starting block has to be Moat House,' she replied. 'Fancy a walk?'

CHAPTER 19

The front door of Moat House was half-open when Kate and Charlie Woo crunched through the shingle to the porch and found Hubert Dunbar sitting on the stairs. He had a glass of what looked like whisky in one hand, and he was still dressed in his pyjamas and a tatty looking dressing gown. He didn't even look up when they stepped into the hallway after receiving no answer to their knock.

'Professor?' Kate asked. 'You okay, sir?'

The scientist threw them a blank glance and took a gulp from his glass. His hand was shaking, and his face was deathly white. 'What do you think, Sergeant?' he said in a low voice and took another gulp.

'We're very sorry for your loss,' Woo said. 'It must have come as a terrible shock to you.'

Dunbar drained his glass and climbed to his feet, leaving the glass on the stair beside him. 'What do you want?' he said in a drab tone that suggested he didn't much care anyway. In fact, he sounded tired and lost. Too tired even to show his usual snappy resentment. Like a man who is witnessing his carefully constructed world slowly collapsing around him.

'We would like to have a chat with you if you don't mind,' Kate said. 'This is my guv'nor, Detective Inspector Charlie Woo.'

Dunbar gave a heavy sigh. 'Well, bully for you, Inspector. I'm surprised you haven't brought the chief constable with you as well. Everyone else seems to have been here in the past few days.'

'I'm afraid we do need to talk to you,' Woo said. 'It will only take a few minutes.'

Dunbar shrugged and waved an arm down the hall. 'As you wish. We'd better go in there. The sergeant knows the way.'

As expected, he led them to the sitting room and dropped heavily into the same armchair each of his offspring had taken turns in occupying previously. Kate and Woo shared the settee.

'I'm surprised you haven't been down to the lake yet,' Kate said as a direct opener.

'What's the point?' he replied. 'Julian's dead, isn't he? Not much I can do about that now.'

Kate was unsurprised by his reaction. It was in keeping with the cold, indifferent persona he had displayed throughout the investigation. But Woo was plainly taken aback by his callous attitude. 'We shall need you to carry out a formal identification in due course,' he said.

Dunbar shrugged. 'Whatever.'

He got up and went over to the cocktail cabinet and poured himself another scotch from a bottle labelled 'Talisker. Single Malt'.

'Can you think of anyone who would want to take Julian's life?' Woo asked.

To the surprise of both police officers, Dunbar emitted a mirthless laugh before returning to his chair. 'Half of Somerset I wouldn't wonder,' he said. 'He was my son, but he wasn't a very nice person. Always poking and prying—'

'And blackmailing?' Kate cut in.

Dunbar stiffened and eyed her narrowly, his brain evidently clearing rapidly of any fog. 'What do you mean by that?'

'Well, he liked to find out things about people, didn't he? Then threaten to make their secret public if they didn't pay up?'

'How do you know that? Who are you talking about?'

'I'm sorry. That's confidential. But he did blackmail you too, didn't he, Professor?'

Both detectives studied Dunbar intently, waiting for a reaction. At first there was no answer and he simply glared at Kate, his pale face flushing slightly. Then he said, 'I don't know what you mean.'

Kate didn't mince her words. 'Did he blackmail you over the death of Howard?'

'And why would he do that? I've told you before, I had nothing to do with Howard's death. It was a damned accident, so there was nothing to blackmail me about.'

Kate shook her head. 'Unfortunately, we don't believe it *was* an accident, Professor. You already know, of course, that a leg from the Brazilian wandering spider you call Martha was found by our scenes of crime team in the locked drawer of your desk, indicating that the creature must have been in the drawer and that it attacked Howard when he put his hand inside?'

Dunbar gulped more whisky. 'It got in through a hole in the back of the drawer, you know that.'

'That is one theory, Professor, but we now believe it may have been deliberately put there by someone who removed the thing from its terrarium for the purpose of harming whoever opened that drawer.'

Dunbar slammed his glass down on a side table beside the settee and jumped to his feet. 'I've had just about enough of these innuendos,' he shouted. 'I repeat I had nothing to do with Howard's death and I will not put up with these scurrilous, unfounded allegations any longer—'

'So what about Gillian George?' Kate continued relentlessly. 'Did he put the squeeze on you because of her?'

For a second Dunbar simply gaped at her, his mouth working silently. 'Gillian?' he almost choked. 'You nasty little bitch. Is nothing sacred to you?'

Kate's expression was bleak. 'Not in a murder inquiry, sir, no.'

'Gillian wasn't murdered. She died from a spider bite—'

'Exactly like Howard then? Funny that, isn't it?'

'No, there is nothing funny about it. It's a question of public record. She died from the bite of a Brazilian wandering spider that somehow got into the rondavel in which she was sleeping.'

'How could that have happened?'

'With the Amazon rainforest right next door, I would say it was an ever-present risk, wouldn't you?'

'The police were surprised she didn't call out for help.'

'So was I when I heard, but she was bitten in the throat quite severely, so the poison could have caused a rapid paralysis, preventing her from functioning properly—'

'As I've just said, exactly like Howard.'

There was a sneer on his face now as he began to gain confidence. 'Yes, just like Howard.'

'Did you know she was pregnant?'

He didn't bat an eyelid this time. 'The police told me after the post-mortem that she was with child, yes. Tragic.'

'Any idea who the father was?'

'How the hell should I know? I employed her as my assistant. What she did in her love life was her own affair.'

'It wasn't you then?'

'No, it damn well wasn't. I'm not in the habit of seducing female employees.'

Liar, Kate thought! But she sensed that she had got about as far as she was going to get with her interrogation. After his initial shock at her aggressive style of questioning, he was firmly back in control, and she guessed he would be a match for anything she threw at him. She played her last card.

'Have you thought that someone might blame you for Gillian George's death nevertheless, Professor? Someone who was close to her who might be intent on exacting some kind of revenge?'

'What nonsense!'

'Is it? You see, there is the possibility that Howard was killed by mistake. That in fact you yourself were the actual target. The target of someone who knew you kept your lab keys and important documents in the drawer of your desk under lock and key. Someone who also knew that it would be the first place you would go to when you started work in the morning. This suggests that whoever killed Howard in error was the same person who probably silenced Julian. Almost certainly because he had tumbled to the truth through his persistent snooping. That person is still on the loose and no doubt still intent on finishing the job they started. In short, you could still be very much in danger.'

'Poppycock!' he retorted, but there was a lack of conviction in his tone and Kate thought she saw a shadow pass across his eyes.

She shrugged and stood up. 'Perhaps you're right, Professor. But you may want to watch your back from now on.'

'You don't take many prisoners, do you, Kate?' Woo commented drily after they had left the room. 'And winding the man up like that could have consequences.'

'I do hope so,' she replied. 'That was my intention. If he is guilty of the murders, there is a chance that he might slip up in some way. If he is not, maybe, just maybe, my word of warning might save his life.'

'Hm. So what have you got in mind now?'

'I think it might be a good idea to take a look in Julian's room. Ten to one whoever stiffed him will have already checked it out to make sure there is nothing there that will lead us to them. But I think it's still worth a look.'

'We don't have a search warrant.'

'I'm not bothered if you're not.'

'Let's do it.'

* * *

The house had the feel of an empty shell when they made their way upstairs. Absolute silence prevailed. There wasn't a sound from any of the rooms they passed. Either Yasmin and Angela Dunbar were having a lie-in, unaware of what was going on outside, which was unlikely as it was approaching ten o'clock, or they had quit the place altogether on some errand or other.

Julian's room was unlocked, and a strong smell of what Kate recognised as cannabis hit them the moment they stepped inside. The place was like a pigsty, with the bed unmade and the curtains only half-closed. Discarded trainers lay on the floor by the bed and several T-shirts and pairs of jeans had been dumped on a chair in the corner.

Kate pointed to a tin lid on a bedside table which had obviously served as an ashtray. Several cigarette stubs with pieces of cardboard in one end lay in the ashtray and Woo grunted.

'He liked his joints,' he commented. 'No wonder the air in here is so foul.'

Kate emitted a hard laugh. 'When I was on the drug squad, the junkies used to smother everywhere with patchouli oil to hide the smell of skunk. Julian obviously didn't care who knew.'

'It could have led to hallucinations though, don't you think? That stuff is lethal. It's known to cause psychosis and schizophrenia. Maybe he didn't actually know who killed Howard at all. It was all in his tortured mind.'

'Then why was he stiffed?'

'Perhaps someone *thought* he had sussed them.'

Kate looked dubious. 'I don't buy that. He may have been some kind of addict, but he was still pretty switched on, switched on enough to be able to uncover guilty secrets and put the squeeze on people as the price of silence—'

Kate broke off and raised a finger to her lips, pointing towards the hallway. But Woo had heard it too. A door quietly closing and the crack of a floorboard outside. Kate waved a hand towards an internal door and they both went for it immediately. They found themselves in an untidy en suite bathroom with a dirty basin and shower cubicle and an unflushed toilet.

Kate wrinkled up her nose in disgust as they froze behind the partially closed door.

The sound of the bedroom door opening, a pause and then footfalls on the thick carpet and a drawer being opened very quietly. Woo touched Kate on the back. She nodded in agreement, then pushed the door of the en suite open.

Angela Dunbar was crouched down by the bedroom cabinet on the other side of the bed, peering into the top drawer. She spun round at the sound of the door opening and gaped at them.

'What the hell are you doing in here?' she exclaimed, jumping to her feet.

'We might ask you the same thing, Angela,' Kate said.

Dunbar moved quickly towards the hall door, but Woo was standing there, blocking the way.

'And who's this arsehole?' Angela spat. 'Fu Manchu?'

Woo sighed at the derogatory reference to his fictitious literary countryman. He had heard all the insults before. 'Not Fu Manchu or Charlie Chan, love,' he said. 'Just plain old Detective Inspector Charlie Woo.'

'My boss,' Kate replied coolly. 'Now, I think you owe us an explanation.'

Dunbar glared at Kate stubbornly. 'I don't need to explain anything,' she said. 'I'm in my own home and can go anywhere I like.'

'Why are you in Julian's room going through his stuff?' Kate persisted. 'And before you answer, you'd better think carefully about what you're going to say. I take it you know Julian is dead, and it is now a murder inquiry?'

Dunbar's eyes widened. 'Murder? Daddy said he was found drowned. That's why all you coppers were here. I didn't know he had been—'

'Oh, he drowned all right, but he had a bit of help.'

Just like before in the hallway, Dunbar's legs seemed to give way and she collapsed in front of them sobbing. Kate guessed it was not out of sympathy for Julian.

She bent over her and very gently lifted her on to the chair where Julian's clothes had been dumped.

'Okay, Angela,' she said firmly. 'Time for the truth. Why were you in here?'

For a moment the young woman continued to cry. But she received no further attention, just silence as Kate and Woo waited patiently for an answer. Seeing this, she glanced furtively at Kate, sniffed a couple of times and began drying her eyes on an embroidered handkerchief.

Kate studied her grimly. She had the measure of Angela Dunbar now. The professor's young, seemingly vulnerable daughter was actually an accomplished manipulator and could play the part of the little girl lost, with tears thrown in, whenever the situation called for it.

'Now, please answer the question,' she said. 'Why were you in here?'

Dunbar scowled angrily. 'What sort of uncaring bitch are you,' she blazed. 'Julian has just died and all you're interested in is quizzing me about why I'm in his room. Don't you have any sympathy at all? I've lost two of my brothers. Can't you see I'm upset?'

Kate was unmoved. 'You hated Julian,' she said quietly. 'You told me he was a psycho who was always creeping around, spying on people, remember?'

'I . . . I didn't hate him. I was just in a bad mood when you spoke to me then. I loved my brother, and I was devastated when Daddy told me what had happened to him.'

'So,' Woo put in, 'knowing the brother you loved so much had been found floating in the lake, why didn't you bother to go to the scene to see for yourself but decided instead to carry out a search of his room?'

Dunbar just stared at him, and Kate could practically hear her mind working with the realisation that her emotional outburst had had no effect. Then, apparently unable to think of another diversionary tactic, she shrugged and capitulated.

'Julian was blackmailing me over the fact that I had been sleeping with Adam,' she said. 'He . . . he followed me to the

188

barn one night and watched us through a gap in the door. Then he found out somehow I was pregnant and demanded money from me or he would tell Father.'

'An excellent motive for murder, then?' Kate said drily.

Dunbar's eyes widened. 'I didn't kill him,' she whispered. 'I'm not a murderess.'

'So why search his room with his corpse only just cold?'

'I was . . . was looking for his diary.'

'Diary?' Woo exclaimed.

She nodded. 'He boasted to me that he had everything written down in it. Dates, times, everything about everybody. I was desperate to get hold of the diary and destroy it before it was found by anyone else.'

Kate believed her. 'Then let us see if we can find it,' she said. 'That might hold the answer to a lot of questions.'

'I can help if you like.'

Kate frowned. 'I don't really think that would be appropriate under the circumstances, do you?' she said.

* * *

'So, nothing,' Woo said an hour later after a thorough but fruitless search of every nook and cranny in the bedroom.

Kate's eyes roved slowly around the room, checking to make sure that they hadn't missed anything. Then she stared at him thoughtfully for a moment. 'The diary isn't the only thing that's missing,' she said and nodded towards a small desk under the window. 'No laptop computer there, yet there's a small printer on the shelf underneath. If you look, there's a power cable and what seems to be a USB cable tangled up on the floor underneath. Furthermore, we haven't come across a mobile yet and he must have had one.'

'There wasn't one on the body?'

'No. I checked when I pulled him out of the lake.'

'Maybe the killer took it off him after killing him?'

'Possibly. Or he paid a visit to this room after the murder to remove anything that might contain incriminating evidence.'

'What about Angela? When we caught her in here it could have been her second visit.'

Kate shook her head. 'I don't think so. Why would she need to do the business twice? She would have done the lot in one go to avoid the risk of getting caught. Anyway, her demeanour was not that of a calculating, cold-blooded killer who had wasted someone a few hours before. She's only a slip of a thing, too. I can't see her having the strength to belt her brother over the head and hold him down in the water until he asphyxiated, can you? No, we're looking for someone else, someone fit, strong and a lot more dangerous.'

'So who then?'

'Your guess is as good as mine. The professor is the only one at Moat House who fits the bill, and I don't see how an outsider could have been responsible. But my instincts tell me that if we don't find out pretty soon, we could be looking at yet another murder.'

CHAPTER 20

The DI's mobile rang as they were heading back down the stairs and stopping to answer it, he left Kate to carry on while he engaged in a short conversation. He caught up with her outside as she waited for him by the parked police cars.

'DCI,' he explained. 'Coroner apparently gave permission for Julian Dunbar's corpse to be collected by the undertakers. But guv'nor wants me "back at mill" pronto to brief him on the new developments.' He grinned. 'Having a fit, I shouldn't wonder. Right when he thought everything was being nicely wrapped up.'

'No problem. I'll liaise with SOCO and the uniform detail if you like and join you later.'

'That would be ideal. But don't you want to get some dry clothes on? You must still be wet through.'

She shook her head. 'Almost dry now. It was only my legs and feet. I'll change once I'm done here.' She yawned. 'Besides, I'd like to have a word with the Matlocks at The Lodge before I leave. It struck me when I last interviewed Josh that he's the sort of character who misses very little. As he's always out and about here as the gardener and odd-job man, he might be the ideal person to tap for information.'

He nodded his approval. 'Excellent idea.' He grinned again. 'Grateful for your sacrifice. I know how much of a terrible disappointment it will be for you to have to forego the briefing with our charismatic DCI.'

She grunted and turned towards the footpath leading down the side of the house. '*Je suis désolée*,' she said, showing off her French.

Kate heard Woo's car drive away as she entered the tunnel leading down the side of the old barn to the lake and she felt the stillness envelop her like an invisible cloak. Twice she stopped after feeling that she was being watched from the gloom on each side. But she saw no one and shortly afterwards she emerged by the bird hide.

'Ah, Kate,' the SOCO manager, Andrea James, shouted from the landing stage, her mobile in her gloved hand. 'I was just going to call you.'

Kate slipped on a pair of nylon overshoes and joined her on the rickety wooden structure.

'More or less finished here,' James said. 'Undertakers have collected the corpse and most of my team have already gone, but I thought you might be interested in this.'

She held out a plastic bag and Kate caught the glimpse of metal. 'Might be nothing, but we found it lying on the edge of the landing stage close to where you say you pulled the dead kid out. Surprised you never saw it. You must have missed it in the dark.'

Kate took the bag and studied what appeared to be some kind of very delicate pendant comprising a plump spider with a green-coloured body and red ruby-like eyes crouching in the middle of a glittering silver, hexagonal-shaped web. It was suspended from a thin chain with a clasp.

She grimaced. 'Not to my taste,' she declared. 'Looks as if it's made of real silver with some sort of semi-precious stone set in the middle, but who'd want something like that hanging around their neck?'

James chuckled. 'Someone obviously liked it,' she replied. 'The thing is, the chain seems to be broken, suggesting it may have snapped after getting caught on something and falling on the ground without the wearer being any the wiser.'

'Or was ripped off in a violent struggle,' Kate commented grimly.

'That's certainly a possibility, but you know how fragile these chains are. They're made of pretty soft metal. It wouldn't take much to snap one. I've worn them myself and it's easy to inadvertently catch them on clothing and other things. Could be a hiker or backpacker was strolling past, stopped to look at the bird hide, and unwittingly snagged the chain on something, snapping it. The pendant could then have become trapped in their clothing, only to fall off with further movement.'

'Or as I've said, whoever killed Julian didn't have it all their own way and the chain broke when he put up a fight?'

'Equally feasible, but with nothing more than a pendant on a broken chain for information, we don't have a lot to go on.'

'Any chance of DNA traces, do you think?'

'Well, prints are out of the question, of course. Because of the design of the thing, there's not enough surface area to yield a result. As for DNA, we'll check that out, but I'm not hopeful. It was lying in a puddle of dirty water which rather limits our prospects for success.'

'Do what you can anyway. But the pendant lying right there at the scene of a violent crime is a bit too much of a coincidence in my book. I can't see Julian wearing something like this, so I'll need to find out who else among the surviving members of his family might have a taste for grotesque jewellery.'

* * *

There was no reply at The Lodge and the curtains were drawn across one of the bay windows. Guessing that Dorothy Matlock would be up at the house preparing evening dinner and Josh would be about somewhere in the grounds doing whatever it was gardeners did, Kate had turned away and was about to head back down the driveway when she heard the sound of a chainsaw starting up. She followed the sound into the woodland at the back of The Lodge and found Josh Matlock in a small clearing, sawing through a fallen tree. He was dressed in a khaki coat, thick woollen trousers and boots and wearing a protective orange helmet and visor.

He wasn't aware of her approaching at first, but then happened to glance round and caught sight of her. He switched off the chainsaw and carefully placed it on the ground beside him.

'Just the man,' Kate said, giving him an encouraging smile. 'Can I have a quick word?'

''Bout young Julian, I'll wager,' he said, undoing the chinstrap of his helmet and balancing it on the fallen tree before propping himself on a nearby pile of logs.

'You've heard, then?' Kate said, watching as he produced a pipe from his pocket and began stuffing the bowl with tobacco.

'Aye,' he said. 'Heard right enough. 'Darned cop cars roarin' past our place at one thirty in the mornin' with them roof lights flashin'. Must have woke up half of Somerset.'

'So how did you know about Julian?'

He lit his pipe and drew on the stem a couple of times before exhaling a cloud of aromatic smoke. 'Left the missus and went up to the house, didn't I? Young copper stopped me goin' any further than end of the drive, but wouldn't tell me nothin', so I went back home. Found out later from the professor that the young lad had drowned in the lake. Murdered, he said.'

He shook his head dismally. 'Knew he would come a cropper one day.'

'Why do you say that?'

He removed the pipe from his mouth and pointed the smoking stem in her direction. 'He weren't a bad lad and he seemed to like chattin' to me whenever he saw me workin' in the grounds. But he be always poking his nose into other

194

folk's affairs, that's why I knew he would go too far 'afore long. It don't do, see. Best to keep to your own business.'

'When I first spoke to you after the kitchen at Moat House was broken into, you said Julian had already told you what had happened. Did he confide in you a lot?'

Matlock pulled on his pipe again but didn't answer immediately. Then he said, 'Didn't really confide in me. Just liked to show how much he knew 'bout goin's on at the big house. I reckons he had no confidence in hisself and wanted attention. I warned him it would get him into trouble one day, but he wouldn't listen.'

'Did he tell you anything about other members of the family. Maybe hint at a few guilty secrets?'

Matlock stood up and reached for his protective helmet. 'Not my place to listen to idle chatter, Sergeant. Now I'd best get on.'

But Kate had no intention of letting him off so easily this time.

'Do you know what he was doing at the lake in the early hours of the morning?'

He sighed and turned to face her again, fiddling with the strap of the helmet. 'Meetin' someone, I shouldn't wonder. I don't think he were into skinny dippin' as folk calls it, and I doubt he were interested in birdwatchin' neither.'

'Meeting who?'

'No idea, Sergeant, I'm only sayin' maybe. As I told you, young Julian didn't tell me much, just boasted he knew things.'

'I don't believe you, Mr Matlock. I think you know a lot more than you are letting on.'

He gave a crooked grin. 'Maybe I does and maybe I doesn't.'

'Well, you need to understand that we are not talking anymore about an accident. This is a murder inquiry, not a game. A double murder inquiry in fact, since we now believe Howard Dunbar was a victim of the same person who killed Julian. If you are withholding information from us, you could find yourself in some very hot water indeed. Even end up as a suspect.'

Matlock thought about that for a second, his grin fading. Then with a frown he placed his helmet carefully on top of the woodpile and said, 'Look, I don't want no trouble with Professor Dunbar. The Lodge ain't just where me and the missus works, it be our home too and we got nowhere else to go.'

'I understand that, Mr Matlock, but as I said to you before, anything you tell me will be treated in the strictest confidence. Just bear in mind that there have been two murders here so far. Until this killer is caught none of you are safe.'

He went silent again, obviously turning her warning over in his mind.

Then he threw a couple of glances around him into the encroaching trees and nodded in the direction of The Lodge. 'Best we go indoors. Ain't no eavesdroppers there.'

A strong smell of baking rushed out to meet them when Matlock pushed through the front door of the little cottage. Kate glimpsed Dorothy Matlock's portly shape through the open door of what was obviously a kitchen at the far end of a short hallway. Her hands were thrust into a mixing bowl on a long wooden table, and she glanced up quickly when her husband growled, 'We got company, Mother,' as he led Kate into a sitting room opposite the stairs to the upper level.

Dropping heavily into a fully-upholstered armchair with faded tapestry covers to one side of an open fireplace, he nodded towards its twin.

'Take the weight off, Sergeant,' he said, looking up as Dorothy Matlock bustled into the room, wiping floury hands down her apron.

'Not preparing tonight's dinner then, Mrs Matlock,' Kate said, giving her a friendly smile.

'The professor give me the day off,' she replied, puffing as she squeezed herself into a third armchair in the half-moon alcove formed by the room's bay window. 'Told me they could manage lunch and dinner on their own for once while all this bad business be going on.' She frowned. 'Now, what be all this about then, Josh?

'Sergeant has some questions for me about young Julian, Mother,' he replied, relighting his pipe. 'But I ain't sure as I can answer any of 'em.'

Dorothy Matlock shook her head sorrowfully. 'That poor young lad,' she said. 'To die like that at his age. Any idea who could have done it?'

'That's why I'm here, Mrs Matlock,' Kate explained. 'To see if your husband can help me with it all.' She stared at him intently, waiting for him to comment. When he didn't, she took the initiative herself. 'Well, Mr Matlock? You said when I started asking you questions outside just now that it was best we went indoors. So what have you got to tell me?'

Matlock threw a penetrating glance at his wife as if seeking her approval. He looked decidedly uncomfortable.

To Kate's surprise, Dorothy Matlock responded immediately to his unspoken question.

'You have to tell, Josh,' she said. 'It be the right thing to do.'

''Appen there be nothin' in it,' he said finally, 'but I'll tell you anyways.'

He scratched the side of his nose with the stem of his pipe, then set it down in an ashtray on the chair arm.

'Fact is, Sergeant, I don't sleep too good. The rheumatis', see. And last night it were really bad. So just after midnight I gets up and goes for a walk around the cottage to try and ease the pain. Then I hears a noise in the woods. Thinkin' it were a fox comin' in after my chickens again, I goes back indoors and gets me twelve bore. But when I goes out again, I sees this figure all muffled up like in some sort of long grey coat with a furry type hood makin' through the trees towards the driveway along our back fence. I creeps round to the front of The Lodge, curious like, and sees this figure come out of the trees by the gates and disappear through 'em on to the lane. A few minutes later I hears a car start up and drive off.'

'Did you see the person's face?' Kate asked, her excitement mounting.

He shook his head. 'As I say, they be wearin' a hood,' he said, 'but I can tell you one thing. From the way they was movin' I would say that it were definitely a woman.'

Kate felt totally deflated. 'Can you remember anything else about them? Did they seem young, middle-aged? Were they tall, short, fat or thin? Anything?'

He shook his head slowly. 'I got the feelin' they be quite slim like, maybe about five feet six or seven, but that's all.'

Kate nodded. 'Well, thank you anyway. If you think of anything else later, I'd be grateful if you'd let me know at Highbridge CID.'

He retrieved his pipe and applied another match to it, climbing to his feet as Kate stood up.

'Sure you wouldn't like a nice cup of tea, Sergeant?' Dorothy Matlock asked, grabbing the arms of her chair to enable her to get up again.

Kate turned towards her with a smile, but her intention to say a polite 'no thank you', abruptly froze on her lips.

The portly lady was dressed in a pinafore over her cardigan and skirt and as she bent forward to lever herself out of the chair, a silver-coloured pendant swung out from under her pinafore on the end of a thin chain. For a few seconds the world seemed to stand still as Kate simply stood there staring in disbelief at the green spider with its tiny red eyes crouched in the centre of the hexagonal-shaped silver web, and she was hardly aware of Matlock's chuckled remark, 'Pretty, ain't it. I made it meself.'

Kate didn't say anything at first. Then she forced a smile and reached forward to take hold of the pendant to examine it more closely before she cleared her throat and asked, 'You say you actually made it? You must be very clever.'

The other chuckled. 'Me? Clever? No way. Went on one of them jewellery courses at the college in Bridgwater and learned how to do it there. I makes all sorts of pendants now.

Spiders, lizards, flowers, trees. You tell me what you wants, and I'll do the rest.'

She pointed to the wall behind Kate. 'There be a few on display over there.'

Kate turned quickly and for the first time noticed the dark wooden cabinet on the wall behind the chair in which she had been sitting. She saw that it contained maybe a dozen different pendants secured to cards attached to the back of the cabinet in some way, possibly with glue. Most were of butterflies, birds and fish, but slap-bang in the middle, as if in a class of its own, was an identical pendant to the one Dorothy Matlock was wearing, the little red eyes of the arachnid gleaming at Kate as if the thing were alive and studying her.

'And . . . and you sell them all?'

'Well, I tries, but I have to admit I ain't sold many yet — maybe only about half a dozen so far and not many folk like the spider design. Gives 'em the creeps, I reckons. In fact, I've only ever sold one of those.'

Kate pricked up her ears. 'Just the one?'

'Aye. Saw me wearin' the pendant couple of weeks back and liked it so much that she had one off me straight away. 'Bout the only person I knows who actually likes creepy-crawlies. But as she practically lives with them all the time that's not really surprisin', I suppose.'

Kate knew even before she asked the question what the answer would be, but she had to ask it anyway.

'Someone local, was it?'

Another chuckle. 'Aye, you could say that. Doc Lawrence be about as local as you can get.'

CHAPTER 21

Kate's mind was in turmoil as she walked in a semi-daze back to her car parked in front of Moat House. Her excitement at the potential breakthrough in the investigation was marred by the realisation that it could have come much sooner had she not been so blinkered at the start. She sat at the wheel for a long time as the shadows began to lengthen and flocks of bats emerged from among the trees. She was lost to reality in a negative, self-destructive mood.

What was the matter with her? The identity of the killer had been obvious from the very beginning. So why hadn't she cottoned on to that fact straightaway? Why had it taken an ugly silver pendant to make the connection for her? Even a rookie detective would have realised that the culprit for Howard Dunbar's murder could only have been Dr Samantha Lawrence. Apart from Professor Dunbar, she was the only person with total, unrestricted access to the laboratory. The only person who could enter and leave the lab at any time of the day and night without attracting attention. The only person who had the necessary skills and experience to handle deadly tropical spiders safely. No one else at Moat House came even close. And if Lawrence *had* killed Howard Dunbar, it was logical to conclude, now that there was the supportive evidence of the pendant, that she had also murdered Julian. A young man whose reputation for snooping made him the most likely person to have stumbled upon the truth.

Kate gripped the steering wheel tightly in a spasm of frustration until she heard her knuckles crack. She had been totally blindsided by the fact that at the time Howard Dunbar had died the biologist was said to have taken two days off, allegedly visiting a sick aunt somewhere. She had committed the cardinal error of failing to check this out. Something so fundamental to any police investigation that it would have been an inexcusable lapse even for a first-year probationary constable. As a result, convinced that the murder of Julian was linked to that of his brother, she had not even considered Lawrence as a possible suspect when the second murder had taken place. The knock-on effect of this had been that despite being an experienced detective sergeant with years of police service, she had faffed about looking for a likely suspect when all the time the real killer was right there in front of her, hidden in plain sight.

No wonder, she thought bitterly, that her colleagues seemed to regard her as flaky and unreliable. Based on her present performance, it was beginning to look as if they were right. If she was going to prove them wrong and redeem herself, at least in her own eyes after her cataclysmic mental meltdown the year before which had put her in the rehabilitation clinic, it was vital that she produced the detection that was required. She had been thrown a possible lifeline in the form of that silver pendant. It was now up to her to make the best use of it.

True to her impetuous nature, she was tempted to get to it right there and then and confront Dr Lawrence head on. Professor Dunbar's cool and collected assistant had no doubt finished for the day and had probably already gone home. But there was nothing to say she couldn't be interviewed in her own cottage and asked if she could produce the pendant. That at least would go some way towards establishing whether the pendant found at the scene of the crime was hers or not.

Yet Kate immediately knocked that idea on the head as soon as it was born, hauling herself back from the brink of another potential cock-up. It was imperative that this stage of the investigation was handled very carefully and in accordance with proper procedures. To start with, the interview would have to be conducted by two officers for corroborative purposes and to meet any safety concerns. There was no telling how Lawrence would react. Furthermore, even if the biologist was unable to produce the pendant Dorothy Matlock said she had purchased, that in itself did not prove anything. Without additional forensic or other evidence, it served only to raise the red flag of suspicion, nothing more. A more subtle strategy was required if this potential breakthrough was to lead anywhere. A case of 'softly, softly catchee monkey'.

Conscious of just how tired she was, Kate fastened her seat belt and started the car. Right, so, the first step was to brief the DI on developments and then home for a shower, something to eat and a good night's sleep. After all, there was no rush. Dr Lawrence had no reason to believe she was under suspicion, and she was unlikely to be going anywhere any time soon.

The thought of going home brought the acid up in Kate's throat once again as she thought of Hayden and the terrible row they had had. In the light of all that had happened at Moat House, she had pushed it to the back of her mind. Automatically, she felt the ring finger of her left hand and found the distinctive mark where her wedding ring had been. She remembered how she had hurled the gold band at her husband in the CID office before storming off like some recalcitrant child. She had said some awful things to him in hot blood and even though she now so deeply regretted them, she sensed it was probably already too late. Hayden was a sensitive, caring soul, who was easily hurt, and he would have taken her harsh words very much to heart. It was likely that he had already packed his bags and gone, leaving her to a cold, empty house and a bare gravel strip where his beloved Jaguar had once been parked. As the bats wheeled above her car and the darkness closed in completely, she continued to sit there with the engine still running, hunched in her seat and sobbing her heart out.

* * *

Charlie Woo was in his office when Kate got back to the police station. He waved her to a chair, then listened carefully to what she told him about the discovery of the pendant by SOCO and the possible link to Samantha Lawrence.

'Good work,' he said. 'That certainly looks promising. But only as far as the murder of Julian Dunbar is concerned. What about Howard Dunbar? I thought you told me she had an alibi for when he was fatally bitten by the spider. That she was away visiting an aunt or something at the time. Maybe the DCI was right all along, and Howard's death *was* an accident.'

Kate looked more than a little uncomfortable as she shook her head. 'The alibi was never checked out. I boobed. At the very start of the inquiry it looked like we were investigating nothing more than a tragic accident, so it didn't seem necessary to verify her whereabouts. After that, I didn't think to follow up on what was claimed.'

'You just accepted it?'

'Not exactly. My focus was on other possible suspects and the issue got sort of lost amidst it all.'

He grimaced. 'Bugger it! Not something I would have expected of you. You're usually so thorough.'

The criticism cut deep, especially coming as it did from her old friend, and she flinched. 'I know. It was negligent and unprofessional. I make no excuses for it. I can only apologise.'

He grunted, then waved a hand dismissively. 'Well, the damage is done now. We'll just have to cover that omission when she is next interviewed. But we all make mistakes. No one is perfect, and you've been through a hell of a lot lately.'

He studied her for a moment, concern etched into his expression. 'Actually, Kate, I have to say, you look like shit.'

'Thanks.'

'No, I mean it. You're driving yourself too hard. If you don't watch yourself, you'll end up with another breakdown. You had a rough time on that last case of yours. You were told by the police surgeon that you needed to slow down and take it a lot easier to avoid a relapse.'

'I'll be fine, honestly.'

'You're far from fine. You're a ghost of the DS I used to know. It may be better all round if I take this case off you. Give you a breather—'

She flared suddenly. 'Don't you dare! I need to see this thing through to the end. It's my lifeline to recovery.'

He thought about that for a moment, then gave a reluctant nod. 'Okay but listen to me. You need to sort yourself out, particularly in relation to your domestic situation. I don't know exactly what's going on between you and Hayden, but it's dragging you both down. As I told you before, I can't have the domestic problems of members of my team interfering with the effective operation of the department, especially when it involves my one and only sergeant.'

She stiffened. 'Hayden has spoken to you, hasn't he?'

He nodded. 'He was in a right state when he turned up late this morning because of the spat you two had last night. He looked totally shellshocked. I told him to take the rest of the day off . . .'

'But there's more, isn't there?'

He sighed. ''Fraid so. He's, er, put in for a transfer to Bristol.'

Kate felt her senses start to swim and she clenched her hands tightly in her lap. 'He's done what?' she whispered.

He gave a half smile. 'Don't worry, I dumped his request in the bin. But you need to get home and straighten things out p.d.q.'

'I think it's too late for that.'

'It's never too late and if you value what you have, it's always worth fighting for. So get off your trim little arse and get yourself home. I don't want to see you again until you and Hayden have resolved your differences and you have had a proper night's sleep.'

She stood up but hesitated. 'Have you told the DCI about us?'

'And why would I do that?'

* * *

The little cottage was displaying just the porchlight when Kate pulled into the driveway behind Hayden's big red Mk II Jaguar. She was surprised to see that the cottage was in darkness. As Hayden's car was there, he had to be at home, so where was he? She glanced at her watch. Eight o'clock. Surely he hadn't gone to bed early just to avoid her?

Her hand trembled as she inserted her key in the front door, dreading the confrontation that might be awaiting her. She could hear the wall clock ticking and see the glowing maw of the open fire as she pushed the door open, but the house was very still. Gently closing the door behind her, she hung her coat up on the hook just inside and turned to survey the room. The voice spoke to her even as her eyes picked out the heavy-set figure slumped in the armchair by the fire.

'You came home in the end then?'

She flicked on the light switch and stared at her husband. He looked awful. His face was pale and haggard, his mop of unruly blond hair even more untamed than usual and his eyes unnaturally bright. He was holding a glass of whisky none too steadily in one hand and as she stared at him, he raised it to his lips and took a sip, spilling some of it down his grubby looking shirt at the same time.

'Do I get one of those?' she asked, nodding towards the bottle on the coffee table in front of him.

He shrugged. 'Glass in the kitchen,' he said. 'Help yourself.'

Her mouth tightened, but she bit back the caustic remark forming on her tongue and went to collect it.

Returning to the living room, she poured herself a stiff measure and downed half of it in a gulp before sitting on the edge of the settee opposite him. She had noticed her wedding ring lying on the coffee table next to the bottle, but she deliberately avoided looking at it as she tried to control the rapid beating of her heart.

'I hear you found another body,' he said suddenly, breaking the awkward silence.

She nodded. 'Julian Dunbar,' she replied. 'Someone drowned him.'

'Well now,' he said, 'poor old Julian.' His voice was laced with sarcasm. 'So he never got the chance to tell you anything then? Who's under suspicion now? You must be fast running out of suspects.'

'Hayd . . .' she began, then abruptly broke off, realising that 'sorry' really was the hardest word to say.

He poured himself another whisky. 'Funny, really,' he said, 'I always thought marriage meant something. You know, exchanging rings and vows and all that signified an entire life together. Seems I was wrong.'

'Hayden, please forgive me,' she breathed, surprised that the apology suddenly came out so easily. 'All those things I said, I didn't mean them. I was just hurt and angry.'

'You said you were leaving me, and you didn't want me anywhere near you,' he accused, his voice rising to a higher pitch. 'You threw your wedding ring back in my face.'

'I know,' she said, her own voice breaking up. 'But I didn't mean it. I . . . I felt trapped and despised by everyone. First the super stopping my acting rank. Then Charlie Woo suggesting I was flaky and unreliable, and Jamie Foster, among others, talking about me and laughing at me behind my back. When you of all people said I was losing the plot and behaving like a neurotic schoolgirl, that just about did it and I lost my temper.'

To her astonishment, she saw tears running down his cheeks. Hayden was actually crying.

'But you called me a weak, lazy bum who slummed around doing nothing,' he choked.

As much to her own surprise as Hayden's and no doubt due to the emotional trauma she was going through, Kate suddenly found herself giving way to a spontaneous outburst of inappropriate gurgling laughter which she was unable to control. 'But you *are* a lazy bum, Hayden!' she exclaimed. 'And you *do* swan around doing nothing.'

For a second he was completely taken aback by her reaction and simply stared at her in disbelief. But then it got to him as well and unable to stop himself, he too dissolved into an uncontrollable fit of hysterical laughter.

In a moment she was across the room and had thrown her arms around his neck in a ferocious hug and both of them were crying and laughing at the same time.

Then finally exhausted by it all, Kate prised herself free of his bear-like embrace and instead settled contentedly on his lap with her head against his chest.

'I'm so sorry, Hayd,' she said, kissing him hard on the mouth. 'Can we start again?'

He beamed happily. 'I can't think of anything I'd like better,' he said. 'Are you going to put your ring back on? Then I think we should celebrate.'

'I agree entirely,' she said and climbing off his lap, she picked the ring up off the coffee table and slipped it back on her finger.

'I'll open a special bottle of red,' he said, getting to his feet.

'Oh no,' she said, pushing him back in his chair and bending down to unzip her boots. 'I have a much better idea.'

'I've got a headache,' he protested.

'Tough,' she replied.

CHAPTER 22

'How are things?' Charlie Woo asked Kate when she walked into the office late the following morning.

Kate's face was grey, and she went straight to the coffee machine without answering.

Woo shook his head. 'Heavy night?'

She poured a black coffee and followed him into his office, slumping into a chair in front of his desk. 'You could say that. But you want to see the other feller.'

'You two back together now, then?'

'*Oh* yes. Very much so.'

Woo settled into his own chair behind his desk. 'Well, that's a relief. So where *is* the other feller?'

She treated him to a ghost of a smile. 'Hayden's off sick. Hurt his back.'

The DI held up his hand in a silencing gesture. 'I really don't want to know anymore, thank you. It's too early in the morning and I haven't had any breakfast.'

Kate chuckled, then winced and cupped a hand round her forehead. 'Got any paracetamol?'

He opened a side drawer and tossed the packet across to her, then raised an eyebrow when she took four.

'Anyway,' he went on, 'the thing is, are you up to that chat with Dr Lawrence this morning?'

She nodded. 'I'll be okay in an hour and a few more coffees.'

He made a grimace. 'That's good of you. You're only nearly two hours late. What's another hour when you're having fun!'

She winced. 'Sorry, guv. I'll be fine, honestly. Anything from SOCO yet about the pendant?'

'Nothing obvious, and they think it's unlikely any DNA traces will be found on the thing because of where it was discovered. As you know, we don't automatically send stuff off to the lab. It's usually dependant on the likelihood of a hit. In this case SOCO feel it would be a costly waste of everyone's time, particularly when the lab is up to its gunnels in work. I therefore decided against it.'

Kate thought about that and shrugged. 'It's a judgement thing, I realise that. So it has to be down to the interview of Dr Lawrence and what that produces.'

He nodded. 'And the ratio of coffee to alcohol in a certain detective sergeant's blood!' he added drily.

* * *

Professor Dunbar treated Kate and Charlie Woo to a sour look when they turned up at Moat House.

'What now?' he said, only partially opening the front door. 'I was on my way back to the lab. You're lucky I heard the bell.'

He was dressed in a white cotton coat like a medical doctor and carrying a cup of coffee in one hand.

'We'd like to have a word with Dr Lawrence if you don't mind,' Woo said.

'What about?'

'I'm afraid that's confidential.'

'Well, she's not here.'

'Oh? Not working today, then?'

He grunted. 'Gone home. Not feeling well apparently.'

'And where is home?'

'I'm not sure I can tell you that.'

Woo's gaze hardened. 'I'm afraid you have no choice, Professor. Unless you want to be seen as obstructing the police in a murder investigation.'

Dunbar scowled. 'Lavender Cottage in the village. She's rented the place.'

Woo smiled pleasantly. 'Thank you for your cooperation, Professor. We should be able to find it.'

'Looks like he got out of bed the wrong side this morning,' the DI commented as he and Kate returned to the CID car.

Kate grunted. 'Situation normal,' she said. 'But I have to say, he did look even more morose than usual. Maybe one of his beloved spiders died.'

Lavender Cottage was easy enough to find. The village was in fact little more than a hamlet, with half a dozen houses, a shop-cum-post office and a gloomy looking church. Kate recognised Lawrence's car immediately. The silver BMW coupé that she had seen outside Moat House was parked on a short gravel strip beside a stone end terrace opposite the church.

They spotted Lawrence at the same time. She was dressed in a blue anorak and black jeans and carrying a suitcase out to the car. As they drew up she raised the boot lid to dump it unceremoniously inside.

'Oh, Sergeant Lewis,' she said, turning quickly in surprise at their approach. 'Are you here to see me?'

'Yes, we are actually,' Kate replied. 'This is my boss, Detective Inspector Woo. Were you going somewhere?'

Lawrence smiled, but the smile lacked any warmth. The biologist looked pale and drawn and she seemed more than a little edgy. 'Oh, nowhere special,' she said. 'Just a couple of days away, that's all.'

'Visiting your aunt again?'

'I beg your pardon?'

'Your aunt. You went to see her a few days ago.'

Lawrence emitted a short, nervous laugh. 'Oh, yes, of course. My aunt. She was, er, sick then, but she's better now. No, I'm just having a break. Going to Stratford-on-Avon actually. Thought I'd take in a Shakespearean play at the theatre. Always wanted to . . .'

'Excellent idea, but before you go, can we have a little chat?'

'But . . . but of course. Come in.'

The front door of the cottage opened on to a tiny living room with a low ceiling, bowed black-painted wooden beams and an inglenook fireplace. A narrow staircase ascended to the upper level in one corner and an open door at the far end revealed part of a galley kitchen. The room smelled damp and musty.

Pulling another suitcase off a floral-patterned set-tee which seemed to be the only item of furniture there, Lawrence said, 'Please do sit down. I'm afraid I can't offer you any tea as, er, everything is switched off.'

Crossing the room to the fireplace, she propped herself on a raised slate shelf on one side. 'So, how can I help you? You haven't found Martha, I suppose?'

Kate shook her head, thinking of the hideous creature and the fangs in the red patch on its belly. 'No such luck,' she said. 'Now, where were you really off to when we arrived, Doctor?'

'Sorry? I don't understand. I've just told you.'

'Well, we've just seen Professor Dunbar,' Woo put in. 'He was of the impression that you came home because you weren't feeling well. He said nothing about Stratford.'

Lawrence coloured up. 'Er, no, it was a spur of the moment decision. I was going to let him know just before I left.'

'Seemed more like you were doing a bunk to me,' Kate contradicted and focused on her intently, watching for the tell-tale sign that, as a trained police interrogator, she always looked for. She wasn't disappointed. It came right then, the sudden nervous swallow and the jerk of the Adam's apple.

'Look, I don't know what this is about,' Lawrence said without denying the allegation. 'But I don't think I have to explain my movements to you, Sergeant.'

Kate's eyes gleamed. She had been expecting that sort of desperate response. Using aggression as a defence when caught out in a lie. It was a classic tactic. But she deliberately didn't press home her advantage. Instead, in an unspoken communication that passed subliminally between the two detectives, she left Woo to home in on the issue as a means of throwing Lawrence off-balance.

'So, exactly why were you leaving in such a hurry without telling your employer?' the DI went on. 'You must admit, it's a bit suspicious.'

For a second Lawrence seemed lost for words. She opened her mouth again as if to say something, but nothing came out and she swallowed even more noticeably than before. Then abruptly she capitulated.

'That horrible man,' she said suddenly, tears in her eyes. 'I . . . I had to get away.'

Kate gave her one of her encouraging smiles. 'Came on to you, did he?' she asked quietly.

Lawrence took a deep breath. 'The man is a pervert,' she said. 'Can't keep his hands to himself. I just can't stand it any longer.'

'But when I asked you a while ago what he was like as an employer, you told me he was, I think you said, dedicated and meticulous.'

She snorted. 'He is dedicated and meticulous, but only where his damned arachnids are concerned.'

'You also indicated you were happy to work for him.'

'I had to say that, didn't I? I needed the job, and he is well respected and a powerful influencer in his field. If he were to dismiss me, I would be finished.'

'Yet you are about to run out on him.'

'I have no choice. It's either that or go to bed with him, and the thought revolts me. Besides, I have already secured another job.'

'How so, without his reference?'

'I am going to work for my previous employer. He will take me back without issue.'

'How can you be so sure?'

She paused a moment, looking guilty again. 'That's where I was when I said I was visiting my sick aunt. I don't have an aunt, sick or otherwise. I was at a job interview, negotiating terms.'

'So you lied?'

'If you like to put it that way, yes, but with good reason.'

'And where was this interview?' Woo came in again.

'I'm sorry, I can't tell you that.'

'Can't or won't.'

She shrugged but didn't answer.

Kate decided to move things on. 'I do like your necklace,' she said, admiring the tiny silver butterfly on a short chain around her neck.

Lawrence looked thrown by the sudden change of tack. 'Thank you, I, er, like wildlife designs.'

Kate affected a frown. 'I gathered you did. I was actually talking to Mrs Matlock yesterday about her hobby making jewellery and I was nearly tempted into ordering one of her pendants. She told me you bought one from her yourself recently, a silver pendant with a spider design.'

Lawrence gave a faint smile. 'Yes, rather unsurprising, I suppose, in view of my interest in arachnids. Unfortunately, though, I seem to have lost it.'

'Lost it?'

'Yes, I remember putting it down somewhere — on the windowsill over there, I thought.' She nodded towards a small leaded pane behind her. 'But I can't find it now. I know I was a bit worried about the clasp. Maybe it came undone and fell off when I was out walking. Bit annoying.'

Kate tugged the plastic bag containing the pendant found at the crime scene from her coat pocket.

'Could this be it, do you think?'

Lawrence's eyes widened. 'Good heavens, but where—?'

'The lake at Moat House, Doctor,' Kate replied, her voice now cold and hard. 'Close to where Julian Dunbar's body was found.'

'Julian? But surely you don't think that I—?'

Kate said nothing. She simply stared at her, waiting.

Lawrence gulped. 'But I've never been to that lake, and I certainly had nothing to do with . . . I mean, why would I want to hurt Julian?'

'You tell us, Doctor. Maybe he was blackmailing you over something in the same way as he seems to have been blackmailing everyone else in Moat House.'

'Blackmailing? That's ridiculous. I would have had to have something to hide, and I am totally innocent of anything.'

'No one is totally innocent, Doctor.'

Lawrence stared wildly from Kate to Woo and back again. 'The pendant must be someone else's.'

Woo shook his head. 'Mrs Matlock said she only sold that particular design to you. Did you tell her you'd lost it?'

'Of course not. I . . . I only bought the blasted thing to please her. Actually I hated it. It was so crude and clumsy, and I considered I was well rid of it.'

'It's easy to say that now, but maybe you panicked when you realised you must have dropped it by the lake, but you couldn't go back for it because the police were there by then.'

Lawrence lurched to her feet. 'It was nothing like that. I only bought it from the bloody woman a fortnight ago and I lost the damned thing somewhere a few days before Julian's death. You must believe me. I'm telling the truth.'

'Please sit down, Doctor,' Kate said firmly and when the biologist sank back on to the shelf, she said, 'Where were you last night, between the hours of midnight and one thirty?'

'Last night? Well, at home here, of course.'

Kate's gaze had wandered around the room, homing in on a long, grey hooded raincoat with a fur-lined trim at the front of the hood that was hanging from a peg behind the front door.

'Your coat there, is it?' she asked.

Lawrence looked bewildered by the question. Even Woo looked puzzled now. 'Well, yes, it wouldn't be anyone else's, would it?'

'When did you last wear it?'

'I'm sorry, what has my coat got to do with anything?'

'Wear it last night, did you?'

'Last night? I don't remember . . . But yes, I think I went for a walk.'

'What time was that?'

'It would have been late. I don't sleep well and usually a stroll helps.'

'Where did you go?'

'Er, I don't know. Around the village probably. There are a lot of footpaths here.'

'Didn't drive up to Moat House then?'

'Moat House? What on earth would I want to go back there for at that ungodly hour?'

'Someone answering your description was seen leaving the grounds of Moat House in the early hours of the morning. How do you explain that?'

There was an abrupt change in Lawrence's demeanour. 'This is absolutely ridiculous. I am not saying anything else without a solicitor.'

'Your prerogative,' Kate said. 'Dr Samantha Lawrence, I am arresting you on suspicion of the murders of Howard and Julian Dunbar. You do not have to say anything. But it may harm your defence if you do not mention when questioned something which you later rely on in court. Anything you do say may be given in evidence.'

* * *

'Very thin ice,' Charlie Woo said when they got back to the police station and Lawrence had been handed over to the custody officer. 'I hope you're able to get a cough out of her, because we've got precious little real evidence to connect her with either murder.'

Kate frowned. 'You unhappy about the arrest?'

'Not at all. We didn't have much option, did we? If we hadn't taken her in she'd have been off on her toes somewhere.'

'Well, we do have some reasonable circumstantial evidence. There's the pendant we found by the body at the crime scene which is obviously hers, and the fact that she can't produce the one she bought from Matlock. We've got witness evidence from Josh Matlock to say he saw someone in a grey coat, like the one that was hanging in her cottage, leaving the grounds of Moat House round about the time Julian Dunbar was murdered. On top of that, she lied about where she was the night Howard Dunbar was killed and refuses to substantiate her claim that she was at a job interview. And don't forget, she is the only person, apart from the professor, who has the necessary skills to handle venomous spiders and with legitimate access to the lab. It all fits.'

He shrugged. 'Agreed. So let's hope we can make it stick as well.'

CHAPTER 23

Donald Dukes was a grey-haired, little man, with a grey face, grey-rimmed spectacles and an even greyer suit. He was wearing a prominent 'Ban the Bomb' badge on his lapel and as the duty solicitor, it immediately became apparent that he was going to be a pain.

'Not much there, I would suggest,' he said after the DI had disclosed their 'evidence' and the little man had had his initial interview with his new client.

The interview in Interview Room 2 at the police station was short and not so sweet, with Dukes constantly interjecting and Lawrence refusing to answer any questions.

In the end, there was no point continuing with the charade and Woo called a halt to the interview, returning Lawrence to the custody officer.

'We need more evidence if we are going to continue holding her,' Woo said to Kate in his office afterwards.

Kate swore. 'The bitch,' she grated. 'And we're so close.'

Woo grunted. 'Are we really?' he said.

'Well, a pendant like the one she is alleged to have purchased was found at the scene of the crime and Dorothy Matlock said Lawrence was the only person she sold that particular design to.'

'Maybe, but we can't positively tie in that specific pendant to her without supporting forensic evidence and that is unlikely to be forthcoming. She claims she lost the pendant, so in the eyes of a court anyone could have picked it up.'

'What about the grey raincoat with the fur-lined hood that was hanging up in her cottage? Josh Matlock saw someone wearing just such a coat leaving Moat House the very night Julian Dunbar was murdered.'

'So what? I expect quite a few people have similar coats and Matlock didn't see the face of the person he saw.'

'Okay, then why has she refused to tell us where she was on the night Howard Dunbar died and why was she about to do a bunk when we went to see her?'

'All very suspicious, I agree, but it isn't evidence. She isn't required by law to furnish us with an alibi for the night of the alleged murder of Howard Dunbar, and she had a reasonable excuse for running out on a man she said was sexually harassing her.'

'But all these things together—'

'Not enough, Kate, as you well know. What we need is more definite evidence, though where you are going to get that from, I fail to see. As a start, I would suggest you go back to Moat House, reinterview the Matlocks and get a statement off Josh Matlock. Maybe something will come out of that. But one thing is clear. We can't hold Dr Lawrence on what we've got. We're going to have to give her police bail, with a requirement to report back here in say a month.'

'And we'll never see her again. She'll simply abscond.'

He shrugged. 'In which case, we'd have to get out a warrant for her rearrest.'

'If we can find her again.'

'That's the risk we'll have to take. All we can do now is get stuck into some more leg work and see what that produces.'

'What *I* produce, you mean.'

'You know what we always say about the job. If you can't take a joke you shouldn't have joined.'

* * *

'No luck?' Hayden asked when Kate dropped back to their cottage to see how he was and to get them both some lunch.

He was lying flat out on the settee, still dressed in his pyjamas, with a cup of coffee on the coffee table in front of him. The television was on displaying a football match. Kate guessed he was on Sky.

'Arrested the professor's assistant, Dr Lawrence, on sus,' she said and brought him up to speed on the investigation.

'Well, that's a turn-up for the books.'

'Yes, but she's denying everything, and she has a bloody brief with her now, so we're stuffed.' She stared at him keenly. 'How's the back?'

'Oh, a little bit better. I think I must have pulled a muscle.'

She stared at him fixedly, disbelief written all over her face.

'So how did you get downstairs?'

'Oh that. Bit difficult, old girl, I must admit. But I managed it in the end.'

She grunted. 'What a brave soul you are.'

'One does one's best,' he replied modestly, then quickly moved on before she could ask anything else. 'But back to your case. If I may say, it's great that the pendant was found at the scene of Julian's murder, but it does strike me as a little bit too convenient.'

'What do you mean?'

'Well, forgive my scepticism, but it is almost as if it was put there for you to find.'

'Who by?'

'Your guess is as good as mine, but in your career so far how often has such damning evidence been left at a crime scene? Very rarely, I would say. Secondly, if the blow Julian received to his head pitched him over the edge of the landing stage into the lake and his assailant then climbed on top of him to hold him down under the water, you would have thought the chain of the pendant would have been snapped in the struggle and fallen into the water, not fallen on to the landing stage.'

'Maybe it snapped in the struggle but didn't actually fall off until the killer climbed back on to the landing stage?'

'Possible, but it's worth thinking about. Also, with reference to the grey coat the intruder was allegedly wearing when Josh Matlock saw them leaving the grounds, did you happen to examine it?'

'Yes, I had a look at it just after the "passion wagon" from the nick carted Lawrence away and we seized it for Forensics to look at.'

'And?'

'It fitted the description Matlock had given to a T. Why?'

'What was it like?'

'It seemed fairly new, but I didn't carry out a thorough examination of it at that stage. I left that to SOCO. Why?'

'Well, if Lawrence *was* the killer and was wearing it when she stiffed Julian Dunbar in the way you suspect, she must have actually been standing or crouched in the lake, holding him down. Even if the coat had more or less dried by the time you managed to interview her, I would have thought it would still have been damp and stained by the muddy water of the lake. Or at the very least, it would have been badly creased. In addition, somewhere in her cottage or in her suitcase there are likely to be her other wet or stained clothes and footwear.'

Kate groaned. 'Shit-sticks! Which means the person Matlock saw leaving Moat House may not have been Lawrence at all. But even if it wasn't her, it still doesn't rule her out as the killer.'

'Agreed, but it rather dents your very circumstantial evidence, don't you think? Furthermore, if she is subsequently able to come up with an alibi for the night Howard Dunbar was murdered, all you are left with is a pendant with a broken chain which you say she claims to have lost anyway. Plus, of course, a possible action against you for wrongful arrest and detention.'

She made a rueful grimace. 'Well, thanks a lot!'

'I always aim to please. Anything else I can help you with?'

Kate was furious with herself when she left the house. She was an experienced DS for heaven's sake. Once again she had cocked up. The trauma and concussion she had suffered on that last case, which had resulted in her breakdown and psychotherapy treatment, seemed to have dulled her wits. She had become half the investigator she had once been, missing important details that were fundamental to the job. She should not have gone back to work so soon, let alone taken on a complicated case like this. But it was too late now. She had no choice, if only for her own confidence and self-esteem, but to see things through to the finish. Somewhere in Moat House there was a ruthless killer. If, and that was a big if as far as she was concerned, it wasn't Lawrence, she was determined to find out who it was. And that meant going back to Moat House, as Charlie Woo had suggested, to see what else she could uncover.

* * *

The lake was not quite as serene as it had been when Kate had last been there. The dark water was being agitated by a strengthening breeze which was sending tiny wavelets towards the bank from the little island on the far side. A shutter over one of the observation windows of the bird hide was rattling incessantly, and the rickety landing stage protested under her feet with a multitude of creaks and groans as she walked along it to the end.

She had no idea why she had returned to the murder scene. Perhaps in some sort of desperate attempt to spot something that may have been missed.

She looked back the way she had come, slowly scanning the trees swaying in the breeze and the severed crime scene tapes writhing in sympathy with them. Why was it they never seemed to be removed from crime scenes after they were no longer needed, she wondered. Was it forgetfulness or just plain negligence? Whatever it was, she was equally to blame for the ugly strips of plastic still being there and she headed back towards the bank she had just left with the intention of removing them.

She saw the figure among the trees at the same moment and froze. It was more like a shadow than anything else, something that moved right to left in the undergrowth, away from the footpath accessing the lake. The hairs on the back of her neck quivered uneasily. She was in plain view of anyone hiding among the trees and for some reason she suddenly felt very vulnerable.

She was being watched. That fact was obvious. Watched by someone who must have seen her arrive and park her car at the front of the house and had then followed her through the woods to the lake. Why?

There could be only one logical reason. To find out why she had returned to the lake and what she was looking for. The mystery person was unlikely to be a press reporter, since as far as she knew the media were not yet aware of the goings on at Moat House. Neither was it likely to be a surviving member of the Dunbar family prompted by nothing more than innocent curiosity. It had to be someone with a personal interest in the circumstances of Julian Dunbar's death.

In short, the killer or someone associated with the crime, who was fearful that a clue of some sort might have been left behind at the scene, and that she might find it. That meant Dr Lawrence might not be the killer after all, but someone else she hadn't even considered. So her own life could now be at risk.

A rook cackled from somewhere among the trees and she twitched at a sudden movement behind her. She relaxed only when she heard the flurry of wings accompanied by the panicky quacking of a duck.

Taking a deep breath, she carefully prised her mobile free of her pocket and gripped it tightly in one hand, ready to call for assistance if necessary, even though she realised that if someone meant her harm, she wouldn't have time to do anything before they were on her anyway.

She forced herself to start walking slowly back towards the bank, making a point of glancing around her all the time to let the watcher know that she hadn't found anything and was still looking. But she kept an eye on the trees at the same time.

Back on the bank, she cast a furtive glance at the spot where she had first glimpsed the figure but saw nothing. Whoever had been there was no longer in evidence. She paused by the entrance to the footpath. The tunnel leading back to the old barn looked even darker in the mid-afternoon light than it had before. She bent down and picked up a short fallen branch, wishing she had brought her old police issue CS gas spray with her.

She stepped into the gloom, increasing her pace and watching for the slightest movement among the trees on either side. A branch cracked twice again but no one showed themselves and she emerged by the old barn seconds later, breathless and with her heart pounding, only then to come to an abrupt halt.

The double doors of the building were wide open, and she could hear grunts and metallic clanking emanating from inside. Curious in spite of herself, she moved closer and peered round one of the doors. A figure in green overalls was bending over the excavator she had seen before, fiddling with something at the side of the engine. She breathed a sigh of relief. It was Josh Matlock.

She coughed to attract his attention and he straightened up, then turned to face her.

'Oh, g'day, Sergeant,' he said with a grin. 'What you doin' here? Bit of birdwatchin' at the lake?'

'Hardly, Mr Matlock,' she replied. 'Have you seen anybody about here this afternoon?'

He wiped his nose with the back of his hand. 'Can't say I have. Why's that then?'

'I, er, think someone was hiding among the trees when I was by the lake just now.'

He frowned and glanced towards the footpath. 'Be one of them hippies I shouldn't wonder. Darned thievin' articles. Al'ays lookin' for things to steal. Want me to take a look?'

'No, no, thank you,' she said quickly. 'They'll be gone now anyway. Actually I was going to call and see you this afternoon. You know, have another chat about the person in the grey coat you saw leaving the grounds following Julian's tragic death. See if I could jog your memory into remembering anything else.'

He shrugged and wiped his hands down his trousers. 'Doubt that, Sergeant, but this darned machine won't start anyway, and I was only just thinkin' of nippin' home for a cuppa. Fancy one too, do you?'

'That would be very welcome, thank you.'

Dorothy Matlock was in the kitchen in her pinafore again when Kate was shown into the sitting room.

'Two cups of tea, Mother,' Josh called as he waved Kate to the same armchair as before. 'Now, what else do you want to ask me, Sergeant?'

Kate pulled out her pocketbook and flicked open a couple of pages. 'You said last time we spoke that the person you saw was definitely a woman. I wanted to ask you how you could be so sure. The figure was in a long, grey, hooded coat, you said, so not much of her could have been visible.'

He chuckled. 'Now then, Sergeant,' he said, 'you're askin' me somethin' there.' His pipe was in his hand again and he began filling it from a worn pouch, spilling tobacco on to the carpet and deliberately avoiding her gaze as if embarrassed.

'Thing is,' he went on, settling back in his chair and lighting up. 'I may be a simple old feller, but there ain't nothin' wrong with me eyes, and I reckons I can tell the difference between a man and a woman even when they got their clothes on.'

'I bet you can,' Dorothy Matlock said, as she walked into the room carrying two cups, a jug of milk and a porcelain teapot on a tray. 'Though you'd prefer the woman's clothes to be off, wouldn't you, you dirty old bugger?'

She set the tray down on a coffee table and frowned at Kate. 'How goes the case, Sergeant? Any clues?'

Kate waited while she poured the tea and nodded a 'yes' when the milk jug was proffered.

'Still ongoing, Mrs Matlock,' she said, watching the milk create swirling vein-like rings in the tea. 'But it's early days yet. We just have to keep plugging away.'

The other shook her head and straightened up again. 'Bad business, though, ain't it? I know Julian weren't the nicest of lads, but what sort of person would creep up behind a young boy like that and not only bang him on the 'ead and push him into the lake, but then hold him down till he drowned? Horrid.'

'A very dangerous person, Mrs Matlock. Someone who has now killed twice and will, I am quite certain, kill again.'

'Lord help us all then. What with murders and poisonous spiders on the loose, I be proper frit.'

'Oh, I don't think you have anything to fear, Mrs Matlock. We believe both Howard and Julian were targeted for a particular reason.'

Matlock brightened a little. 'Well, that's a relief anyway,' she replied, then abruptly changed the subject. 'Thought anymore about my pendants then, Sergeant? You seemed proper took with the one I sold Doc Lawrence. Pity she's gone and lost hers. Don't s'pose it's been found anywhere, has it?'

Kate hesitated, trying to be tactful. 'Sorry, Mrs Matlock, but nice as they are, I don't think they're quite my style.'

'No matter, me duck,' Matlock replied. 'You probably don't like spiders. As I said to you before, a lot of other people don't neither.' She laughed out loud. 'Though it's the real ones I worries about. All of them legs and that. Ugh!'

But Kate was not really listening anymore. Something was nagging at her, something which must have been triggered by what Dorothy Matlock had said. An elusive fragment of conversation. Maybe just a word or a phrase that had jarred on her before being consigned to her subconscious. She was hardly aware of the woman's voice droning on and on in the background and she stared at her with her brows puckered in concentration as she tried to home in on what had struck such a discordant note with her. Then in a sudden flash of mental neon she had it, and it was at this point that she froze.

How the hell did Dorothy Matlock know the precise details of Julian Dunbar's death, apart from the fact that he had drowned? That information had never been given out. Furthermore, how did she know Dr Lawrence had mislaid her pendant when Lawrence herself had clearly stated she had not told her she had lost it?

As her brain struggled with the implications of it all, Josh Matlock's gaze focused on her as if he could read what was in her mind. Then releasing another wisp of smoke from the corner of his mouth, he withdrew his pipe and smiled almost sadly. 'Bit of a clanger you dropped there, Mother,' he said quietly. 'I reckons you said a mite too much this time, don't you? Ain't that so, Sergeant?'

For a few moments Kate was too shocked by what had inadvertently been revealed to say or do anything. These two lovely, homespun characters were her murderers? It didn't seem possible. They were the last people on earth she would have suspected. Yet, after Dorothy Matlock's slip-ups and her husband's reference to the 'clanger' she had dropped, there could be no doubt about it.

'Thing is, Sergeant,' Josh went on, 'we can't have you tellin' nobody 'bout what you just found out, can we? Not 'afore we done what we have to do to the old professor.'

Kate continued to stare at him, her senses re-sharpened by his ominous words. So Dunbar *was* the target after all. Had been all along. And now these two knew that she knew. She swallowed hard, fully appreciating the grave danger she was now in. They had already callously murdered two people, so they certainly wouldn't lose any sleep over killing her even though she was a police detective. The pair were in a catch-22 situation. They really didn't have any choice.

She was conscious out of the corner of her eye that Dorothy had moved away from her and was standing by the door. Her mouth went dry. She was trapped and about to die.

CHAPTER 24

Josh leaned forward slightly. His face had lost its kindly, country bumpkin look, and his gaze was now cold and hard.

'So, Sergeant Kate Lewis, what's to be done, d'ye think, eh?' he said softly.

Kate tensed in the chair. She was a fit young woman, police-trained in self-defence. She reasoned that she was easily a match for Dorothy, who had to be in her sixties at least and was well overweight. Josh was another story. Although maybe a bit older than Dorothy, he was a manual worker, probably had been all his life, and she guessed he packed plenty of muscle. But he was still sitting down. Maybe if she moved quickly before he could make it to his feet, she could barge Dorothy aside and get out into the hall . . .

At which point Josh released his familiar chuckle, though no mirth registered in his eyes. It was as though he had been reading her mind again.

'You'll never do it, missy,' he said. 'Mother might look like a silly old fart, but what you don't know is that, like me, she be ex-army, and quite a tough old girl, too. See, we got this nice little number here on account of the fact that we served in the regiment with the previous owner, Colonel Buxton.'

'You won't have it much longer if anything happens to the professor. You'd be killing the golden goose,' Kate retorted.

He shook his head. 'Oh. I don't think so. Whoever takes over after, they won't be able to throw us out. Them new laws on tenancies won't let 'em. Anyways, why would they want to? We ain't done nothin' bad and they couldn't run this big place without Mother and me.'

Kate could no longer see Dorothy. She was outside her peripheral field of vision. She had no idea where the woman had gone, but she didn't dare turn her head to look round in case it served to confirm what Josh had suspected she was thinking and precipitated a reaction.

Instead, she went for a tactic she had used a number of times before in her career when she had faced a similar perilous situation. Staving off the inevitable as long as possible by continuing to talk.

'Why did you kill Howard and Julian?' she said, trying to control the faltering note in her voice.

'Now that's a big question, missy,' Josh replied.

'We be wastin' time, Josh,' Dorothy protested from somewhere near the door.

Josh withdrew his pipe from his mouth and placed it carefully in an ashtray on the arm of his chair. 'Now, now, Mother,' he said, 'don't be so impatient. I think that after all the hard work the good sergeant here has put into this investigation she has a right to hear the truth of it.'

Like the true egotist, it was evident that he was enjoying what he saw as his moment of triumph, and Kate felt a sense of relief that he had fallen for her ploy. But she knew she couldn't keep the distraction going for long. She would have to think of something p.d.q. before she ran out of questions, or he got tired of answering them.

'What you don't know, Sergeant,' he went on, 'is that all this has been about Gillian George, the professor's previous assistant—'

'Poor little love,' Dorothy interjected again, drawing a censuring look from her husband as he continued.

'Fact is Gillian were the only daughter of Dorothy's sister, Mavis, and six years ago, when Gillian were eighteen and at uni, Mavis and her husband, Bill, had a car accident. Bill were killed outright, but Mavis survived for a couple more days afterwards. We made a promise to her 'afore she passed that we would see Gillian right. We sort of looked out for her from then on, helpin' her with money and such like. Gillian later got her degree in biology and got into somethin' to do with spiders, like the professor here—'

'Arachnology,' Dorothy put in smugly.

'Aye, that be it. Anyways, she got took abroad on some job to do with that. And she come home again lookin' for another job just as Professor Dunbar moved in here after the old colonel's death. Thinkin' that were a stroke of luck, we got Gillian to apply for a job with him. But in case he thought it were all a fix we made her promise not to tell him she were our niece, so he never knew.'

He scowled. 'It were a while after Gillian got the job that we found out what he were really like, but by then Gillian had started havin' an affair with him and she wouldn't listen to us.

''Course, then she goes to Brazil with the dirty old bugger, don't she? The next thing we knows she's dead, and pregnant, too, we finds out later. Papers say her death be an accident, but we knows that it's nothin' of the sort. He done her right enough by puttin' that thing in her bed to start with, or my name's not Josh Matlock.'

To keep things going, Kate took a chance and cut in. 'You can't know that for certain.'

He stared at her, his eyes practically smouldering with hate. 'Can't I? Well now, missy, I says I can. See, little Gillian phoned us couple of days 'afore she died on one of them satellite things, tellin' us he had put her in the family way and that she were goin' to tell him but was scared what he might do. And we know what he done after that, don't we?'

'Why didn't you pass all this on to the police?'

'Police?' he practically spat. 'And what would they have done, eh? We couldn't prove nothin' and the professor bein' one of them big knobs with friends in high places, nowt would have happened. So me and Mother here decided we would sort him out ourselves and make sure he got same as poor Gillian.'

'But then it all went wrong.'

He nodded. 'Aye, that it did. Mother were cleanin' the professor's lab once a week, so she learned his routine like. She knew that the first thing he done in the mornin' were to open the locked drawer in his desk to get his charts and things out, so that's where I puts the spider. We knew it would run off and hide somewhere after, so no one would suspect it were in the drawer to start with. It would then have all gone down as just an accident. 'Course, what we didn't know was that Howard had planned to break into the lab hisself, so he copped it instead of Hubert. That spoiled things, which were a real pity.'

Kate still couldn't see Dorothy, but sensed she was some-where close behind her and her flesh crawled. She would have to make her move soon. She eased herself forward slightly in the chair, then tried to cover up the move with a blurted, 'But . . . but how did you get into the lab without a key?'

'Key?' He chuckled again. 'I don't need no key, missy. Show the sergeant, Mother.'

There was movement behind Kate, and she heard a drawer open. Then a leather zipped wallet landed in her lap.

'Open it,' Josh directed.

Kate did so, trying to control the tremble in her fingers. Inside was a curious assortment of long, thin, steel tools, some toothed or hooked at the tips, others bent like a den-tist's probe.

'Picklocks,' she said without thinking.

He grinned now. 'Aye, you be dead on there, Sergeant. I been a naughty boy, see. When I left the army and got married, Mother here opened up a pet shop. But I needed a real career, so I took up an apprenticeship as a locksmith. Then I spent a few years screwing houses. Good times I had then, too. But I come within a whisker of bein' caught on one partic'lar job and give it all up for good. But I never forgets me skills and there be very few locks I can't open even now. The lab has just a basic Yale and that give me no problem at all when I done that job. As for the desk drawer, a child could've sprung that and relocked it after, same as I did.'

'But what about the spider?'

His grin broadened. 'It's only deadly if you're careless, and I got experience handlin' critters like that when I served with the regiment in Belize in the eighties. That's 'afore we all got slung out after they got full independence, like. Bit of a borin' postin', that were, so we run a book on catchin' black widers and Brown Recluse spiders without gettin' bit. Got quite good at it, too, and when Mother opened her pet shop after we was both demobbed we done quite a trade in exotic spiders.'

'I thought Mrs Matlock was scared of them?'

'What like you, you mean? Not her. She just said that, didn't you, Mother?'

There was no reply and Kate caught him exchanging glances over her shoulder with Dorothy who was obviously lurking behind her. She was running out of time and the pair of them still hadn't relaxed their guard which is what she had been counting on.

'So why Julian?' she said, moving her right hand surreptitiously along the arm of the chair to curl around the padded edge to help with leverage when she was ready to make the break for the door.

Josh scowled again and a distant expression stole into his eyes. 'Knew too much, did that silly lad,' he murmured. 'Tried to warn him 'bout his snoopin', but he never listened. Then I were workin' in the side room of the old barn the afternoon 'afore he died, and I sees him come in. But he don't know I am there. I keeps quiet, like, and hears him on his mobile to you sayin' he knows who killed Howard and tellin' you to meet him by the lake that night.'

He shook his head. 'He were a bit funny with me when I were chattin' to him in the grounds couple of hours 'afore that. As if he were feelin' guilty over somethin'. So I sussed he had somehow found out 'bout Mother and me and were goin' to spill the beans. I couldn't be sure, like, but I couldn't take the chance neither. So I waits for him that night and takes him out 'afore he even knows I'm there. Horrible job it were, too. He fought like a demon for what must have been five to ten minutes till he drowned.'

Kate tried not to think about that. 'And you planted Dr Lawrence's pendant at the scene to frame her for the murder?'

'Not right away, no. That be Mother's idea. See, quite by accident the mornin' 'afore young Howard copped it she finds the doc's pendant with a broke chain lyin' on the floor of the lab when the professor opens up for her to clean the place. The doc were away visitin' her aunt for a couple of days, so knowin' the pendant could only be hers, Mother puts it in her pocket intendin' to mend it and give it back to her when she comes in again. Then after I done Julian, Mother hits on the idea of droppin' the pendant at the lakeside to frame the doc. So I rushes back and puts it there, prominent like, for your lot to find. I only just gets away again, too, 'afore you turns up, with half the constabulary.'

He sighed almost with contentment. 'But I have to say, you was a big help to us poppin' in at The Lodge yesterday. That give Mother the chance to tell you about the doc buying the pendant. We needed you to know Mother sold the thing to the doc so it would tie her into the crime scene, see, and 'afore your visit we hadn't quite figured out how we was going to do that. We couldn't just say it outright as we weren't supposed to know it had been found by the lake.'

'And how *did* you know it had been found there?'

He grinned again. 'I creeps back through the woods early this mornin' and sees it gone, so I reckons you must have it. Then later on I follers you and that Chinese guy you was with to the doc's house and sees you nick her. With the story I'd made up about the prowler in the grey coat I'd seen the doc wearin' a few times and what we'd fed you with about the pendant, I knew then Mother and me be home and dry.'

He sighed. 'But 'course, Mother then has to go and spoil things just now by sayin' too much, don't she? Which makes you a bit of a liability now, don't it, Sergeant?'

Kate swallowed hard under his stern gaze. 'And I suppose it was you I caught sight of in the woods when I went there just now?' she said quickly.

He nodded. 'Sees you goin' past the old barn, so I decides to keep an eye on you. But I shoots back 'afore you returns to the barn after.'

He reached for his pipe again with the nonchalance of a man settling down in front of the fire to read the Sunday newspaper.

'So there you have it, Sergeant,' he said quietly and with a disturbing air of finality. 'As clear a confession as you'd ever have got from anyone. Pity you won't be able to use it.'

Kate stared at him, her gaze now wild and desperate.

'I warn you,' she blurted, putting on a brave front, 'my colleagues know I've come here. If I'm not back soon they'll be all over you.'

Josh nodded. 'Be too late by then, missy, won't it? You'll be long gone, and who'd suspect two old fuddy-duddies like me and Mother here of doin' anythin' nasty?'

Kate felt physically sick. Fate had called time. She had no more questions left to ask and they were now going to kill her. She had no choice but to make her break for the door before it was too late.

And as if to galvanise her into doing just that, it seemed Fate had also chosen that very moment to throw in some diversionary support. The old brass bell at the front of The Lodge suddenly jangled loudly with all the cacophonous panic of an old ironclad's call to action stations. As Josh's head jerked round in the direction of the sound, Kate saw through the bay window that there was a woman standing outside, staring around her with obvious impatience as she waited for someone to come to the door. It was Angela Dunbar.

What the young woman was doing there was irrelevant to Kate at that precise moment. Maybe it was just a social call. All that mattered was that it provided just the distraction she needed, and she launched herself forward with every fibre of her being.

But she was cruelly outplayed. Even as she erupted from the chair, a strong arm encircled her neck from behind, slamming her back down again. Dorothy! Then a sweet smelling pad was pressed over her nose and mouth. Seconds later a black hole opened up before her and she knew no more.

* * *

Distant voices. Muffled. Indistinct. Kate was floating in a black void. Half in, half out of consciousness. She was dizzy and nauseous, her mouth so dry that she felt like the inside of her cheeks were cracking open. She was really hot, yet she couldn't stop shivering. She opened her eyes but saw only more darkness with just a faint gleam beginning to expand in its midst. She was lying on her side on a hard floor with her arms secured behind her back. She tried to move but her wrists seemed to be held together in some sort of unyielding restraint that bit into the flesh, and her ankles were tightly bound.

What had happened to her? Where was she? She was confused, disorientated and unable to think rationally following the effects of the powerful anaesthetic. Then gradually the fug in her brain began to clear and she remembered it all. Josh Matlock's confession. Angela Dunbar turning up at the crucial moment. The pad impregnated with what she guessed was probably chloroform being held over her nose and mouth by Dorothy Matlock. She strained against whatever it was that was confining her wrists and heard a metallic rattle. It was as she had suspected. They had used her own handcuffs on her, and crackly plastic tape had been wound around her ankles.

At the same moment the tiny light she had noticed spread into a strip light bolted to the ceiling. It revealed that she was in a small, windowless room with an iron spiral staircase ascending to a wooden door in the far left-hand corner.

Obviously a cellar of some sort. Steel shelving holding tools and a variety of boxes and tins occupied the whole of one wall. There were a couple of glass aquariums standing on a table in another corner, one empty and the other containing a thick layer of soil and some rocks and greenery. Hooks had been fixed to the low ceiling and she felt the waves of nausea return when she saw the bloodied corpses of rabbits and pheasants hanging from them in a neat row, the sightless bulging eyes of the nearest furry carcass glaring at her accusingly. The room, which was a shiny grey colour, was heated by two radiators and was exceptionally warm, smelling of new paint. But at least as far as she could see there were no cobwebs or spiders.

As she lay there on the floor, still futilely flexing her hands behind her back, there was the loud metallic 'crack' of a key turning in a lock. The door at the top of the spiral staircase was thrown open and Dorothy Matlock appeared. She was carrying a large plastic bag in one hand, and she deliberately flexed it several times on her way down. Kate didn't need to be told how the pair planned to dispatch her now. Suffocation wouldn't cause any injuries and it wouldn't leave any awkward traces either.

'Comfy, m'duck,' Dorothy mocked as she descended the stairs. 'Good of you to bring those handcuffs with you in their nice little pouch. It saved us a lot of trouble.'

Kate managed to get herself up into a sitting position with her back against the wall. 'You'll know just what trouble is if you do anything to me,' she bluffed. 'You won't like spending the rest of your days in Holloway at your age.'

'Who's going to know what I done?' she sneered. 'Josh has already found a nice boggy part of the moat to drop you in after you've took your last breath—'

'So, he's left you to do the dirty work for him then, has he?' Kate threw back, trying to avoid looking at the plastic bag.

Matlock simply shrugged. 'Josh and me, we does everythin' together,' she said. 'Always have. And he be doin' his bit with good old Hubert right now.'

Kate's eyes widened. 'The professor? What do you mean?'

'Obvious, ain't it? No point just snuffin' out his lights. That's too good for Dunbar. He needs to know why first, and Josh and me thought he should suffer the same horrid end as poor Gillian did. Sort of an eye for an eye, like.'

'You mean you're going to use one of those spiders on him?'

'Not just one of 'em, sweetie-pie, but same sort of horror what bit Gillian. I think he called the ugly thing Martha.'

'But Martha ran off after attacking Howard and she still can't be found.'

Dorothy chuckled. 'That's what everyone were supposed to think, m'dear. But my old Josh, he be a clever bugger. He were there in the lab that night and had only just popped that nasty little monster out of her tank into the desk drawer and locked it up again when he hears Howard stickin' his key in the front door what Josh had locked behind him.'

She sucked in her breath. 'Josh told me he hid in the little room where all them spiders is kept, and he hears Howard break the winder and start pullin' out loads of drawers and that. Then there were this awful scream, and he finds him on the floor of the lab, rollin' about somethin' dreadful with the spider hangin' on to his neck. Proper horrid, Josh said it were. But he managed to grab the thing with the professor's special gloves and net and dropped her into one of them little lab boxes used for movin' the creatures about in. He then come home with her, and we stuck her in that old fish tank over there what we'd brought back with us when our pet shop business folded. All nice and convenient.'

Kate's blood ran cold in spite of her own predicament, but she could see no movement in the aquarium containing the substrate and greenery, so guessed the spider was gone. 'Convenient?' she echoed. 'And you both just left Howard there, writhing in agony?'

Dorothy shrugged again. 'What else could we do? The lad were already in a bad state and would have died anyway.'

Kate didn't say anything for a moment but studied her with a look of disgust as something else dawned on her. 'But he didn't just leave, did he?' she said finally. 'The venom wouldn't have worked that quickly, would it? So, Mr Matlock calmly sat there waiting for it to spread through that poor boy's body, having already smashed the antivenom vials in the cabinet so that they couldn't be used. He only left when he was sure Howard would no longer be a problem.'

Dorothy snorted. 'Well, Josh couldn't risk Howard tellin' folk that he'd been in the lab too, could he? It would've ruined everything.'

Kate shook her head in contemptuous disbelief. 'You pair are some pieces of work,' she breathed.

Dorothy scowled. 'We're doin' this for Gillian,' she retorted, 'and no one asked you to poke your nose into things anyways.'

She was standing right over Kate now, the plastic bag held open in front of her and a sadistic grin forming on her chubby face.

'So, there you have it,' she said, 'Now, I must get on. Josh'll be back 'afore long and he'll expect me to have done as good a job as he done. Not be wastin' time gossipin' down here.'

Kate wriggled away from her along the wall on her behind, but it was futile. Dorothy just walked slowly after her. 'Now then, m'dear, make it easy on yourself. It'll all be over in a tick.'

She waited until Kate was trapped in the corner, then bent over her.

'Pity you come round from the chloroform,' she continued. 'I were hoping all this could be done while you was still under, but I got interrupted.'

Then as Kate twisted her head in all directions to frustrate what she was about to do, Dorothy slipped the plastic bag over her head and held it tight around her neck with both hands.

CHAPTER 25

In seconds Kate was struggling to breathe. The bag was misting up so that even Dorothy's hateful face had begun to disappear. She tried desperately to grab part of the bag with her teeth. To tear a hole in the thin plastic, but she couldn't get to it. There was mounting pressure in her head. She was aware of her heart thudding away. Seemingly beating against the inside of her skull like the mad, frenzied beat of a bongo drum. The world was fading fast. Coloured lights flashed on and off all around her. Her lungs were going to burst. She needed air . . .

Then suddenly she was gulping in great lungfuls of it as the bag was ripped off. Her head was spinning, and she felt sick. The lamplit room with its iron staircase sprang into place through a patchy mist. She heard a voice shouting at her as if from far away and someone was shaking her roughly by the shoulders.

'Kate, breathe! For God's sake, *breathe*!'

A figure was bending over her, tearing at the plastic tape binding her ankles. Not Dorothy, but someone else she couldn't quite make out . . .

Then her eyes abruptly clicked into focus, and she was staring at Angela Dunbar's white face.

'I'm so sorry, Kate,' Dunbar sobbed, unwinding the last of the tape. 'None of this was supposed to happen.'

Kate stared wildly about her. 'But where's . . . ?' she began, then glimpsed the prostate figure of Dorothy Matlock on the floor facedown a short distance from her. There was blood dripping from a wound on the side of her head and what looked like a broken chair leg lying nearby.

'It . . . it was the only way I could stop her,' Dunbar choked. 'I had to hit her. Do . . . do you think . . . ?'

Kate looked again at the woman who had just tried to kill her and unsurprisingly showed no sympathy whatsoever.

'Never mind her,' she replied. 'See if she has a key to these.' She pivoted round towards the young woman to show her the handcuffs.

Matlock groaned and stirred slightly as Dunbar gingerly went through her pockets, shortly producing the little key with its distinctive tag.

Kate bent forward to allow her to unlock the cuffs, then let her help her to her feet. She stood there for a moment with her shoulder up against the wall. She felt groggy and nauseous and had to wait for the circulation to return to her arms and legs.

'So, you're in on this with these two?' she said, staring at the distressed young woman with undisguised revulsion.

Dunbar dissolved into a flood of tears. 'I didn't mean for Howard or Julian to die,' she wailed. 'It was Father I was against. He . . . he murdered Gillian and we were so much in love—'

'You were in love with *Gillian*?'

Dunbar wiped her eyes on the sleeve of her anorak. 'I . . . I am — was — bisexual,' she whimpered. 'At least, I thought I was. When Gillian died my world collapsed.'

'And you wanted payback?'

'At the start, yes. I already knew from what Gillian had told me that the Matlocks had got her the job here and were looking after her.'

'So you went along with their plan to kill your own father? Or was it maybe *your* plan?'

She shook her head fiercely. 'They approached me with the idea, telling me that Gillian's death couldn't have been an accident, but that Father must have killed her. I knew about his reputation with women and that Gillian had dropped me because she was having an affair with him, so it all seemed to fit. I was so bitter at the time that I just went along with what Josh and Dorothy said they planned to do.'

Kate pushed herself off the wall as the feeling gradually returned to her legs. Then carefully bending over Dorothy, she grabbed her arms and handcuffed them behind her back.

'Until Howard and Julian were murdered,' she said over her shoulder to Dunbar.

Dunbar broke into another sob and sank down on to her haunches against the wall, staring down at the floor. 'Howard's death was an accident,' she replied, 'and believe me, I had nothing to do with what happened to Julian. I . . . I came over here earlier to tell the Matlocks I was done with it all when I saw you through the bay window sitting on the settee after I'd rung the bell. I changed my mind then and decided I should confess everything to you instead of talking to the Matlocks before anyone else got hurt. No one answered the door, so I ran off and hid in the woods to wait for you to come out.'

Kate straightened up, wobbled slightly, then steadied herself, turning to face Dunbar. 'But you came back.'

'When I saw Josh leave some time afterwards and you didn't come out again, I realised you were in trouble. The front door wasn't locked, so I slipped inside. Then I heard voices and traced them to the door leading to this cellar. It too was unlocked, and Dorothy was so engrossed with you she never heard me creep down the stairs. I grabbed the first thing I saw which was the broken chair leg and . . .'

'Well, I'm bloody glad you did. But how long did you wait after Josh had left The Lodge before you came in here?'

'I don't know. Maybe an hour. I know I was getting very cold, and I almost gave up.'

Kate grimaced. 'Shit. So he has an hour's head start. Now I need to ask you, was Josh carrying anything when he left the house?'

Dunbar nodded. 'A small cardboard box.'

Kate closed her eyes tightly for a second. 'Bloody hell, he's got Martha with him. I ought to have guessed. He's gone after the professor. Have you got a mobile on you? When the bastards put me out, they took my personal mobile as well as my job radio.'

Dunbar shook her head. 'I left mine in my room.'

'Well, there's no time to search for mine now. I've got to find the professor before Josh does. Do you know where he's likely to be?'

For reply, Dunbar simply screamed, 'Watch out!'

But Kate was too late. She had broken another cardinal rule by turning her back on her prisoner. Somehow Dorothy Matlock had managed to haul herself to her feet, using just the strength of her legs and thighs. A truly powerful woman, it seemed, despite her apparent age and weight. Her shoulder slammed into Kate, pitching her forward into the wall she was facing. Dazed but still upright, Kate staggered back round to face her, but Matlock was no longer there. She was running at full pelt across the cellar to the spiral staircase despite her hands being handcuffed behind her back.

Kate recovered and stumbled weakly after her, inwardly cursing Dunbar for just sitting there crying. But Matlock's luck was about to run out. She only got halfway up the spiral staircase towards the door before it happened. Whether she lost her balance because of the handcuffs or tripped over her own feet, it was impossible to say. But one minute she was thumping up the narrow, open pattern treads and the next she had lurched sideways into the handrail. Perhaps due to her weight, she took part of the flimsy rail with her and with a wild scream plunged over the edge and smashed into the concrete floor.

From the way her bloodied, broken head was twisted round in a pool of still escaping blood and brain matter,

241

it was patently obvious that she was quite dead, but Kate didn't waste too much time confirming the fact. She knew full well that time was not on her side. Leaving Dunbar still sobbing on the floor, she raced up the stairs and through the wooden door without a single glance behind her. There was only one thought in her mind. Would she get to Hubert Dunbar before Josh added him to his list?

* * *

The phone rang as the second half of the recorded soccer match began. Hayden grabbed it irritably from the arm of the settee beside him. He had moved it there from its usual place on the small table by the stairs for convenience just in case someone chose to interrupt his afternoon's entertainment rather than because of his alleged bad back, and he nearly knocked over the glass of beer standing beside it.

The caller was the DI and he sounded worried.

'Is Kate with you?' he asked.

'She was, guv,' Hayden responded truculently, turning the sound on the television down, 'but she's gone now. Why?'

'Just got back into the office and no one seems to have seen her. Tried to raise her for a sit' report, first on her job radio and mobile through Control, then her personal mobile, but she's not answering. The GPS tracker says she's still at Moat House.'

Hayden frowned, as he tried to remember what Kate had said to him at lunch. 'Then that's where she must still be.'

'Well, it's where I assumed she would be, continuing inquiries.'

'But why more inquiries? She told me Dr Lawrence was in custody for that job.'

Woo sighed. 'Yes, but we had to release Lawrence on police bail for further inquiries. We had insufficient evidence to charge her. Problem is, we have actually telephoned Moat House and spoken to the professor. But he says he hasn't seen her at all. That means no one has heard so much as a whisper from her since she left the nick at lunchtime.'

'But she must have left here well over four hours ago.'

'That doesn't sound good. I'm leaving for Moat House right now.'

Hayden didn't even bother to reply. Miraculously achieving a complete recovery from his bad back, he erupted from the settee at a speed that would have put an Olympic athlete to shame, heading for the bedroom at the top of the stairs to pull on some clothes . . .

* * *

There was the sound of feet stumbling along the driveway behind her. Kate glanced briefly over her shoulder as she ran through cold, driving rain, cursing the sudden change in the weather. Angela Dunbar was only yards behind her, no doubt preferring to stay close to Kate rather than remain in the cellar with Dorothy's corpse.

She reached the gravel hardstanding in front of Moat House within minutes. The house was ablaze with light which was good, but there was no sight or sound of life when she charged through the open front door into the hallway. Angela collided with her as she stopped abruptly to listen.

'What—' Dunbar began but broke off when Kate turned on her with a sharp, 'Ssh!'

She need not have bothered. The house seemed held in the grip of a heavy, sepulchral silence, broken only by the rattle of the rain against the windows.

'Where the hell is everyone?' she breathed.

Dunbar was crying again. 'Apart from me, there's only Yasmin and Father left now,' she whimpered.

'Right,' Kate continued. 'Let's get some help.'

Turning back to an old-fashioned telephone on a table by the front door, she picked up the receiver from its cradle and lifted it to her ear. 'Dead,' she muttered. 'He must have cut the sodding wires. Come on, let's check the lab first. It's the most likely place.'

Dunbar shook her head fiercely, her eyes wide and terrified. 'I'm not going in there.'

Kate nodded, realising that she had no right to expect her to. 'Then go up to your room and lock yourself in. Got it?'

More head shaking. 'Josh could be up there. He'll kill me too if he knows I've helped you.'

Kate controlled her frustration with an effort and nodded towards the sitting room. 'Then go in there and hide somewhere. But hurry!'

She watched the young woman disappear inside the room, shutting the door behind her, then headed along the passageway to the kitchen and the door leading out to the courtyard and the so-called annexe.

The rain had reduced to a fine drizzle and a faint, smoky moon was beginning to emerge. But much of the courtyard remained in shadow which also cloaked the windowless front of the building at the far end.

The place appeared to be in darkness. Not even the faintest bar of light showed in the cracks down the sides or under the door. A low wind had arisen, stirring the fallen leaves that were scattered across the courtyard from the encompassing woodland. It caused the branches of a cotoneaster shrub covering part of the inside wall to scrape against the rough stonework like skeletal fingers.

Kate shivered as she remembered the day the professor had shown her the terrariums in the side room of the laboratory and the eight-legged horrors crouching inside, their black, soulless eyes fixed on her with unblinking intensity. She thought of Howard Dunbar and the hideous creature that had raced out of the drawer and up his arm like something out of a nightmare. Her senses began to swim, and she was forced to clutch at the kitchen door frame for support as the shakes started in her legs and she began to break out into a cold sweat. She couldn't go in there. Not with *them*. What if

Josh was in there with that thing in the cardboard box? What if he had released it and it was scuttling about in the gloom?

Coward, a voice in her head mocked. *You don't deserve to be in the force.*

She gritted her teeth. She *wasn't* a coward. She had proved that enough times in the past. She would tackle anyone or anything. But spiders . . . they were something else. She thought for the umpteenth time of the old shed in her childhood and her stepfather's sneering laugh. He was long dead, but he was still mocking her from the grave. Still enjoying the fear he had engendered in her and the phobia that had become hardwired into her psyche as a result.

Cursing his very memory, she took several deep breaths and forced herself to calm down. Then willing herself forward, she left the kitchen doorway and crunched her way across the forecourt to the lab. The door was unlocked. She opened it slowly, peering into the gloom beyond and suddenly remembering she hadn't even got a torch. She fumbled just inside the door, found a switch and flooded the place with pale flickering light.

The lab was empty. She frowned. That was something she hadn't expected. She stepped inside and advanced a few paces, only to stop dead almost immediately. The bottom drawer of the desk, which appeared to have been repaired, had been pulled out slightly, the chair in front of it turned sideways as if to allow someone to stand up. Moving closer, she saw that the laptop computer was on, exhibiting what appeared to be some kind of bar chart on the screen. Beside this there was an open A4-sized notebook, with a pair of glasses and a ballpoint pen resting on top of it. It was plain that someone had been sitting at the desk working there up until very recently. The professor? So where was he? And why had he left without bothering to put anything away or lock up?

Sudden movement out of the corner of her eye. She wheeled round. Something small and dark had just raced across the floor past the desk and disappeared in the gap between two filing cabinets. She glanced quickly at the internal door to the side room that housed the terrariums. It was half-open. The hairs went up on the back of her neck and her skin prickled unpleasantly. What the hell had she just seen? It had looked hairy and very much like . . .

Very carefully she turned around and moved towards the outside door. She got halfway and then came the flash of something moving very fast to her left. She felt her legs sag slightly, then almost at the same moment she released a slightly unbalanced, relieved laugh as she saw exactly what it was. A mouse. It had been nothing more than a bloody mouse. She was still laughing inanely as she quit the laboratory and re-joined the courtyard, but her laughter soon died.

The scream was slightly muffled, but unmistakable for what it was, and it rose higher and higher in pitch, until it ended in a long, gurgling moan that was abruptly cut off. It was one of the most blood-curdling sounds she had ever heard, conveying a sense of abject terror, and it came from somewhere not in the house, but in the woods behind the laboratory. The old barn! It would have to be, wouldn't it?

The side gate leading from the courtyard into the grounds stood wide open and Kate went through at a run. Wet tree branches slapped her face as she followed the track around the back of the so-called annexe to where it joined the path from the house leading to the lake. A crack of light showed down the middle of the double doors which had evidently not been closed properly. She pressed her face against it, straining her eyes to see inside. She could see nothing but flickering light, but as she stood there, she heard the sound of childlike whimpering, and the hard voice of Josh Matlock speaking over them.

'. . . So you see, Professor, it's only right that you should suffer the same fate as poor little Gillian, but me and Dorothy felt we should first have the little chat we've just had, to make you understand why you've got to die, to give you time to repent.'

'No, no,' a second voice, scarcely recognisable as belonging to Hubert Dunbar, pleaded in a choking moan. 'Please not that. *Please!*'

There was a sneering laugh. 'Oh, but I have to, Professor. It would hurt Martha's feelings if I didn't let her say hello to you.'

Kate stared desperately around her in the strengthening moonlight, once again conscious of her perilous situation. She was alone, unarmed and facing a ruthless killer driven by a fanatical desire for revenge. She needed some sort of protection, however basic, to even the odds. She spotted a length of steel pipe lying on the ground and tiptoed over to pick it up, and it was as she turned back to the barn that she heard a repeat of the anguished scream that had drawn her there.

Muttering a short prayer, she hauled one of the doors open and ducked through.

* * *

Sticky weaves trailed across her face and clung to her hair from the cobweb-festooned beam above her head. Sudden heat and the rich, sickly smell of burning paraffin instantly engulfed her. The lamp Kate had seen before on the top of the up-ended beer barrel had been lit and was glaring at her like a single yellow eye from the midst of the dancing shadows it had created around itself. Its light fell directly on to the glistening white face and rolling eyes of the man lashed to the metal bed frame. The professor! It also revealed the gnome-like figure of Josh Matlock bending over him. He had a small cardboard box held in both hands and was plainly in the act of tipping the contents on to Dunbar's twisting, writhing body.

The scene had all the terrifying ingredients of a Gothic horror film. But for Kate, knowing the awful thing that the box contained, it also represented the sum of all her fears, temporarily numbing her brain and freezing her limbs into a Gorgon like paralysis. Then as Matlock spun round, his face twisted into a malevolent snarl, several quivering hairy legs suddenly thrust their way out of the partially open end of the box. This was the trigger that overruled everything else, galvanising Kate into action.

Where she got her courage from in such a nightmare scenario was unclear. Whether it was the impulsive response that was such an integral part of her make-up or simply the years of police training that now kicked in, the fact remains that the dynamics of the situation were dramatically reversed.

Forcing her frozen legs to work, she lurched towards Matlock, swinging the lead pipe in her hand and slamming it into the box just as the spider's body began to emerge. The blow sent the box flying across the barn, consigning it to the inky shadows, but things didn't work out quite so well for Matlock. Somehow the spider parted company with the box at the critical moment and attached itself to the sleeve of his coat. Even as he frantically shook his arm to dislodge the creature, uttering an agonised cry before it dropped to the ground, Kate realised he was too late. It had bitten him.

'Stay where you are,' she shouted as he stumbled towards the door. 'It could be anywhere now.'

'Then it's all yours,' he snarled. Before she realised what he was going to do, he charged through the doorway out into the wind and the rain. The next instant she heard the door crunch shut and the sound of something slamming into place on the other side. Her mind flashed back to the day Josh had first shown her and Hayden the barn. She remembered too late the long wooden arm slotted into two hooks on the outside of the doors to hold them shut.

That arm had now been slotted back into place once again, but with them shut inside. Left to share the claustrophobic darkness with the most venomous spider in the world.

* * *

Hayden arrived at Moat House at the same time as Charlie Woo and a convoy of marked patrol cars with flashing strobes. A dishevelled Angela Dunbar was waiting for them on the front doorstep, being comforted by Yasmin Dunbar in a silky, black kimono.

Within minutes the house and laboratory had been searched and after a harsh interrogation of Angela Dunbar, heavy boots headed rapidly back along the driveway to the main gate and The Lodge.

They found Josh Matlock without much difficulty. He was sitting on the floor of the cellar with Dorothy's bloodied head in his lap. But there was something seriously wrong with him. His whole body was shaking, and multiple beads of perspiration were running down his face which seemed to be contorted in pain. Unbeknown to the DI, it was half an hour since Martha had sunk her fangs into his arm and the arachnid's powerful toxins were already flooding through his veins to cripple him. He showed scant interest in the police officers when they burst through the cellar door, and at the same moment he released a long, agonised groan, doubling over to vomit on the floor.

To his alarm the DI saw that Matlock's right hand was curled round the body of a shotgun lying on the floor beside him.

'It's all over, Mr Matlock,' he said quickly, motioning the other officers back through the cellar door behind him. 'So don't do anything silly.'

Matlock raised his head to look up at him and issued a ragged cynical laugh through tightly clenched teeth. 'All over, you say?' he said, in a halting, rasping voice. He hauled the shotgun off the floor with a shaking hand so that the stock was resting on the floor between his outstretched legs and the double barrels were pointing upwards at a sharp angle. 'You're spot on there, feller, it be all over right enough. Mother's dead and I got bit. But I ain't goin' the way Howard went.'

Then groping for the weapon with his other hand, he forced the barrels under his chin and pulled both triggers, pebble-dashing the ceiling with his brains in a multitude of rich colours.

* * *

The doors wouldn't budge. Kate used every ounce of strength she possessed to try and force them open. But it was pointless and in the end she had to give up. As far as she knew, there was no other way out of the barn, and she had no intention of searching for one with Martha lurking somewhere in the inky blackness. Her only hope was that Hayden, Charlie Woo or someone at the nick would have started to wonder where she was after all this time. That they would come looking for her when they got no response after calling her up. She glanced at the luminous dial of her wristwatch. She'd been gone for over four hours now. Surely someone would have started to worry? But what if they hadn't?

She tried not to dwell on the issue and concentrated instead on trying to free the professor, peering at the floor all the time for any sign of stealthy movement. Fumbling in her pocket for the clasp knife she always carried with her, she bent over him and started cutting through the tape binding his ankles. He said nothing. Just stared at her, whimpering and moaning like a small child, his eyes so big in the white mask of a face that they resembled over-sized marbles. Plainly, his horrific experience had affected his mind and he was no longer the arrogant, self-assured scientist he had once been. He only seemed to be aware of her when she started cutting the tape securing his wrists to the bed frame. His whimpering suddenly ceased, and his freed hand shot out and gripped her arm with surprising strength.

'Martha's here,' he said in a conspiratorial whisper, rolling his eyes and throwing a couple of anxious glances around him. 'Watch out. She's a wicked girl.'

Then he was back to whimpering and muttering to himself.

His chilling warning couldn't have been less welcome to Kate. When the next moment there was the sound of rustling in the gloom behind her, she instinctively whirled round in the direction of the sound, her skin crawling. But it was too dark beyond the pool of light cast by the lamp to see anything.

The familiar shakes returned to her legs, and she felt the perspiration starting to run in rivulets down her face and neck. She knew the signs only too well. She was close to hyperventilating and losing control. That couldn't be allowed to happen. She had to keep her head. To somehow get herself and the professor out of the barn to safety. Though how she was going to do that was not clear to her at that precise moment.

More noises, though they were too loud for a spider. She guessed they had been made by rats or mice. But then there was a frantic, scrabbling and a sharp agonised squeal, followed by absolute silence. She remembered the mice in the laboratory cages and felt sick. Martha?

Forcing back the panic rising within her, she hurriedly finished cutting through the tape binding the professor's other wrist and helped him up into a sitting position. But there was no response from him afterwards. He simply sat hunched on the edge of the bed frame, holding a muttered, one-sided conversation with himself as if she no longer existed. A conversation that was no longer intelligible. Something had obviously snapped in his brain. Something that may have been developing for quite a while over the guilt he had probably had to live with since Gillian's death. But in his present state he was of no use to her and more of a liability than anything else. Just what she didn't need!

For the first time in her career since her ordeal in the previous nightmare case which still haunted her, she could see no way out, and it was at that point that she felt something brush against her ankle. Springing back with a wild cry, she collided with the barrel holding the paraffin lamp, sending it crashing to the floor. The spurt of flame that erupted from the shattered glass cut a fiery trail across the barn, igniting everything inflammable in its path. This included the petrol in the tank of the mower which almost immediately exploded, propelling fiery embers in every direction.

Within seconds the bales of straw or hay at the back of the barn went up with a loud 'whoosh', despite their apparent sodden state. The hungry, yellow flames were soon climbing the wooden walls to ignite the roof's thatch. Dense smoke filled the barn and Kate and the professor were soon gasping and choking in its midst.

Throwing herself against the double doors again and again Kate desperately tried to force them open, but it was useless. They gave a little, only to then spring back into place. Where Dunbar had gone Kate had no idea and she was past caring anyway. The smoke was so dense now that she couldn't see a thing and her lungs felt as if they were on fire like the barn.

She was going to die this time for sure. Asphyxiated, then burned to a crisp in a raging inferno. She couldn't breathe and there was a weakness in her legs that was worsening by the second. Her head felt as if it were going to burst open. She was about to pass out. Then she was on the floor, and she didn't care anymore. She was done. Through with struggling against the inevitable and resigned to an acceptance of death.

Fiery tongues were now spreading from the back of the barn and reaching out for her. If only she could die before they got to her . . .

Then sudden light, a thunderous roar and she was enveloped in burning embers as a powerful force seemed to propel her through the air. She slammed into the ground, gasping, coughing, vomiting and someone was rolling her over and over in some sort of thick cloth.

Bright moonlight. Hands stripping off her clothes. Bitter cold freezing her skin. A worried face peering intently into hers.

'Kate?' Hayden's voice barking at her. 'My God, are you okay?'

She was lying half-naked on a patch of grass with other faces all around her, gawking and grinning. Someone wrapped a coat around her bare shoulders as Hayden helped her to sit up. Her coat, blouse and trousers were in a pile beside her, badly burnt and still smouldering.

The barn was just a skeleton. Its gaunt frame showed through the smoke and the dying flames, reminding her of the pictures she had seen of the flesh-stripped ribs of an animal carcass on the African veldt. It had gone up in minutes like a torch and Kate realised just how lucky she had been to escape such an inferno. But she had not got off entirely scot-free. She was beginning to feel the intense soreness of the burns she had undoubtedly suffered and dreaded to think what her body was going to look like in a few hours.

'You were actually on fire when you were blown out of there,' Charlie Woo explained, nodding at her pile of clothes. 'When we opened the doors the strong currents of air that were sucked into the blaze must have created something like a miniature firestorm. What firefighters call a backdraught.'

He grinned. 'Still, it was nice of you to light up the barn like that to tell us where you were.'

Kate didn't see the joke but shivered with cold, her teeth chattering like castanets. Then the next moment she started as something else occurred to her. 'What about the professor?' she blurted. 'He was in there, too.'

Woo exchanged glances with Hayden, and it didn't go unnoticed. 'He's not—?' she began.

Woo shook his head. 'Miraculously not,' he said, nodding towards a group of uniformed figures gathered round someone on the ground two to three yards away. 'But he's suffered some nasty burns and he seems to be completely off his head. The lads are keeping him there until the paramedics arrive.'

Kate tried to get up, ignoring the further looks she got. 'Listen to me, all of you,' she said in a rush. 'Our killer is Josh Matlock, the bloody gardener. He locked us in there with Martha, then fled the scene. But he won't last long without antivenom treatment. The spider gave him a nasty bite.'

She yelped when Hayden placed a firm hand on her shoulder over her burns, preventing her from standing. 'He's actually beyond any form of treatment now, old girl,' he said. 'He obviously couldn't face the prospect of what the toxins would do to him and blew his brains out with a shotgun.'

Kate sank back down on the grass. 'So, it's finally over,' she said. 'We're done.'

'Not quite,' Woo said, adopting a stern expression. 'There's the small matter of how Dorothy Matlock came to be lying dead on the floor of a certain cellar with a broken neck and a pair of handcuffs on her wrists.'

'She just slipped,' Kate said wearily.

'Slipped?' Woo echoed. 'Well, I hope the jury will see it the same way.'

'Jury? But . . . but it was an accident. She was running away, and she fell.'

He seemed perplexed. 'Hm. That's what they all say, isn't it? "Sorry, guv, but she slipped".'

'But . . . but it's the truth.'

Woo suddenly released a chuckle and held up his hand to cut her off. 'Yes, I know it is. I was being cruel. Angela Dunbar told us everything.'

'And you still kept it going?' Kate breathed. 'You shit-bag. You unfeeling, piss-taking shitbag.'

'And that, Sergeant Lewis,' he finished, 'will cost you a lot more than just one single malt in the bar.'

AFTER THE FACT

Kate awoke suddenly. For a moment she was confused by the fragile sunlight stealing into the room through the open blinds and the white sheets on the bed, unsure of where she was after her dreams of spiders and burning barns. Then she remembered, gave a relieved sigh and eased herself up into a sitting position against the headboard, propped up by a couple of pillows. The smell of cooking wafted up to her from downstairs and moments later Hayden appeared in the doorway carrying a laden tray.

He grinned when he saw she was awake. 'How's the injured soldier?' he quipped and set the tray down on her lap.

It was a week since the terrifying incidents at Moat House and she had once again been put back on sick leave to enable her to recover from her ordeal. Her physical injuries had not been serious. A few painful burns, some cuts and abrasions, but nothing more. She had been very lucky and was discharged from hospital after being detained for just one night's observation.

But her fragile emotional state was another matter. The clinical psychologist the force had insisted on her seeing was highly critical of the fact that she had been allowed to return to work so soon after the trauma she had endured on her last case.

'You need several more months' rest,' he told her. 'Notwithstanding the concussion you suffered when you were locked in the boot of that car, you have recently experienced more trauma in your job than most people experience in a lifetime and there is a cost to that in terms of your mental wellbeing.'

'You mean I'm heading for the nuthouse,' she said.

'No, I'm not saying that at all. But what has happened is that the traumas you suffered in your last case have had the effect of triggering the release of other unpleasant memories that you have kept buried in your subconscious for years and these have assumed an exaggerated prominence in your mind — your arachnophobia for instance.'

'I've always been scared of spiders,' she replied dully.

'Yes, but that fear has become centre stage in your thinking exactly because of your mental state, and you will need time and possibly some specialist clinical treatment to put that problem back in the box.'

'To hell with that!' Kate replied. 'I've had my fill of trick cyclists, thank you.' Then she promptly walked out, leaving him gaping after her.

'So, what's the news back at the mill?' she said to Hayden, eyeing the burnt offering he had set in front of her. She was unsurprised by his lack of culinary skills, but she said nothing to avoid hurting his feelings and began nibbling at the cremated rashers of bacon and solid fried egg.

He sighed and propped himself on the edge of the bed.

'You were fast asleep when I came home last night,' he said, 'so I didn't like to awaken you. But it seems Dr Lawrence disappeared as soon as she was released from custody on police bail and it looks like she's gone abroad, so I don't think we'll be seeing her again any time soon. Angela Dunbar was arrested after her admission of involvement with the Matlocks, but she got hold of a QC brief and promptly retracted her statement. DI doesn't reckon we've got enough to charge her with anything, but the file is being sent to the CPS for a decision anyway.'

'And the professor?'

He shook his head. 'Still away with the fairies and not amenable for interview. He's currently in a special hospital being assessed, and the feeling is he's almost certainly going to be committed under the Mental Health Act in the end.'

'So we'll never know for certain whether or not he murdered Gillian George?'

'Probably not. But it's all water under the bridge now anyway, and if he did, he's certainly going to pay for it in the future by spending the rest of his life in an institution.'

'With the "delightful" Yasmin Dunbar inheriting Moat House and becoming the lady of the manor, I suspect.'

'Very likely as she too cannot actually be tied into any crime.'

Kate laughed without humour. 'I hope she enjoys sharing her future solitary life with all the ghosts that must be lurking in the shadows of that house.'

'Not to mention the spiders,' he added, then snapped his fingers. 'Oh yes, and it seems the IOPC have been appointed to look into the circumstances of the case to make sure we handled things properly.'

She grimaced. 'Bloody rubber-heelers looking for scalps,' she said, referring to the investigators of the Independent Office for Police Conduct.

He frowned. 'It's not that at all, but you knew this would happen, especially as a result of Dorothy Matlock's death in handcuffs. It's automatic. Super doesn't believe it will go anywhere, though, and ironically Angela Dunbar has backed up your statement on the circumstances of Matlock's dive from the stairs, so you're in the clear.'

She shrugged. 'Who cares? I won't be in the job much longer anyway. I said I would resign after this case was over and that's exactly what's going to happen.'

He grunted. 'And what are you going to do instead? You're a bit too old to be a "trolley dolly" for British Airways and even if you could get a job at Tesco, I don't think you'd enjoy sitting on one of their checkouts.'

'Maybe I'll set up my own private detective agency. You know, investigating unfaithful husbands and dodgy salesmen.'

He sighed heavily. 'Now you're being silly. This job is the only thing you've ever known and personally I can't see you in any other role.'

'So I stay on as a damaged DS with everyone looking for the right moment to stick a knife in my back, is that what you're saying? You know as well as I do that now I have been tainted with mental health issues, promotion to DI will never happen. I'm stuck in a groove and that's it for me until I retire.'

He placed a hand on her knee over the sheet. 'Would that be so bad? A DS running a team, pulling in the bad guys, with a nice pension at the end of it all? You could do a lot worse.'

'And what about "Maverick" and "Go it Alone" Kate? How do I get rid of those slurs?'

'You don't. You're a darned good detective and everyone knows it, so you just carry on doing what you always do.'

'And what's that when it's at home?'

'Catching villains and annoying the hell out of the powers that be. What could possibly be more satisfying?'

'Hm. A lot more than hunting for poisonous spiders, I suppose.'

He laughed and was then suddenly serious. 'Talking of which, at the start of this business you did say that you would tell me why you developed such an irrational phobia about God's little creatures.'

'I said I would tell you about it one day, when I'm ready.'

'Well, how about telling me now? It's seems to me to be as good a time as any.'

She hesitated, then abruptly released her breath in a sigh of resignation. 'Okay, okay. But the details remain between the two us. Promise?'

'It's a deal. Scouts honour.'

She grimaced and her eyes clouded over for a second. 'I was a child when it all happened,' she began. 'I was living just outside Ilford in Essex with my mum and dad and my twin sister, Linda. You remember Linda?'

He nodded grimly. 'Of course I do. She was murdered by that swine, Twister, during Operation Firetrap, when he mistook her for you.'

She took a deep breath. 'Brutally put, but yes, that was Linda, and I will never ever forget what happened to her . . . Well, Linda had always been something of a rebel, and she went off the rails completely when she was about eleven after getting into bad company. When my father tried to bring her to heel, she ran away, got into drugs and became addicted to cocaine. She was eventually picked up by the police and ended up in care after being caught burgling houses to feed her habit. It broke my father's heart as he adored the pair of us, and he died of a stroke within months of her being put away. Then about a year or so later my mum met Maurice, a very attractive and outwardly personable man who could have charmed the knickers off a nun. She was totally besotted with him and though I saw through him and realised that he was only after the money Dad had left her, she wouldn't hear a word against him. Not even when he started coming on to me within weeks of their marriage, touching me up and trying to get me drunk. Then one night just after my thirteenth birthday, he actually cornered me in my bedroom, threw me on to my bed and tried to rip off my nightdress—'

'Gordon Bennett!'

'Even at that age, though, I had very sharp nails and he soon let go when I raked his face with them. But he explained away the marks I left on his cheek by telling my mother he had caught me smoking pot, even producing one of his own joints as "evidence" and claiming I had attacked him when he'd taken it off me. Because of my mum's experience of Linda's drug taking and the fact that she was so infatuated with Maurice, she chose to believe him instead of me and she let him cart me off to lock me in the old woodshed at the bottom of the garden as a punishment.'

She shivered. 'The shed had only one small window and was very dark inside. It was also infested with spiders. Shut in the gloom like that for several hours with those bloody things crawling all over me was a pretty traumatic experience for a kid of my age, I can tell you, and I screamed the place down. But my terrified reaction served only to stimulate my stepdad's perverted mentality and from that day on he shut me in the shed whenever he felt like it, telling my mum it was a punishment for some alleged misdemeanour he had dreamed up.'

'And your mother just went along with it all?'

She shook her head sadly. 'By then she too had sussed him out, but it was too late. She was not a well person and very much in fear of his violent temper, so she hadn't the strength or the will to do anything about it.'

Hayden looked horrified. 'So things just carried on as before?'

'For a couple more years, yes, but then I took it on myself to do something about it. I crept out one night while Maurice was in a drunken stupor and burned the garden shed to the ground.'

'You did *what?*'

She shrugged. 'It was all I could think of doing at the time, but I needn't have bothered. Maurice died in a pub brawl just months later and my mum and I lived quite happily after that until her death from a stroke, like my father, just before I left university. What I experienced in that garden shed all those years ago, however, has never gone away. It left me emotionally scarred and while I have managed to somehow pack the memories away in my subconscious, they are still there, waiting to resurface, as they did with this case.'

She treated him to a tired smile. 'So, now you have it all, Hayd. I'm afraid you've not only married a wicked arsonist, but one with a screw loose to boot.' She patted his arm indulgently. 'But don't worry, no one ever found out I torched the shed, so there won't be a police raid or men in white coats knocking on our door to cart me away any time soon.'

He shook his head with sudden irritation. 'This is no time to be flippant, old girl—'

'Why, you going to turn me in?'

'Don't be stupid, Kate. I'm talking about your mental state. You need help with this arachnophobia thing.'

She shook her head. 'That's what the shrink told me, but it ain't going to happen. I played the game at the clinic because I had to for the sake of my job, but there is no one less amenable to that sort of counselling crap than me, so I'm done with it all. I'll manage my problem in my own way from now on.'

He looked far from happy, but after much chewing of his lip, he capitulated with a heavy sigh. 'Well, if you're sure . . .'

'I've never been more sure of anything in my life.'

He brightened up. 'Well, since dear old Martha was nicely barbecued in that barn, at least you won't have to worry about spiders hiding in sheds or under the bed anymore, will you?'

She glanced a little uncertainly across at the window and the remains of a web fluttering in the breeze from the left-hand corner. 'Let's hope you're right.'

'Of course I'm right. I'm never anything else, am I?'

* * *

The sunlight cheering Kate's bedroom hardly touched the wooded grounds of Moat House, leaving much of it in a strange, misty gloom. That included the burnt-out shell of the old barn and the patch of incinerated woodland surrounding it which now resembled a blackened heath.

It also included the empty, shadowy rooms of the house itself where curtains remained partially pulled across windows and the sonorous ticking of the grandfather clock in the hallway was the only sound to break the otherwise sepulchral stillness that reigned.

Yasmin Dunbar was now the sole remaining resident following the night of terror the week before which had committed the professor to a local mental hospital and sent her stepdaughter, Angela, packing. But she was not unduly perturbed by the fact. She had had the remaining spiders in the laboratory collected by a colleague of her husband, and she intended leaving Moat House herself just as soon as she had managed to tie up some legal details with her solicitor and put the place on the market. In the meantime, she was quite happy to have the house to herself. She wasn't fazed by thoughts of ghosts lurking in dark corners and she felt completely relaxed as she slipped into the frothing suds of her bath, a glass of Hubert's excellent wine in one hand.

Martha liked the bathroom too. The radiator and the rising steam gave it a hot, humid feel after the days and nights she had spent under bricks and in deep holes in the ground outside. It reminded her of home in the Amazon rainforest. Her escape through the split timber in the back of the barn had been little short of miraculous. But Martha didn't know anything about that. After all, she was only a simple arachnid. But she was very keen on setting up home in this great big house with its dark rooms and ready supply of cockroaches and mice. She was extremely curious about the bare arm dangling over the side of the bath, though, and she crept slowly towards it, her dull soulless eyes seemingly fixed on the red painted nails and the glittering, gold band on one finger that seemed to draw her on . . .

THE END